MURDER

IN

TOY TOWN

Peggy & Frank —
All the best —
Jennifer Taylor Wojcik

Jennifer Taylor Wojcik

ISBN: 9781796890082

ISBN 13:
Library of Congress Control Number:

MURDER IN TOY TOWN

Other Books by Jennifer Taylor Wojcik

FROM DAY ONE
DAY AFTER DAY
THE FINAL DAY: ALL CLEAR
"WORN SANDALS" The Missing Years of Jesus

CHAPTER ONE

St Petersburg, Florida
February 2000

Dusk was approaching - that time between late afternoon and early evening when you need your headlights more to be seen than to see. Traffic was winding its way home from the workday, and both Interstate 275 and U.S. 19 were heavily saturated with commuters. He had decided to get off Interstate 275 at Gandy Boulevard and use a short-cut to get home.

Headed west, within a mile he maneuvered two quick right turns off Gandy, onto the route that would take a good twenty minutes off his commute.

The street had developed into a sort of frontage road, paralleling the Interstate, and encompassing several industrial sites. While the street was well-traveled during the day, there was light traffic at night. The street was off the beaten path even though it ran by Toy Town – the 240 plus acre landfill that had been in the Tampa Bay Area news so much lately.

The landfill came into being in 1960, and since then had been up for sale, posted for development and petitioned to be cleaned up and closed all within the last few years. Toy Town had become its moniker and the Pinellas County Crackers said the name came from the small, portable 10' x 30' trailer that used to *guard* its front entrance. It eventually included a site designed for pilots of model (toy) airplanes to safely take off and land. This part of Toy Town was well attended by young kids, their parents, and some not-so-young toy airplane enthusiasts.

Toy Town had become a mammoth operation, servicing all household recyclable items, offering safe disposal of batteries, electronics of all types or sizes and a free drop off point for any resident who presented proof of their Pinellas County residence. Painfully aware of misplaced debris that fell from trucks carrying it to the site, Toy Town's service center sent crews out intermittently to pick up errant rubbish that accumulated on or along the street known by the locals as Toy Town Road. It could have been – and probably should have been, a full-time job.

He'd driven this stretch of road many times and was familiar with its nuisances. Inevitably, there always seemed to be at least a couple of bags of trash that had either fallen off a truck or blown off one that could impede traffic on this otherwise open road.

Anyone who used this stretch of highway was used to seeing debris strewn on both sides of the street or often stuck in the middle of it, and tonight was no exception

Approaching him – heading southbound - was a large dump truck that appeared to be traveling at a high rate of speed. It was not until he got closer to the oncoming trucks that he saw the second truck now attempting to pass the first. He instinctively swerved to the right to avoid a head-on collision. Tim narrowly missed the oncoming truck, saw it hit a large black bag, forcing the bag up into the air and ultimately into his car.

Immediately stopping, Tim got out surveying the damage the garbage bag had caused. Swearing under his breath, he checked the driver's side front fender which was now bent, noted his headlight was broken and looking around, saw that neither truck had bothered to stop, least of all slow down. As he looked in the direction the trucks were traveling, he saw nothing but their tail lights dimming in the distance.

Walking back to the driver's seat, he heard a siren and saw approaching blue lights. It was a Florida Highway Patrol cruiser, and it was headed for the shoulder behind his now-distressed vehicle. He was thankful for the timeliness of the officer, and walked toward the back of his vehicle to meet with him. He could at least give the policeman a description of the two trucks that had sped away after hitting the bag of garbage, and nearly causing a head-on collision. He knew the officer would have had to pass these two trucks in route to this location.

Immediately Tim recognized that he would not be shaving any time off this commute, but little did he know what had just happened, much less that he was now in the thick of it. Tim Tyler was in for more adventure than he had bargained for.

CHAPTER TWO

Tallahassee, Florida
1995 – Five Years Earlier

Heather Howell was the epitome of a self-made woman. She had progressed from a brilliant criminal attorney with a stellar record, to now serving as a criminal investigator. While some might see that as a lateral move, Heather had more than earned her stripes in corralling and convicting one of the most elusive underworld criminals of the time.

Heather had worked with agents from the FBI, CIA and Secret Service. She had earned their respect and fluently spoke their language. Through her innate power of discernment, she caught onto things quickly, and then researched them to prove her senses were on cue.

To say Heather Howell was well-connected was an understatement. Her previous law practice had made her a household name among the Florida Bar Association members, Supreme Court Judges and in particular thugs she had convicted. But, she had vowed to uphold the law and to seek justice for anyone who had been wronged. In her estimation, there were worse consequences than being hated by criminals.

In 1990, Heather opted to enhance her skill set while working on the Carmine Lorenzo case. In that situation, she had been retained by Matthew Winters, whose family endured years of suffering and stalking by Lorenzo's crime syndicate. Matt Winters was also practicing law, ably aided by Police Detective Peter Sutherland, and both of these professionals had made an indelible mark on Heather. They had become comrades whose single goal was to stop the tyranny of the Lorenzos, and they had accomplished that and then some.

After a well-deserved vacation at the end of the Lorenzo trial, Heather secured her Private Investigator's license. Taking a course in fire arms and defense training, she then purchased a hand gun and obtained a concealed weapons permit from the state of Florida.

At that juncture she called both Matthew Winters and Pete Sutherland, inviting them to lunch. Once the obligatory catching up was done, Heather announced her intentions to her compatriots. Both men looked blankly at her. Neither Matt nor Pete offered a comment.

"Guys" Heather questioned. "Have you nothing to say?"

Pete said, "We knew you'd switch careers. The lawyer stuff is just too *plain* for you Howell."

"Excuse me" said Matt. "Are you saying lawyers are plain? I'm not *plain*, and I'm an attorney."

"You're both right. And Matt, you're an attorney doing an investigator's job legally. I will too." said Heather. "I learned so much from the two of you, and our mental sparring and brainstorming sessions was a rush."

Matthew said, "We made a great team Heather."

Pete retorted, "And now our little chickadee is going to leave the nest! Here's to you Howell!" as he raised his drink.

"Thanks guys, and there's just one more thing...I've decided to make a new start somewhere else in Florida." Both men fell silent.

Having friends who taught at Stetson University & College of Law in St. Petersburg, and knowing several local criminal attorneys, Heather opted to relocate to the Tampa Bay Area. While it had been the home of her latest crime bust, the climate was more temperate than the Panhandle, and the Bay Area was a larger metropolitan market where she felt she could more readily establish her newly expanded career.

Heather Howell spent most of her waking hours marketing herself as a PI (Private Investigator) with a specialty in criminal investigation. By joining all the appropriate organizations and charities associated with her new career, she had gotten off to a good start.

She made sure she was invited to or involved in every civic organization. She joined the Chambers of Commerce, in Tampa, St. Petersburg and Clearwater. She distributed business cards everywhere she went, and was fastidious in consistently making the best possible first impression.

Her experience as an attorney gave her instant credibility. She had most often served clients on the prosecution side of the law, mainly because she took great pride in seeing those who broke the law handed justice. Now she was looking at things from a different perspective; she knew there were prospective clients that needed a strong defense, and with her investigative skills honed, Heather knew she could handle either side admirably.

Initially, Heather marketed herself from her home, a three bedroom, two bath condominium she had leased in downtown Tampa. Within a few months, her client list started to develop in earnest. She called every criminal attorney in the Bay Area, and scheduled face time with them. Not stopping there, Heather met with large defense firms as well as the small boutique firms within the tri-city area. She also made it a point to get to know each District Attorney in the tri-county.

Heather Howell submitted her resume to the local bar associations in Hillsborough, Pinellas and Sarasota Counties, emphasizing her credibility as an expert in criminal investigation and convictions. And while her experience leaned toward the side of prosecution, she had experience in the defense side of the law as well. Given a preference she opted for prosecution, but realized that the constitutional right of the accused was *innocent until proven* guilty.

Once her client list began to expand, she considered moving to a professional office complex, but opted to forego that overhead at this juncture. And because her zip code already defined her as being in *Downtown Tampa*, she saw it as a non-recoverable (and as such a needless) expense. The Private Investigator side of the business was doing well, but most of her activities were "out" of the office rather than "in".

As her marketing efforts paid off, Heather was invited to speak at civic and charitable dinners, fundraisers and the like. This not only put her in the presence of the media, it helped bolster her credibility as an authority on the subject of criminal investigation.

Heather Howell had worked long and hard and was now poised to take full advantage of her carefully calculated and well-executed plan. Howell Legal Services & Investigations was not only born, it was becoming a household name.

CHAPTER THREE

Tampa, Florida
1997

Tampa was one of the fastest growing cities in the country, as well as in the Sunshine State. Commerce was growing exponentially, the Port and its ancillary waterways were thriving, and talk of a new Convention Center had become a reality. Adjacent to the Convention Center, a plethora of restaurants, clubs and retail shops opened in what was named Harbor Island. Accompanied by a luxury hotel and a monorail tram called a "people mover", guests could be transported from Harbor Island over the bridge to the convention center and back.

More luxury hotels were predicted to open as developers and investors took a long hard look at the land in and around Tampa Bay, specifically downtown.

Multi-millionaires like Donald Trump were seen lunching with City Development Council members, and rumors of a new hotel were born.

As interest grew alongside reports of permits being issued for hoteliers, the sports industry followed suit. Tampa had become home to the Buccaneers – an NFL team add-on. The National Hockey League ultimately developed the Tampa Bay Lightning hockey team that required the building of an arena. Nearby St. Petersburg sported a major league baseball team – The Tampa Bay Devil Rays, and for racing enthusiasts, there were two dog tracks and one thoroughbred horse track. When one added a never-ending array of water sports to the mix, Tampa Bay had it all. Sunshine, water, balmy temperatures and breezes off The Gulf of Mexico made Tampa a highly desirable destination for business and tourists alike.

As interest grew, so did the need for improved roads, airport facilities and the like. Transportation needs created jobs, homes and businesses. It was an economic boon and a wonderful time to settle in the Bay Area of Florida.

Heather Howell had her finger on the pulse of the community. She knew the right people and seemed to be at all the right places at the right time. She was however a professional, and an unmarried female. While the area was progressing, the old southern culture, ideologies and biases were still very much rooted in Tampa Bay.

Tampa had a female mayor named Sandy Freeman who pushed the glass ceiling, and by all reports, was doing a great job. It was a start at breaking traditional mores. Heather Howell wanted to break new ground as well, and as her case work became more publicized, so did Howell Legal Services & Investigations.

CHAPTER FOUR

St. Petersburg/Clearwater, Florida
February 20, 2000

Timothy Tyler was known as an all-around good guy. Everyone who knew him called him Tim – those closest to him often referred to him as *Timbo*. That nickname came during middle school when there was more than one "Tim" in his guy squad and they needed to make a distinction between them. While he didn't love the nickname, it had just stuck and he dealt with it.

Tim had grown up in central Florida and had spent most of his adult life living in the Bay area. Leaving only long enough to serve in the Army, Tim had really never thought of living anywhere else. He loved the weather, the ability to be on the water for recreation, and he had a good job in St. Petersburg.

Tim was a middle manager in the Information Technology Department for the Pinellas County Humane Society. There he oversaw and developed computer programs in support of the animals taken in, housed, treated and adopted out of the center. Tim had assisted in developing the "chip" method of animal identification, and was pivotal in getting Pinellas County's chip program activated.

His training in IT, along with his profound love of animals made him excel in his position. Tim was the "go to" guy at the office. He maintained his team's work space in the shelter's adoption center, to be closer to those they served.

Tim Tyler had never married. He owned a modest home in Clearwater that he shared with his best buddy – a German shepherd rescue (of course) named Tattoo. Tattoo was about three years old when he came into the shelter. He had been abused physically, was severely malnourished and in deplorable condition.

To see Tattoo now, you would never know he was the same animal. Tim had lovingly cared for, attended to and trained Tattoo and he was now a happy, healthy five year old German shepherd.

In the Army, Tim had been assigned to the K9 unit where he specifically worked with the German shepherd breed. There he learned the proper training techniques ranging from hand signals and commands to one-word voice commands. Training these animals was rewarding for Tim, and the most difficult part of his job was seeing them off to work with someone else once they were sufficiently trained.

While he had an affinity for shepherds, Tim loved all dog breeds. And as unusual as some thought it to be, Tim loved cats as well. He had even considered adopting a kitty as a playmate for Tattoo, but he had not yet acted on that urge.

Being a stand-up kind of guy, Tim had never had even a brush with the law. He admittedly drove too fast at times, but hadn't had even so much as a speeding ticket. Now he found himself staring into the eyes of a Florida State Policeman, his own car damaged, and a bag of garbage along side of the road that he had obviously hit.

###

"Good Evening officer" Tim said, leaning on the back of his car.

"Evening" replied the trooper; "It appears there's been a bit of a run-in here. I'll need to see your driver's license, registration and insurance card please."

Tim nodded, handed his driver's license to the officer and told him he would retrieve his registration and insurance from the glove compartment in the car.

"I'll walk up to the car with you" said the officer "and please don't make any sudden moves."

Tim was surprised at the remark but assumed the officer was exercising additional caution and following protocol. The two walked to the passenger side of Tim's car and Tim slowly opened first the door, then the glove compartment, retrieving the paperwork and handing it over to the officer.

"So, Mr. Tyler, what exactly transpired here?"

Tim told the officer exactly what had happened, including a fairly thorough description of the two dump trucks that were approaching him at a high rate of speed.

"And where were you going Mr. Tyler?"

"I was on my way home from work."

"Do you always take this route?" the officer asked.

"Not always, but occasionally. I take this route when Interstate 275 is backed up to Gandy Boulevard. Driving this route cuts off a bit of time in getting to US 19." Tim replied.

"So you were in a hurry to get home, sir?"

"Not particularly, but moving slowly is preferable to sitting at a stand-still on the Interstate." Tim smiled.

"And at what rate of speed were you traveling when you allegedly met these dump trucks?"

"I was probably going 35 or 40 miles per hour."

"Probably – but you aren't sure?"

"I am sure I wasn't speeding, sir. And officer, the trucks would have been the ones you passed on the way here. They were speeding off in that direction," Tim said, pointing south.

"Okay, Mr. Tyler. Let's have a look at the damage to your car. We'll need to fill out a report for your insurance, right?"

The two walked to the front of Tim's automobile. Using the policeman's flashlight, they first inspected the driver's side front fender and light, finding a large dent in the fender and a broken light fixture. Tim watched as the patrolman made notes.

Looking closer, the policeman ran his fingers lightly across the surface of the dent picking up a sticky fluid.

"What is that?" Tim asked.

"There is a wet, sticky residue here that will require testing to determine its origin," said the policeman. "Mr. Tyler, what exactly did you *hit* with your vehicle?"

"As I told you officer, there was a large black garbage bag that was struck by one of the dump trucks and the edge of my vehicle when I swerved to avoid a head-on collision." Tim was becoming weary and felt this was sounding more and more like an interrogation.

"And where is this bag of garbage now, Mr. Tyler?"

"I assume it's on the side of the road" said Tim. "I didn't look for it; I stopped to see what the damage was to my car when you arrived."

The officer was silent, but was shining his flashlight along the sides of the street. Sure enough, there was a large black bag in the ditch. When the officer saw it, he immediately radioed for backup.

Within a matter of minutes another FHP vehicle came to a stop on the other end of Tim Tyler's vehicle. The two patrolmen conversed outside of Tim's earshot. The latest patrolman on the scene walked over to the black bag and opened it. It did not contain garbage. Inside was the bloody body of a woman.

"Mr. Tyler, I am placing you under arrest..." were the last words Tim remembered hearing that night.

CHAPTER FIVE

Tampa, Florida
February 21, 2000

"Howell Legal Services & Investigations" Shirley said professionally and yet with a warm, welcoming tone in her voice.

Shirley was a god-send. She was in her mid-forties, skilled and a person who took pride in her work. She had been a receptionist and an executive assistant to both a judge and a criminal attorney, and knew how important that first connection to the outside world really was. When someone needed to speak to an attorney, a judge or a private investigator, they weren't in the mood to be put on hold, summarily responded to or put off.

Howell Legal Services & Investigations now took up residence in a rehabbed office structure in Hyde Park, located on Tampa's South Side. Heather felt very comfortable in these surroundings and in leasing the entire building, had room for anticipated growth.

Heather's office was simple in its décor and a pleasant atmosphere where she could meet one on one with her clients. She created a conference area where more formal meetings or depositions could be held. A small office was created across from the conference room that allowed opposing counsel privacy as needed.

The reception area was comfortable and well-appointed. This was Shirley's domain, and everything she needed was at her fingertips.   Heather had invested in the latest computer technology

and software and spared no expense in making Shirley as comfortable as possible.

Shirley had taken evening courses while she worked, and had received a degree that qualified her as a paralegal.   This made her all the more useful at the firm, and Heather Howell was fortunate to have such a dedicated person on staff.

"Ms. Howell" said Shirley "Timothy Tyler is on line one and needs to speak with you immediately. He has been arrested on charges of homicide." Shirley had accurately screened the call and prepared Heather for what she was about to hear.

"Thank you Shirley" Heather said, promptly answering the call. "Good morning, this is Heather Howell."

Tim Tyler's story poured out over the telephone line. Heather heard the confusion and abject desperation in his voice. "Will you agree to represent me, Ms. Howell?" Tim asked.

"Mr. Tyler, are you currently in jail?" asked Heather.

"Yes, I am. My car was also impounded. I have to appear in court this afternoon and need to have someone represent me."

"Mr. Tyler, I am an attorney and can represent you as your counsel. I would like to get the details of exactly what happened, your recollection of the particulars and then we can discuss what services I offer that would best suit your needs. For now, tell me where you are being held and I will come there so that we can talk before your arraignment."

"Thank you," said Tim. "I am in the Pinellas County Jail on 49th Street. How soon can you get here?"

"I'll be there by noon. Hang tight Mr. Tyler."

Heather hung up the phone with her mind weaving various scenarios she had envisioned while hearing Tim Tyler's hurried explanation. She would be meeting with him soon, and if her instincts were on point, was eager to sink her teeth into this one. She buzzed Shirley to add the appointment at the Pinellas Jail to her calendar.

Feeling confident that the firm would take the case, Shirley had already researched Timothy William Tyler. She told Heather the information obtained so far was on her computer for review.

"Thanks Shirley – good job as usual. Will you also request arrest records, speeding violations, anything pertinent to Timothy Tyler. Check both state and local data bases for anything and everything he's had a license for or been a part of? I need to know as much as possible before the arraignment. And, can you get information on the Jane Doe who was killed?"

Heather immediately reviewed the information on Tim Tyler. Based on the data alone, she was putting together a sketch of him. She then went onto the Florida Highway Patrol (FHP) site to obtain the official report. That's when the hair stood up on the back of her neck.

CHAPTER SIX

St. Petersburg, Florida
Jane Doe, the Deceased

"Jane Doe" was a white female believed to be in her early to mid-thirties. The Medical Examiner had *unofficially* told the police that Jane Doe apparently died from "blunt force trauma" to the upper body; a cause of death that was as broad as one could be. The autopsy would narrow the results but that could take up to six weeks to complete.

The only other information readily available and provided by the Medical Examiner & Coroner's office was that based on blood pooling, rigidity and amount of body decomposition she had been dead for roughly eight to twenty-four hours.

This left the FHP and the St. Petersburg police department with the task of determining the identity of Jane Doe. Priority one: who she was, and then who had both a motive and an opportunity to kill her.

Checking through all reported missing persons in the area had netted no results. No one matching the description of Jane Doe had been reported in Pinellas, Sarasota or Hillsborough counties. The search then widened to encompass other counties near Pinellas, and if nothing popped, they would issue a statewide search.

With the state police, the St Petersburg Police and the County Prosecutor's office in search of Jane Doe, they collectively turned up nothing state-wide. The State Prosecutor took over now and ordered a search through the nationwide data base for missing persons. If anyone had reported this individual as missing, it would appear here.

CHAPTER SEVEN

Heather Howell's Office
Tampa, Florida

Heather had procured information on Tim Tyler, but it was only a baseline from which she would prepare a complete profile and timeline. After meeting with Mr. Tyler at the Pinellas County Detention Center, she agreed to represent him at his hearing that afternoon, where she managed to have Tim released on bail.

Heather had agreed to meet with Tim Tyler in her office the following morning.

Having gained virtually no information from the prosecutor during the arraignment, Heather was told simply said the defense would have their discovery within the parameters of the law; 30 days before the trial date.

The Next Morning

Shirley greeted Tim and handed him a new client form to complete. He promptly did so and returned it to the reception desk. Returning to his seat, he smiled at Shirley and thanked her.

Within mere minutes, Heather Howell was ushering Tim back to her office. She would spend as much time as necessary with him to find out as much as she could about the man, the situation he was in and intuitively gain insight into what kind of individual (in her estimation) he was.

The two talked for nearly two hours. While Heather always worked off a prescribed list of initial interview questions, she quickly got to the heart of the matter; Tim's side of the story.

After acquiring Tim's permission to record his statement, she simply initiated the recording with the date, time, place of the statement, all who were present, and the charges that had been entered against Tim Tyler. Tim was then asked to state his full name, address, place of employment and his date of birth.

Heather had explained to Tim that if he ever needed a break or questioned anything, he should simply raise his hand and she would stop the recording. Tim agreed and began sharing his version of what happened on the night he was stopped by FHP and arrested.

He began by stating that he was leaving work on the day of the incident, and found I-275 North to be in a traffic bottleneck south of the exit to Gandy Boulevard. He then described his new route to Clearwater, as well as his reasons for taking that route. Tim gave a clear and concise timeline of the events surrounding his arrest. He then stated that while he knew his vehicle had come in contact with the black bag, he was confident that he was the *second vehicle* to have struck the object.

Stating that his memory was clear, the approaching dump truck had struck the bag first, pushing it into and ultimately off the front of his car. Tim raised his hand, and Heather stopped the recording.

"Is there a problem" Heather asked?

"I just remembered that the truck was in my lane – headed straight toward me and that's when I saw the black bag coming at me as well." Tim explained.

"That's the reason we relive the scene – before it gets too far from memory." Heather said. "Are you ready to go on?"

"Yes" Tim said and continued.

"Is there anything in particular that you remember about the truck?"

"It was speeding. It seemed that he saw me and hit his brakes, and then he seemed to speed up again. The truck was huge and coming straight at me."

As Tim continued, he noted that the first FHP Officer arrived within a couple of minutes after the accident occurred.

"Did either of the trucks stop?"

"No – neither of them stopped. Before I could decide what to do, one of ultimately two FHP Officers arrived."

He gave a detailed description of both officers who came to the scene, including their names. When he finished he simply said, "I couldn't believe I was being arrested and carted off to jail. My car was impounded and I was taken to the Pinellas County jail's holding cell. There I was fingerprinted, searched and given an orange jumpsuit to wear." He again raised his hand.

Stopping the recording once again, Heather asked Tim if there was anything else he wanted to say. An exhausted Tim Tyler simply shook his head.

Recognizing his distress, Heather said she had a few questions she would like to ask him if he was up to it. Tim agreed and Heather proceeded on the record.

"Mr. Tyler, were you speeding when you struck the bag on the highway?"

"No ma'am and I told the officer I was driving at 35 to 40 miles per hour when that occurred. That is well within the speed limit for that stretch of highway."

"Did you purposely or willfully strike the black bag on 28th Street North on the night of February 20, 2000?"

"No, it was accidental."

"Did you have any knowledge about the content of that bag?"

"No, I assumed it was debris – garbage."

"Did you place anything – any object – person or thing, in that bag?"

"No – I did not."

"Were you asked to identify the Jane Doe found in the bag?"

"Yes, I was asked, but I had never seen her before."

"Did anyone ask you if you were injured in the collision with the bag?"

"No."

"Did the FHP officers open your trunk?"

"Yes."

"And did they ask your permission to do so?"

"No."

"Did anyone examine the interior of your car at the scene?"

"Yes – the FHP officers looked through the inside of the car before the tow truck and the crime scene investigators arrived."

"Did the officers ask permission to look inside your vehicle?"

"No. The only thing they asked for was my driver's license, registration and proof of insurance. I provided them with all of those items. The registration and proof of insurance were in my glove compartment, so I had to retrieve them."

"And the officer or officers allowed you to do that?"

"Yes – it was just the first officer – Blair. He instructed me to make no swift movements and he walked me to the passenger side to retrieve the papers from my glove compartment."

"Did you find that odd, Mr. Tyler?"

"Yes I did. I felt like I was suspected of something illegal – like they thought I had a concealed weapon or something."

"And did you ask about why they were acting oddly?"

"No. I complied with what I was told to do, and assumed the policeman was just being cautious."

"Last question for now Mr. Tyler, did the FHP find anything inside your car or car trunk that was deemed concealed, suspicious or illegal?"

"No."

"Thank you. We will now stop the recording. The elapsed recorded time is one hour and two minutes."

Tim appeared exhausted. Standing, he poured himself a glass of water from the pitcher on the table and politely asked Heather if she would like some as well.

"No, thank you. I know questions like these can be tedious, but you handled them very well," said Heather.

"I have nothing to hide Ms. Howell. As I said yesterday on the phone, I've done nothing wrong. I just can't figure out how this got out of hand so quickly. One minute I'm driving home from work, and within the blink of an eye I'm charged with homicide – murder for goodness sake." Tim was now pacing in front of Heather's desk. "I wonder how many automobiles have hit garbage bags, boxes and the like along that roadway. I'll bet we would both be surprised at the number. It almost always has debris of some sort in or along the street."

Heather said, "Tim, it isn't *necessary* that I believe in your innocence to represent you, but I would suggest that you hire a Private Investigator. There are a lot of 'unknowns' here. In order for anyone to prepare a defense for you, we have to establish a timeline that includes where and how Jane Doe was killed; how she ended up in a garbage bag on the side of the road; who the dump truck drivers were; why they were racing one another down the highway; and what if anything they had to do with the incident. It's my belief that you were at the wrong place at the wrong time, but my belief won't keep you out of jail."

"Does that mean you think I should hire a *separate* attorney?" Tim asked.

"Not necessarily, but that is entirely up to you. Being an attorney with criminal experience on the prosecution side gives me an advantage in that I know what can or cannot be used as evidence in a defense trial. In other words, I won't do or say anything in an investigation that could taint or corrupt the evidence. That prevents information from being thrown out of court or worse, never heard in court. As I said, this decision is yours alone."

"Then I would like to retain you as my PI *and* as my defense attorney." Tim reached out his hand to shake on the deal.

"I'm pleased to be in a position to work with you Tim. Do you have any questions for me at this time?" Heather asked.

"My only question is the amount of money I need to give you as a retainer?" Tim asked.

"My retainer is Ten-thousand Dollars, and once that retainer is absorbed, we will bill you on a fee for time basis. The rate will depend on the nature of the work; obviously a lesser rate for research and a higher rate for hearings and/or meetings and depositions. My assistant Shirley will provide you with a packet of information which explains our fees in detail. Look it over and if there is anything you need clarified, just call."

"Thank you, Ms. Howell. I am relieved to be in capable hands." said Tim.

"Thank you, Tim. Shirley will give you copies of everything we have discussed. I will be in touch with you as soon as we have additional information on your case, but in the meantime, should you think of anything else that I should know, call. Oh – and it would be best that you refrain from discussing the case with anyone else. If the police or anyone from the media contacts you, please refer them to me without comment."

Heather took the first opportunity to review the tape recording of Tim Tyler's version of what transpired on the night of February 20, 2000. She then compared Tim's version to the official police report and highlighted discrepancies or things that were unclear.

Crime Scene Investigators had been called to the roadway after Tim's arrest. There the CSI team looked for tangible and visible signs that could in any way have been related to the incident. There were distance measurements taken from Tim's automobile to the black bag. Tire marks from Tim's vehicle were observed as a sudden swerve toward the shoulder of the road and skid marks from his vehicle were noted prior to the swerve. There were no skid marks ascertained from either of the trucks who were paralleling one another and meeting Tim's car. CSI had noted an oil leak that occurred in the right southbound lane, and traces of oil that moved to the middle lane and then back to the right lane.

With her red highlighter, Heather marked that statement since it indicated that Vehicle two was the leaky oil truck, and had indeed overtaken Vehicle one in the same area Tim Tyler had reported meeting the dump trucks head on.

That also told Heather that Vehicle two was the truck that *initially* struck the black bag containing Jane Doe. Heather's task was now to find a dump truck in a large metropolitan area where literally thousands of them roamed the roads; one which was leaking oil - may or may not have sustained damage, and was traveling that particular stretch of road on February 20, 2000.

Then the next question – why were the police looking only at her client? Heather made a note to talk with the County Attorney's office asking that very question.

CHAPTER EIGHT

Tim Tyler
Clearwater, Florida

Tim was relieved to pull into his garage and watch the door close slowly behind him. He was emotionally exhausted but believed he had found the right person to help him sort out this utterly ridiculous yet horrendous legal situation.

With today's events running through his mind, Tim unlocked the door to the house to naturally find Tattoo lying in his bed next to the kitchen door.

"Tattoo, novas" Tim said. Immediately the German shepherd was off his bed and sitting at Tim's feet. "Hi big guy, I could hardly wait to see you." Tattoo had waited for the command, even though his entire body was shaking in delight at seeing his pet parent. Tim did not want Tattoo jumping up on people due to his size and innate instincts. Had Tim waited more than a minute without giving the command, Tattoo would have barked and then he would have attacked. This command identified a friend to Tattoo and would insure any intruder would be dealt with appropriately. Being a responsible pet parent meant that training was the best gift a pet parent could provide.

Commands between pets and pet parents were like passwords are to user names. Tim knew commands had to be unique to the situation and that consistency was imperative. Without proper training, Tattoo could have become an oversized lap dog, or a fierce and treacherous attacker. With training and consistency, Tattoo could be both.

The bond between Tim and Tattoo was something to behold, and the responsible pet parents of the world share that with their animals. Without hesitation, Tattoo would lay down his life for

Tim's and vice versa. They were the best of friends, family to one another and each exhibited unconditional love for the other.

Having now had his mood brightened, Tim took Tattoo for his nightly run and afterwards the two settled in for dinner and relaxation. The day had been stressful. Reliving the drive home on February 20th felt more confusing with each passing day, and Tim had wondered more than once 'why me?'

He had to trust his instincts about Heather Howell and her skills. At the moment, she was the only person standing between his incarceration and his freedom.

CHAPTER NINE

Heather Howell's Office
Tampa, Florida

The dump truck search began with an inquiry on the Internet. In the old days, PI's had to research phone directory listings as one starting point. Not only was that prone to human error and incomplete at best, it was outdated before it was printed. Internet technology had superseded every other source by combining speed, accuracy and data base information that related every area of "dump truck" businesses together.

Then there was always the "motor vehicle registration" which was more accurate that other sources, and now it was available online.

The search turned out to be voluminous. In Tampa Bay, there were some one-hundred eighty five companies that leased or owned dump trucks, and the registered vehicles' listing was in the 'hundreds of hundreds' range. Heather wasn't deterred by any of this information. She would simply narrow her online search; tighten the parameters and lower the number.

Her father asked her once 'how do you eat an elephant?' to which she replied, 'I don't know, how?' The answer from her dad was straightforward and simple - 'one bite at a time'. She had long carried that lesson with her, which came in particularly handy at a time like this.

One bite at a time is how she approached every new challenge, and by afternoon's end she had culled the list to roughly one hundred. Just because a truck was owned and licensed to a Tampa Bay Area owner did not mean it was operated locally. As her research progressed, she learned about the special licensing that commercial truckers were required to have. That tidbit could cull the number even further.

Leaving little to chance, Heather formed a list of city and county workers who had any connection to the dump site in Toy Town. From that, she prioritized them by position, length of service and basic overall knowledge of the facility. With that, with Shirley's help, she would develop an interview schedule. She was confident that there was a plausible connection between the site and the incident, and someone there probably knew something. Fair or not, finding that connection had *become* her job.

Because her client's case had become front-page news, Heather was sure that the owner or operator of the one or more dump trucks that traversed that road on 02/20/2000 would be repairing or replacing their damaged vehicle to avoid any association or suspicion.

To narrow the results even further, Heather compiled a detailed list of "body" shops that specialized in semi-tractors, haulers and dump trucks. She also compiled a list of junk yards specializing in salvaged truck parts. And, she intended to follow up over the next days and weeks in the event "the" truck had been temporarily pulled out of service.

As it happens with most any research, there is a learning curve that an investigator must surpass. With dump trucks and haulers, that curve was a steep one. But, as a result Heather Howell now knew more about these vehicles than she cared to, but in the course of boning up on these behemoth trucks, she learned that they have inherent dangerous characteristics – all of which she would mention in court should it come to that.

Heather's father had taught her many things about life. Probably the most important lesson he had taught her was that "you don't know what you don't know". That took some time to sink in, but once it did, it made the investigative process a lot more interesting. When stuck on something Heather would ask herself the question – what don't I know that I need to know?

All of this information led Heather to a new set of questions for her client. She now needed to know (based on what she had now learned) what kind of dump truck had Tyler encountered that night. Were the two trucks alike in size? Were they different in configuration? She had come to know that there were 4-axle trucks with a lift axle, a 4-axle with two steering axles (and larger than the first) and how did these compare to a very basic 4 x 2 dump truck used for payloads of 10 metric tons? Without knowing these details, all else was merely speculative. Heather decided to print out various types and sizes to assist Tyler in his recollection. Again, Heather knew he could not accurately define something he didn't know much about. Perhaps the photo samples would spark a memory.

Heather had most likely found the appropriate dump truck type in her early research, but went further to learn about the larger truck varieties including the European Union Heavy trucks, Semi-Trailer end dump trucks, transfer dump trucks; truck and pups dump truck," Superdump" trucks, Dump trucks equipped with plows. Roll-off dump trucks, an articulated dump truck or hauler and more.

Heather's philosophy was too much information was always better than too little information. She assimilated photographs of all of these makes and models to show her client. Perhaps this would help him identify the "type" and/or model of the trucks he came so close to on 02/20/2000.

CHAPTER TEN

The On-Scene Officers
02/20/2000

The Florida Highway Patrol program is highly regarded and offers some of the best training for its Troopers. Their jurisdiction encompasses the entire state. When summoned by local city or county authorities, FHP takes precedence over their jurisdiction.

On the night of February 20, 2000, it was Florida Highway Patrolman Daniel Blair who arrived first on the scene. Blair, a 10 year veteran with the FHP is a white male, who stands six feet two inches tall and weighs in at two hundred twenty pounds. His assigned patrol for the past several months included 28th Street North as well as the surrounding area. Blair drove an easily identifiable FHP Marked Cruiser.

When Blair radioed for backup on February 20, it was FHP Officer Darrell Dunn who responded. Dunn, a black man stood six foot one and weighed two twenty five. He was a fifteen year veteran of FHP and had received several commendations. Dunn drove an unmarked FHP vehicle and was often called in for backup on calls of a "sensitive" nature; namely suspected drug busts, raids, hit and run incidents, homicide and so on.

It had been Darrell Dunn who opened the bag on February 20th, which resulted in the arrest of Timothy Tyler. And while Dunn had just arrived on scene immediately prior to that, he apparently asked very few questions of Tyler. Most of the interrogation at the scene was done by Daniel Blair.

The police report supported that Dunn asked Tim only a couple of questions including, whether or not he had been drinking, using recreational or prescribed drugs, and if he knew the identity of the victim (in the bag) or the driver(s) of the dump trucks that allegedly forced him off the road.

According to Tim's statement, the officers conferred privately before Dunn retrieved the garbage bag and its contents. That discussion was not part of the official report and Tim Tyler was not privy to their discussion. Heather Howell wanted to know more about that exchange.

Daniel Blair was a single man. While he had been married for a few years, he had recently divorced and seemingly had thrown himself into his work after the divorce became final. He had never had disciplinary action taken against him, but had been questioned by Internal Affairs (IA) on more than one occasion. The circumstances surrounding the IA questioning were based on accusations of harassment; two from females who in separate instances claimed sexual harassment and one from a male from whom Blair demanded a breathalyzer.

Dunn was married with two teenagers and by all reports was a seasoned officer with a good record. There were no cases that required Internal Affairs investigations related to Dunn.

CHAPTER ELEVEN

Toy Town
March 2000

In the past few days, workers who manned Toy Town and its active as well as dormant landfills were abuzz with the arrest of Tim Tyler. No longer did the crew joke about the birds that perpetually filled the skies of Toy Town, nor did they complain about the incessant odor coming from the tubes anchored into the ground to allow escape of the built up methane gases. Today the topic of conversation was about the body that had been discovered. Speculation ran rampant about how and where the body had been found, and many of the crew wondered where the now infamous "black bag" had come from.

Heather Howell had compiled a list of Toy Town employees and set up interviews. Most of the workers at the facility were none too eager to get involved, but some who were morbidly curious wanted to step right up. Heather's interviews were succinct and to the point. For accuracy and with their permission, she recorded every interview. A court stenographer took care of that task with ease and Heather got the transcripts at the end of each day.

One of Heather's early questions was about Jane Doe. Heather produced a composite sketch of the woman. Did anyone know her? Did they remember ever seeing her or someone who resembled her? To the last person, the response was "no".

Heather gleaned a lot of potentially useful information from the employees of Toy Town. In addition to the city/county vehicles that delivered garbage and other debris daily, Heather got the company names of many of the dump trucks who were licensed to use the facility. That narrowed her list substantially, although she knew better than to think it was all inclusive.

She learned that Toy Town took 'sensitive' debris such as electronics, paint, solvents, batteries etc. from residents of Pinellas County – with proof of residency. That area was restricted and closely monitored for adherence to city, county and EPA codes.

While Heather's research turned up numerous 'ideas' from Toy Town employees all too willing to provide their opinion, she was faced with a plethora of what ifs. The variables had grown out of proportion, but being an experienced PI, Heather decided to take stock of the various scenarios and follow where the facts led her.

Her interviews ended with the plant's top managers. They provided her with a list of approved/recognized 'vendors' and the trucking companies who frequented their plant. She learned that Toy Town kept a log of each truck's arrival time and load quantity. This information could prove to be golden.

Heather secured the log from February 20, 2000. She knew from the coroner's initial findings that the corpse was believed to have expired within eight to twenty-four hours of discovery. That timeline covered virtually all of February 20.

Heather asked the plant managers for a list of private citizens who had made drop-offs that same day. That list was readily provided and contained some fifty plus people who had access to Toy Town on February 20 in addition to the regular delivery trucks.

Heather thanked the Toy Town managers for their cooperation, adding that she might have supplementary questions, or need additional information at a later date. They assured her they would cooperate fully.

CHAPTER TWELVE

Howell's Notes & Analysis

Here were the facts: Anyone who lived in Pinellas County could obtain access to Toy Town proper. While they were monitored for their specific drop-off, the monitoring ended there. These guests were not continuously monitored from the drop-off to the exit. And any employee, part or full-time had unrestricted access to the site. Errant "garbage" ended up along the roadway on any given day, falling off garbage trucks, blowing off flatbeds or even pickup trucks. "It" – the black bag - would not have been suspicious in its own right.

Anyone with access to Toy Town on February 20, 2000 could have dropped the black bag containing the body of Jane Doe.

What Heather did not know was: Did someone associated with the facility know Jane Doe? Did they have a reason to kill her? And if so, was it accidental or planned? What if Jane Doe was still alive when she was stuffed into the black bag? The coroner had originally indicated blunt force trauma as the cause of death, but she *could* have been alive (but unconscious) when her body was placed inside the bag. That would mean pre-meditated murder, but by whom?

Jane Doe could have been killed *anywhere* and transported inside the garbage bag. The intent could have been to simply leave the bag at or near the Toy Town site.

Heather ran through other possibilities as well. Perhaps an accident occurred, someone (the perpetrator) panicked and not thinking clearly, opted to try and dispose of the body and any evidence.

Once a positive ID was made for Jane Doe, Heather could look for connections to anyone working at Toy Town. Until then, she would have to ask a lot of questions of a lot of people – including those she had spoken with previously.

The coroner's official autopsy report was not yet available, but there had been no indication that Jane Doe was sexually molested or traumatized. That in and of itself ruled out a lot for Heather, but again, it was something that had to be followed up on.

There would be a break in the case; Heather had seen it happen many times in the past. Someone or something would slip and the indicators she looked for would become apparent. Diligence in finding the facts had to be coupled with a great amount of patience.

The agenda for the next day would be to follow up with the coroner's office and then check with the police to see if any leads had come forth about Jane Doe's true identity. She would also review the transcripts from the employees and management of Toy Town.

As her "to-do" list lengthened, Heather astutely recognized her need for another pair of eyes, and another set of trained hands. She needed help with the detailed investigation that this case demanded.

CHAPTER THIRTEEN

Heather Howell's Office
Tampa, Florida

Tim Tyler waited as patiently as he could for Heather Howell to meet with him. She reportedly had some news to share and he was more eager than fearful to hear what she had to say.

Shirley had offered him something to drink, but Tim opted for nothing. He had politely taken a seat in the waiting room and tried thumbing through a magazine. When Heather buzzed Shirley to say she was ready to see Tim, he literally leapt out of his chair.

Walking Tim back to her office, Heather made small talk. This made Tim nervous and gave him the feeling he was not going to like what he was about to hear. When Heather closed the door behind her, she shared her news.

The coroner's report was in and so was a lead on the identity of Jane Doe.

Tim nodded his head and said simply, "ok, what have we got?"

Heather succinctly reported that Jane Doe was believed to be a Ms. Amelia Ann Blake of Cincinnati. Ms. Blake apparently had few relatives; none of them close, and had last been seen at her job on the 13th of February.

"Tim, have a seat. Have you ever heard of Amelia Blake?"

"No, I have never heard of or known anyone by that name. I don't know anyone from Cincinnati for that matter." Tim responded.

"Here's what we know about her to date: Amelia Blake worked at a waterfront tavern on the Ohio River, just south of Cincinnati. She was a part-time bartender, part-time server and hostess, and had been employed there for several months."

"So is the identity confirmed? Do they know it is Amelia Blake?"

"We believe it is she, but we will know definitely when DNA results confirm it."

"It seems even more gruesome now that there is a name that goes with the body" Tim said shaking his head. "That probably sounds weird, but while we were calling her Jane Doe, it didn't seem quite as real."

"I understand, Tim" said Heather. "It's not as if you have encountered these situations before. Unfortunately, I have become somewhat desensitized to the morbidity that goes with these cases. While I have no emotional connection with the deceased, I do take my responsibility seriously in finding out how they died and bringing the perpetrator to justice. That much I can contribute, and hopefully prevent this sort of thing from happening again. I feel that I have a responsibility to them *and* to you as my client."

"Thank you."

"Yes, of course. Now as to the coroner's report, I am waiting for a final and complete copy to be sent over to me, but the overall result is that the forensic pathologist agrees that blunt force trauma was the cause of death. I would caution you to recognize that while this is a broad and common cause, it neither condemns nor exonerates you. "

"Blunt force trauma is routinely involved in cases classified as accidents, as well as in cases of suicide and homicide. Almost all transportation fatalities – including those involving motor vehicle collisions, pedestrians being struck by vehicles, airplane crashes, etc. are classified as blunt force trauma. It can be caused by being struck by a firm object, like a fist, crowbar or bat or from blast injuries. One can fall from a height and die from blunt force trauma, so you can see this is a very open-ended conclusion. It's a lot to absorb. Do you have any questions Tim?"

"Not at this time."

"Ok, then I'll continue. With a forensic autopsy, particularly when blunt force trauma is confirmed, the pathologist or coroner look for any 'patterning' that may be evident on the body. The pattern of a wound may well indicate what object was used to inflict the injury. In some cases, blunt force trauma may cause internal lacerations or damage to the soft tissues. It may also cause dislocated or fractured bones. If the forensic pathologist picked up any trace patterning, or if there was additional internal trauma, it will be included in the final report. "

"That's a long way of saying that we have to dig deeper into the official autopsy report to find out exactly what happened to Ms. Blake. It is likely that her death resulted from a combination of external and internal trauma. We will have to wait and see what the full report shows."

"I'm eager to know Ms. Howell."

"I am as well, Tim – I should have the profile of the autopsy in a couple of days. By the way Tim, do you have any friends or acquaintances who may know Amelia Blake – or even a woman named Amelia? I ask because Blake may not be her maiden name."

"I'll give that more thought," said Tim "but I don't recall knowing anyone named Amelia. If I come up with anything, I'll let you know immediately."

"Of course, thank you. I really don't have anything further at the moment Tim. Do you have anything we should discuss or any questions for me?"

"I'm just curious to know if you learned anything at Toy Town."

"Actually, I learned a lot about recycling and reclamation, who has access to the facility, but nothing that has as yet produced results. I have several interviews to go over, but nothing to report yet. I assure you I will let you know if I find anything promising." With that Heather stood and walked Tim out of her office to the lobby. "See you soon, Tim."

"Thanks Ms. Howell." Tim smiled and turned to leave.

No sooner had Tim left her office, Heather received a fax transmittal report with a photograph of Amelia Blake. It had come to her from the Greater Cincinnati Police Department. As Heather perused it quickly, she asked Shirley to request a copy of Ms. Blake's police records – if there were any, and requested that Shirley find out where she banked. She would have to subpoena Blake's bank records.

Sitting at her desk, Heather looked closely at the grainy black and white faxed photo of her latest Jane Doe. She could not help but wonder why no one missed this woman, or if they had, hadn't bothered to report her absence. What a sad state the woman must have lived in.

Brought back to the present with the buzz on her telephone, Shirley was calling to give her an update.

"Heather, the Coroner's office called and said they will be messengering the autopsy report on Jane Doe this afternoon."

"Thanks Shirley. Let me know when it arrives, please? And make an extra copy for me to mark up?"

"Certainly, my pleasure."

Heather returned to the interview transcripts from Toy Town's personnel. This time through she would cross-reference anyone who might have an Ohio connection in their background.

As she poured through the employees' transcripts, nothing really jumped out at her. She then turned to the management interviews and although it wasn't a big thing, it was *something*. There was one middle management level employee who had previously worked in Ohio. He had mentioned it in reference to the procedures' manuals that he had introduced and ultimately implemented in St. Petersburg.

'It was the way we did things in Ohio, and it saved the facility a ton of money'...Edwin Miller had said...

Heather made a notation on her pad to obtain more information about Edwin Miller. And, to avoid singling anyone out, she would request resumes for all of the managers employed at Toy Town.

Picking up the telephone, she dialed Toy Town's office and made the request. After speaking to the Human Resources representative, Heather was promised file copies of each of those resumes.

CHAPTER FOURTEEN

Florida Highway Patrol
Tampa, Florida – April 2000

Nothing was considered routine in the FHP office. Every day something new crept up marring what might have been a great day at work. For veteran officers like Daniel Blair and Darrell Dunn there were special challenges. In addition to their own responsibilities, they were expected to spend time with the less experienced assigned to the Tampa FHP division.

Mentoring young officers had its own challenges. They were typically graduates from college as well as having completed specialized training in their particular field. Frequently the freshly inducted officers resented being shadowed by their more experienced counterparts, and were naïve (or brazen) enough to mouth off.

Both Blair and Dunn acknowledged the authority newbies felt because they now wore a badge. They could recall the sudden sense of power and influence they experienced as a "sworn officer of the law". It was pride on steroids and for some that exuberance lasted for years.

Having had years of experience, a seasoned officer was basically allowed to handle newbie situations in their own way. If a newbie mouthed off, he might end up having to wash the cruiser and wax it by hand, or spit-shine shoes. Some vets even resorted to making them ride in the back seat, while others simply reported them to the chief and let the system handle it.

Daniel Blair basically tried to avoid working with the newbies. He appeared to believe it was a waste of time, and felt he would be better used on patrol alone or partnered with a more seasoned officer. And, because of the harassment issues he had been given more mentoring time rather than less. It was his own punishment for tying up Internal Affairs, even though he had been exonerated in those cases.

Blair, born in New York and coming to Florida after graduating from college, had expressly disliked the cold winters. After coming to Florida ten years ago, he met and married a woman from Tampa. After only four years of marriage, she sued Daniel for divorce stating their marriage was irretrievably broken; a catch-all cause that required little if any pertinent reason. It was the fastest way out of a marriage that two people no longer wanted.

Blair fit the stereotype for a 'high-strung' northerner. While extremely intelligent, he wore his knowledge like a shield but wielded it like a saber. Not prone to back down from a challenge, he was a "leave no prisoners" sort of fellow. He often acted on impulse rather than caution that led to some awkward situations. Bottom line however -- Blair was a good officer and had a positive rapport with his fellow patrolmen.

Darrell Dunn appeared to take everything in stride. He was easy-going by nature and by all accounts enjoyed his career. Working with the younger officers could be a challenge if you let it become one, but raising two teenagers simultaneously was providing first-hand knowledge about what youth assume they know and can do. He felt he was better prepared for the newbies than some of his counterparts.

Dunn had been born in Florida and had wanted to be a police officer for as long as he could remember. He had graduated from college and from the police academy and was well-know and admired by his fellow officers.

Blair and Dunn had developed a professional kinship over their tenure at FHP. It had come from working the same shifts, backing each other up on tenuous situations, and using their individual skill sets to apprehend criminals. Dunn was forever involved in drug busts and Blair was often called to assist. It was the perfect combination of 'good cop/bad cop' – a tactic often used to elicit an admission of guilt or to secure the name of an accomplice.

Unlike most local law enforcement agencies, FHP was more of a one-man to one-car patrol. Training and experience taught them to call for backup when the officer felt it was warranted. Neither Blair nor Dunn risked being overpowered, incapacitated or worse. When a threat was sensed, the backup request was issued without hesitation.

That had been the situation when Blair radioed for backup the night Tim Tyler had ultimately been arrested on homicide charges. Whether sensing danger or just needing corroboration of the situation, an officer will call for assistance. Obviously, Blair wanted another officer on scene, whether or not he had 'sensed' Tim Tyler might give him a problem.

Blair and Dunn had filed their separate but not disparate reports for February 20. Blair's report indicated that he was 'tipped off' by an unidentified informant and raced to the scene on 28th Street North. The tip indicated that vehicles were swerving on the roadway and traveling erratically at a high rate of speed.

Dunn's report reflected his arrival time on the scene. It was within ten minutes of Blair's request. Dunn had also issued a data base inquiry on Tim Tyler's license plate and driving record upon arrival.

Both Blair's and Dunn's reports included the arrest of Tyler, a call for the CSI team to assemble, impounding orders for Tyler's vehicle and a call to the Pinellas County Coroner's office for pick up of the body. Police personnel were on scene until the following morning. The roadway was closed to through traffic – which was standard operating procedure when a fatality occurs.

The incident happened early enough to make the eleven o'clock news. Blair and Dunn had both received telephone calls from the local newsrooms, but referred the inquiries to their Public Communications Officer. That individual had prepared a non-descript press release giving only the basic information known at the time of the release. Tim Tyler's name was not given to the media, nor was there any description of the contents found in the bag.

CHAPTER FIFTEEN

Heather Howell's Office
Tampa, Florida

Having recognized the enormity of the information she would need to gather for this case, Heather opted for a second opinion as to how best to handle it. She picked up the phone and was pleased when she heard his voice on the other end of the line.

"Matt Winters".

"Matthew – it's Heather. I'm glad I caught you answering your own phone!"

"Well, Ms. Howell, it happens to be 6:30 pm here in Gainesville, and I'm relieved that it isn't Mrs. Winters calling to remind me of that. What are you up to?"

"I need your opinion on a case – a big case. Let me tell you about it…"

Heather related her well appointed, but abbreviated synopsis of the Tim Tyler case to Matthew. After he asked a few questions and got some clarification on a few points, he affirmed Heather's suspicion that she needed help on the fact-gathering, and could use input from another investigator on the findings.

"I wish I could clone Pete Sutherland" said Matt, "but he's one of a kind."

"Would you run this by Pete and see if he has a recommendation for me? He may know someone in the Tampa Bay area that could be useful."

Matthew, with his humor intact answered, "I will, but you know that means that we're all in this case together. You'll have to send me a couple of dollars to retain me and now Pete. Can you handle that?"

"Bill me and I'll process it" teased Heather. "Thanks."

"I'll talk with Pete tomorrow and one or both of us will call you back, post haste. Goodnight Heather."

CHAPTER SIXTEEN

Barbara Blake – Mother of the Deceased
Covington, Kentucky
April 2000

Uniformed officers of the Covington Police Department rang the doorbell of Barbara Blake's home. Mrs. Blake came to the door promptly, and seeing who was on the other side of the door opened it and said "Is there a problem?"

The officers asked to enter the residence, and sitting with Mrs. Blake told her that her daughter, Amelia Ann, was deceased.

Staring intently at the floor, Mrs. Blake asked what had happened to her daughter. The officers gave her little information other than the body had been discovered near St. Petersburg, Florida and had been identified at long last through dental records.

"You should tell me how this happened," Mrs. Blake said, "I have a right to know."

"You do Mrs. Blake. At this time all we are at liberty to say is that she died of suspicious circumstances which are under investigation in Florida."

"And her body? Where is Amelia's body?"

"Ms. Blake's body is currently at the Coroner's office in St. Petersburg, pending completion of the autopsy."

"Autopsy? Who authorized an autopsy? Not me, and I'm the only next of kin she has." Mrs. Blake was agitated and wringing her hands.

"I'm sorry Mrs. Blake, but in circumstances such as this, an autopsy is ordered to determine identity, then the next of kin are notified. There is no other way to handle a 'John or Jane Doe'."

"Well since you are so sure that this 'Jane Doe' is my daughter, I want her remains sent here immediately. And I also want a detailed explanation of what happened to her – from the chief of police in St. Petersburg and the chief of police here. Do you understand?"

"We will contact the Coroner's office on your behalf ma'am and have Amelia's body returned to any mortuary you choose."

"Leave your cards and telephone numbers. I will contact the funeral directors and let you know where my daughter should be sent. Now if you would leave me alone with my questions, angst and disbelief, I would very much appreciate it. I'll see you out officers."

CHAPTER SEVENTEEN

Autopsy: Jane Doe NKA (now known as) Amelia Blake
Tampa, Florida
Heather Howell's Office, April 2000

While not her preferred reading material, particularly first thing in the morning, Heather Howell grabbed the autopsy report as soon as it hit her desk. She perused first the highlights and then the detail.

The main things Heather looked for initially was protocol – was the body encased in a body bag or evidence sheets for transport; were photographs taken before the body was removed from the wrapper; was there a record of evidence immediately taken off the body, i.e., hair samples, fingernails, fibers, paint chips or other foreign objects collected; and had an x-ray been taken while Jane Doe was still encased?

These things were imperative as crucial evidence could be taken from the body if done in a timely manner. This too, was the responsibility of the coroner, and should anything be left out, it could have an effect on the findings.

Next, Heather looked for the x-ray report and saw it was there. She scanned the general description of the body: white female, brown hair of shoulder length, brown eyes, approximately 32 years of age and no recognizable birthmarks or tattoos. Heather noted that the body had indeed been fingerprinted, and an additional set of x-rays had been done of the teeth to assist the authorities in determining identity.

She noted that the coroner had taken "scrapings" of tissue matter from underneath the victim's fingernails. No further explanation was given as to its origin nor was there any additional description.

Next would be the internal examination – not to be read by the faint of heart. Heather did not skip a word, fearing she might miss something that the forensic pathologist had not missed.

Reading about the dissection of the organs, the detachment of the larynx, esophagus, various arteries and ligaments was inconsequential. Severing all the organs' attachment to the spinal cord as well as the bladder and rectum, the pathologist could then remove the entire organ set for closer investigation. Heather noted that organs were weighed and tissue samples taken. These would subsequently be viewed under a microscope and their significance would be indicated in the conclusion of the report.

Before moving on, the pathologist reported that Ms. Doe was apparently pregnant at the time of death. Based on size and composition, the fetus was approximately fifteen weeks along in development.

The contents of the stomach were examined and weighed. This indicated that Jane Doe had been dead for merely hours prior to discovery.

The skull was examined and after cutting away the scalp, the skull was cut open, exposing the brain. The brain was then removed and examined. Examination of Jane Doe's brain showed definite signs of trauma. The skull had been struck by a long cylindrical object, leaving behind deep tissue damage to the occipital portion of the brain. The autopsy showed that the spinal cord had remained intact, but the membrane known as the *tentorium* (a membrane that connects and covers the cerebellum and occipital lobes of the cerebrum) was partially severed.

Heather made this note in the margin: *The simple translation here was that Jane Doe's brain was only loosely connected to the spinal cord after the initial blunt force trauma occurred.*

Reading further, Heather noted the process had taken approximately four to six hours, including the paperwork she was reviewing.

CHAPTER EIGHTEEN

Forensic Pathology & Autopsy Report
Dr. Edward Moray, MD, Pathologist

"Jane Doe, a 32 year old, pregnant white female died as a result of blunt force trauma. Ms. Doe had progressed approximately fifteen weeks in pregnancy, and based on several factors including stomach and intestine contents, rigidity and lividity, the time of death was mere hours prior to discovery."

Ms. Doe died as a result of having been struck with a cylindrical object that appears to be between eighteen and twenty-four inches in length. The circumference is most likely between one and one half inches to two and one half inches, and based upon the impression, is most likely made of heavy wood or iron. The force of this object cracked the skull, partially severing the tentorium membrane, thereby loosening the brain from the spinal cord, and allowing movement of the brain within the skull cavity. This would not however, in and of itself, necessarily cause or result in *immediate* death."

"There are two events that should be noted: 1) Ms. Doe may have been alive at the time she was placed in the black garbage bag. The insult to the body, accompanied with restricted air could have resulted in her death; and 2) Reddening of the skin occurred with abrasions to the lower back, buttocks and legs, without ecchymosis (bruising) indicating that some severe impact of these areas most likely occurred post mortem."

"One of the greatest challenges of an autopsy is in examining the wounds, and the case of Jane Doe is no different. Homicide cases like this one demand careful and thorough examination of the injury that caused death. Due to the lack of further physical evidence, the official ruling from this office must be blunt force trauma from an unknown source with the characteristics, size, dimension and shape as noted above. These findings are represented by the clear imprint marking on the nearly severed tentorium. The following photographs of the brain of Jane Doe reflect the markings and impression left by that cylindrical object."

Attachments: X-rays of brain, fetal position in womb of decedent, and organ photographs.

Opinion

Time of Death: Body temperature, rigor mortis, plus stomach contents approximate the time of death between eight and twenty-four hours prior to this examination. Based on that timeline, death could have occurred as early as 6:00 pm on February 19, 2000 or as late as 9:00 am on February 20, 2000.

Immediate Cause of Death: A) Blunt force trauma; and of note **B)** streaking/reddening/abrasions of torso without ecchymosis occurred post mortem; causation consistent with being struck by vehicle(s).

Manner of Death: Homicide

Remarks: Decedent was approximately fifteen weeks pregnant without apparent complication at the time of her death.

###

Heather's telephone rang and without hesitation she picked it up. "This is Heather Howell"...

"Is this 'the' Heather Howell?" It was Pete Sutherland calling from Gainesville. He was in the office of Matt Winters and had Heather on speaker phone. "You're on speaker with Matt here too."

"Well guys, I was beginning to think you were waiting on that retainer to call me back."

The two men laughed.

"We're actually calling with good news." Matt said.

"Yeah" Pete interjected, "I have a buddy down there who worked as a detective for the bureau. He's semi-retired now, but still as sharp as a tack and according to his wife, needs something to do to get him out from under foot."

Matthew said "That's Pete speak for he'll work cheap and he's thorough."

"That sounds perfect. Who is he and how soon can I get him on board?"

"His name is Steven Oliver Bascom, lovingly known as a real SOB, but only to those who try to hide something from him. I'll give him your telephone number and ask him to contact you right away."

"Thanks Matthew. Thanks to you as well, Pete. I appreciate the referral and am eager to meet with him. Will you two be briefing him?"

"No – since we're non-gratis here, we'll leave that to you."

"Ok, the check is in the mail. Later boys."

Buzzing Shirley, Heather updated her on things to calendar and to request that she get any/all information she could on Amelia Ann Blake of Covington, KY/Cincinnati, Ohio since that positive ID had been made on Jane Doe.

CHAPTER NINETEEN

Amelia Ann Blake
Covington, Kentucky

Named after her great-grandmother, Amelia, and her grandmother, Ann, young Amelia Ann Blake was born a blessed child. Her mother Barbara, at age 35, gave birth to her first and only child. She had not planned to have any children, despite the pleadings of her husband, William.

Barbara Blake was no ordinary woman. She was a school teacher, and married to William (Bill) Blake, a successful politician in Kenton County. By all accounts, the Blake family was considered a part of Covington's upper middle class.

Amelia felt the pressure of success from an early age. Coming from flourishing stock, Amelia knew she was expected to be as good, if not better than her friends, beginning with scholastic performance. She knew that when grades came out, an "A" was expected; a "B" meant she was slacking, and a "C" was an automatic grounding - all privileges suspended.

Although Amelia had a great relationship with her father, good grades were an issue on which he would not bend. While not always in agreement with his wife, Bill Blake held strong to the rules laid down by Barbara. Amelia rightfully assumed his rigidity on grades had everything to do with her mother's influence, and less to do with her own performance.

Amelia was a precocious child, well liked by her teachers. Her classmates vacillated between jealousy and admiration, never quite finding middle ground. One classmate started a rumor that Amelia was adopted, and as if that were a bad thing,

Amelia left school crying that day. The first person she asked about it was her father, running to him for assurance and consolation.

Amused that this old-as-the-hills rumor was still being tossed around in public school, Bill Blake was careful in handling this delicate subject with his daughter. He deftly explained how he planned and prayed for a child for months and even years before Amelia was conceived. He assured Amelia that she was of his own flesh and blood and that she need not worry about hurtful rumors at school.

Amelia was appeased by her father's explanation, but knew that he would share what had happened with her mother. Sure enough, after dinner Barbara spoke to Amelia about it saying, "You should know better than to think that we would have adopted you and not told you about it. You're a smart girl. The next time someone says something like that to you, use your head instead of bothering your father, ok?" The only thing Amelia could do was nod her head.

Having been upset, then relieved at her father's comments, Amelia was now blaming herself for everything that had happened. Her mother was right, she was a smart girl. And she took that to mean that she shouldn't ask her father or mother stupid questions. That was the day she pledged to figure things out on her own – as best she could.

With one unwitting statement, Barbara had negated all of the carefully chosen words he used to console their daughter. Words that meant she was cared for, loved, wanted and blessed. The meaning that resided in Amelia's memory was "you're smart enough to handle it yourself".

Unfortunately, Amelia Ann Blake would never be the same. After internalizing that *message*, she then allowed it to dictate and shape her life. And unfortunately, her mother never intentionally meant to impart that message.

Amelia's father, Bill, died when she was only eighteen years of age. She had entered Mount St. Joseph University in Cincinnati the year before his passing, and was working at the Cincinnati airport as a part-time server in one of the restaurants.

A private, catholic college, Mount St. Joseph University was Amelia's first choice to attend. It was a co-educational college, and was located in an unincorporated community near Amelia's home.

Mount St. Joseph originated in 1920 by the Sisters of Charity of Cincinnati, and had a reputation for high quality education and experiential education. It had long been known for its personalized attention from faculty and staff, and appeared to be the perfect fit for Amelia.

Having not chosen a major, Amelia pursued basic academic required courses and her schedule was quite full. Working part-time had been her decision as well, and was acceptable as long as her grades did not suffer.

Now that her father had passed, Amelia wondered about her future at Mount St. Joseph. Tuition was expensive, scholarships weren't readily available and her future looked ominous. While her concern overwhelmed her thoughts, Amelia opted not to involve her mother.

There was a whirlwind of attention and activity surrounding the days of mourning for the loss of William Blake. Amelia and Barbara were inundated with neighbors and friends who came to their aid in handling chores like cooking, cleaning and serving.

The flags at the Kenton County government buildings were lowered to half-staff in honor of William Blake. The Memorial and High Mass services were at capacity and all county government employees were in attendance. William Blake was interred in the Linden Grove Cemetery on Holman Street in Covington. After an intimate gathering of close friends and family at the Blake home, the public display of grief ended.

Privately, Barbara and Amelia continued to grieve; separately, distinctly. Barbara turned to work for consolation; Amelia turned inward. Feeling lost and abandoned, Amelia began to study less and added extra hours to her part-time position.

Ultimately, Amelia had to leave Mount St. Joseph University and sought full-time employment as a server. Confiding in her mentor and friend Sister Agnes, Amelia pledged to earn enough money to come back and finish her coursework at Mount St. Joseph.

Amelia and her mother were estranged and saw each other only when it was required. One such time was the reading of William Blake's Last Will and Testament at his attorney's office in downtown Cincinnati.

Barbara Blake was positioned across the large, mahogany conference table from her daughter, Amelia, in the attorney's conference room. The stillness was eerie and neither of the Blake women chose to make eye contact with the other.

When William Blake's attorney entered the room, he was accompanied by two other counselors and a stenographer. After expressing the firm's sympathy, to both Barbara and Amelia, they began.

In essence, Barbara Blake was given full right of survivorship for the home, furnishings and one of the family's two automobiles, plus a two-thirds share of the life insurance policy. Amelia would receive a one-third share of the life insurance and one of the automobiles, free and clear of debt. William had set up a trust for Amelia in the amount of thirty-thousand dollars, fully escrowed and redeemable upon her thirtieth birthday.

The attorney then handed Barbara Blake an envelope containing a letter from her husband. Separately, he gave Amelia an envelope believed to be a letter as well.

Papers were fully-executed, being signed by all parties and the meeting was over.

Amelia looked at her mother and simply said, "I will move all of my belongings out of your house this week."

Shaking her head in either disgust, disillusionment or both, Barbara said "Fine."

And within a few days, Amelia went to her childhood home to pack her things and spend a few minutes reminiscing about the good times she had had there. Arriving while her mother was working, Amelia had time to walk through the house uninterruptedly. She smiled as she entered room after room, but wept when she opened the door to the master bedroom closet.

There were her father's belongings: shirts, suits and ties, his golfing clothes and the horribly beat up Cincinnati Red's baseball hat Amelia had given him one father's day. Without regret, she reached for it and packed it among her things.

Packed and ready to leave, her mother Barbara arrived.

"I was just leaving."

"I see. Do you have everything?"

"I hope so; I don't plan to come back. I'll just be going now."

"Sure, that's what I figured you would do; cut and run."

"Mother, I know I'm doing what you want, and it's also what I need to do. I have no doubt that you will be fine."

"If that's the way you want it, I won't say another word."

Amelia walked out of the house brokenhearted.

Several years later and after a handful of jobs working as a bartender and/or server, Amelia Ann Blake took a job as Hostess for the well-known floating restaurant *Mike Fink's*, located on the Ohio River in Covington. This popular eatery and riverfront landmark featured a central raw bar and "riverfront" seating throughout. This job was the most prestigious of Amelia's career, and she was thrilled with her good fortune.

Mike Fink's was a yacht-like restaurant housed in The Showboat Majestic, and moored on the banks of the Ohio River in Covington, Kentucky. Tourists and locals alike enjoyed waterfront dining with a view of the Cincinnati Red's Baseball stadium and skyline of the city.

Reservations were highly recommended and a "wait" was probable even with a reservation. People loved the atmosphere almost as much as the food. Its décor was purely nautical – like that of a fine, old yacht, complete with all the quirks of a ship.

Amelia worked well with the staff, always being courteous to them as well as those who came there to have a cocktail after work, or have a dinner. She was probably closest to Melanie – affectionately called "Mel" – a bartender at Fink's. They were roughly the same age, though Mel had been married and had a child who she was supporting with little or no help from the child's father.

Mel shared the same work ethic as Amelia and often had an after-hours drink together as they worked to close the restaurant. They had become close friends as a result, and trusted each other with their thoughts and feelings on a number of issues, including (of course) men.

Amelia loved her job at Mike Fink's. She made conversation with the guests easily and politely, and had an uncanny memory of names and faces. Regulars and tourists were impressed by her ability to cater to the crowds, and if a wait occurred, Amelia would always make amends by offering free cocktails, complimentary snacks or a discount good toward their next visit.

Amelia was well received and well-compensated. The manager at Mike Fink's knew he had made a wise choice, and constantly received positive reports on her courteousness and ability. Amelia regularly received gratuities from the customers as well.

She was approaching her thirtieth birthday, and financially, she was doing well. Amelia had saved some money, rented a nice apartment in Cincinnati, and now hoped with the influx of money from her trust fund, she would feel secure enough to find a relationship.

Amelia had dated, but had mostly platonic relationships to this point. While she didn't have a strong sense of wanting children, she felt she should consider it now rather than later.

Regardless, there was no one who claimed her interest or aroused her romantic desire making the point moot.

Being raised in the Catholic Church, Amelia knew she had one shot at marriage. She also knew she probably should have children, but feared her own mother's shortcomings would be her own. Currently, Amelia was content with her life, but if someone came along, she would pay attention. Otherwise, she would just keep on doing what she had been; no expectations – no disappointments.

Within a week of making that internal decision, she met him, and everything changed.

CHAPTER TWENTY

Heather Howell's Office
Tampa, Florida
Attorney Notes

Having read and reviewed the autopsy report, two things gave Heather the encouragement she was looking for; the notation that a "cylindrical object" appeared to have caused the blunt force trauma to Amelia Blake's skull and the pathologists' finding on *time of death*.

Taking the size factors into account, the weapon could have been a tire iron, a tool handle, a broken cue stick, a night stick or even a police baton. That list wasn't all inclusive, but each fit the description. In any event, it might be enough to clear Tim of the felony charge he currently faced. But where was the murder weapon, and who had wielded it against Amelia?

The next obvious conclusion was that Amelia Blake was struck by this cylindrical object before she was placed in the black garbage bag. Whether or not she was alive when inserted in the bag still remained unknown. The Coroner's report reflected the opinion that Amelia could have been dead when she was placed in the bag. It was the old adage of 'dead bodies do not bleed'. The report said the abrasions on the torso 'did not cause bleeding' (sic).

But the question about the genesis of "matter" extracted from underneath Amelia Blake's fingernails was not described or defined further in the report. If it included skin tissue, hair or other genetic material, it could indicate that Amelia engaged in a struggle with her attacker. That "matter" could provide the DNA belonging

to the killer. And on the subject of DNA, there was no mention of DNA being extracted from the fetus.

The Coroner's conclusion on time of death certainly worked toward creating at least reasonable doubt for her client, Tim Tyler.

Heather asked Shirley to call Tim and have him come in to see her.

CHAPTER TWENTY-ONE

Meeting with Tim Tyler
April 2000

Heather was smart. She knew that there was still an uphill battle to get Tim absolved of all the charges he was facing, and she never intended to give a client false hope.

When Tim arrived, Heather asked him to sit at the conference table with her. On it, she had placed a copy of the coroner's report, including the requisite drawings that accompanied the document. Giving Tim the "gist" of the report, Heather showed him the photo of the head injury that Amelia Blake sustained. She related the statements about a cylindrical object and told Tim the official cause of death had been determined as this blow to the head.

Tim's eyes lit up. "Then they can't say I did that! I never saw the woman."

"True" said Heather, "but the autopsy can, and may be challenged."

"What do you mean?"

"While the coroner states cause of death as blunt force trauma, and mentions the impression left by a cylindrical object, opposing counsel will no doubt bring up the fact that Amelia may have been alive in that garbage bag, until the bag was struck by a vehicle. The coroner's information alone will not exonerate you."

"But I didn't hit the bag first!" Tim stated firmly. "The garbage truck that was passing the other one hit it tossing it up into the air and down onto my car."

Heather continued. "What we have to do now is find out who was driving the truck – the one that caused you to swerve to the right, struck the bag first and sent it reeling into your car. I've been researching trucks and haulers that frequent Toy Town and I have photos that I want you to review. That may jog your memory.

"I don't know of anything more I can tell you about it." Tim was obviously weary of reliving that night and its ugliness.

"Tim, I want you to close your eyes and envision the events of that night. I want you to tell me what you see in your mind's eye. Tell me anything and everything that comes to mind."

Tim began. "It was dusk. I was driving north. I saw a large dump truck barreling toward me in my lane. He was passing another dump truck and I saw him hit the bag. I hit my brakes and swerved to miss the truck. That's when the bag struck the fender of my car."

"Tim, did you notice anything unusual about the truck that was approaching you? Did you see markings or any writing on the vehicle?"

"Not that I remember. I do remember thinking it was a huge truck – you know, bigger than most garbage trucks that I've seen."

"Good job Tim. That could be helpful. I want to show you photographs of different types of trucks. You look at them and tell me if any of them resemble the truck that caused you to swerve off the road."

"Ok, I'll take a look."

Heather walked to her desk and secured the folder with generic photographs of dump trucks and haulers. Tim perused them carefully. He came to the photo of the EU 4-axle truck with 2 steering axles and he stopped.

"That one – it was like that one."

"You're sure?" asked Heather.

"Yes, definitely I am sure."

"Ok Tim, look at this one, please." Heather showed him the US 4 axle with lift; a more commonly used garbage truck.

"No ma'am, that's not it. That may have been the type truck he was passing, but I'm positive, it was the other one – it was significantly larger than the one he sped around."

"Thank you Tim. Is there anything else you can recall that might help?" Heather asked.

Tim just shook his head.

"If you think of anything, no matter how small, call and let me know, ok?"

"I will, I promise. Thank you for all you're doing."

###

The search for a dump truck had been narrowed, thanks to the photographs. If they were going to prove Tim's innocence, they had to find that truck as well as its driver.

Heather hoped that having Tim's recollection of the type of vehicle would narrow the search significantly. She would elicit Shirley's help in finding out how many of that model was registered in the Bay Area, and to whom they were registered.

Just as she was adding a note to Shirley's To-Do list, she was alerted to a call from Steven Bascom.

"Heather Howell" she said as she answered her phone.

"Steven Bascom here Ms. Howell; I was referred to you by Peter Sutherland and Matthew Winters."

"Yes, sir; I am very pleased to hear from you. Could we arrange a meeting to discuss the particulars of what my office is looking for?"

"Yes, Ms. Howell, I can meet with you at your convenience. I live here in Tampa, and am familiar with your firm."

"Excellent. Does tomorrow morning work with your schedule – say nine o'clock?"

"Perfect. I will be at your office by nine sharp. Thank you. Goodbye."

"Goodbye."

Heather was trying to decide whether to get her hopes up or not. Bascom sounded pleasant enough – polite and to the point. He didn't sound like a clone of Pete Sutherland with his quick wit, but then Pete would never have initiated a telephone conversation with a prospective employer by being witty. She shook her head at her own thoughts, and decided she had accomplished all that she could for one day.

It was time for relaxation and something to eat. After penciling in Bascom on her calendar, she turned out the lights and headed for the parking lot.

Travelling home, Heather opted for a stop at a pub called **Just Us Bar & Bistro** – a popular bar hangout for attorneys, stenographers and process servers. You could occasionally find a judge or two sharing a cocktail there as well. When she walked in the door she immediately recognized her friend Bob Zee sitting at the bar.

"The last time I saw you Bob, you were sitting right here." Heather chuckled. Bob stood, gave her a friendly hug and pulled out a bar stool for her.

"I've actually showered and changed a few times since then. I thought you'd found a new watering hole."

"No, I've just buried myself in work lately."

"Big case?"

"Yes and it seems to get bigger with every passing day."

"Want to chat about it?"

"Want to? Yes. Can I? No."

"Just answer one question – if you can. Is it the murder in Toy Town?"

"Wow. Now it has a name? Yes, that's the one."

"Wish I could help. Your first drink is my treat. Maybe that will help."

"Thanks Bob, you're a dear."

Bob motioned for the bartender and ordered a martini for Heather. "Dirty – shaken, please Melanie."

"Gee Bob; you seem to know all the bartenders by name."

"Yeah, Mel is new. She just moved to Tampa a couple of weeks ago. She's a great bartender – been doing it for years and has worked at some pretty sweet places."

Melanie placed the martini in front of Heather with a napkin and a side plate with two cheese stuffed olives. "Enjoy" she said as she smiled.

"Thank you, Melanie is it?"

"Yes. My friends call me Mel."

"Welcome to Tampa, Mel. My name is Heather Howell, and this is a delicious martini."

"Enjoy Ms. Howell – nice to meet you."

Turning her attention back to Bob, Heather asked him if he knew or had ever heard of a man named Steven Bascom.

Bob said "The name sounds familiar, but I'm not sure I know him. What does he do for a living?"

"I hear he's a retired detective. He allegedly worked for one of the three letter bureaus prior to retirement. I'm meeting with him tomorrow."

"I love the way you say things...'allegedly'... only attorneys talk like that Heather. And I'll bet you say things like that on dates, don't you?"

Smiling and sipping she said, "guilty!"

CHAPTER TWENTY-TWO

Florida Highway Patrol Offices
Tampa, Florida
April 2000

Heather Howell had issued an order of deposition for FHP officers Dunn and Blair relating to the case again Tim Tyler. The receipt of that summons was no surprise to either of them.

The officers conferred briefly about the summons. Dunn appeared to be nonchalant about receiving it, while Blair, seemed aggravated.

"What a monumental waste of my time," said Blair. "This case seems to be pretty cut and dried to me. Why can't they just admit the case report and let us do our jobs?"

"Come on Blair," said Darrell Dunn, "you know the routine. The attorney is trying to make a name in town and from what I hear, she's a by-the-book kind of lawyer – dots all the I's and crosses all the T's. She doesn't want any surprises in court, so she's deposing us. It's not a big deal."

"Perhaps," said Daniel Blair, "but it's just a pain in the butt to rehash what's already in our reports. Besides, I don't think she's going to get him out of this mess without time in jail."

"We'll see" said Dunn. "I'm out of here for forty-eight hours, stay safe. I'm going fishing with the kids. It should be fun."

"Yeah, enjoy."

CHAPTER TWENTY-THREE

Heather Howell's Office
Tampa, Florida

Shirley was actively pursuing all of the EU 4-axle trucks registered in Hillsborough, Pinellas, and adjacent counties in the Tampa Bay Area. So far she had found about ten companies who had one or more of these vehicles licensed.

Reporting her findings to Heather, Shirley added that she had supplied company addresses and telephone numbers.

"Excellent work Shirley," said Heather. "I very much appreciate your attention to detail."

"If you want help contacting them, just give me a script to follow and I will gladly assist you in the telephone calls."

"Thanks Shirley. I'll let you know what I need. By the way, I'm expecting a gentleman named Steven Bascom any minute. Just let me know when he arrives please."

"Trust me" said Shirley, "I can hardly wait for him to get here."

###

Not surprisingly, in Heather's review of the owner's list, she did not recognize even one company name. Then again, she had never had the need to hire a dump truck. That made her think about who *would* have occasion to use dump trucks. They were certainly expensive vehicles to purchase, and her assumption was that if one needed their services only on occasion, one would lease the mammoth vehicle. Her father's voice echoed in her head: *one bite at a time.*

"If" this was premeditated murder, as Heather had surreptitiously decided it must be, then a dump truck and a land fill was a pretty clever means to dispose of "a bag of garbage". That scenario would mean that Tim Tyler was simply in the wrong place at the wrong time. It could have been anyone on that street. And perhaps Tim and his vehicle were merely complications to the original plan.

Heather decided that these telephone calls should be handled personally. Shirley was terrific and very capable, but Heather wanted to note any hesitancy or reluctance on the part of the truck owners.

"Ms. Howell, Detective Bascom has arrived. Shall I bring him in?"

"Thanks Shirley, I'll come out to greet him."

CHAPTER TWENTY-FOUR

Steven Oliver Bascom
Retired Bureau Detective

"Detective Bascom; I'm Heather Howell. Thank you for your promptness. Let's get started." Turning to Shirley, "will you hold my calls while I chat with Detective Bascom, please?"

"Of course, may I bring you coffee?"

Bascom simply nodded his head. "That would be great, thanks" Heather said as she and Bascom took the short walk to her office.

"Please have a seat."

"So Detective, please tell me about your experience and your career."

"Long story short Ms. Howell; I served with the FBI for twenty years before moving to the Secret Service for the last fifteen years. I was and am a detective and have a good record of service with both bureaus. While I am 'retired' I have time to devote to private interests."

"And how much did Pete and Matt tell you about the case I'm working on?"

"When Pete mentioned that you were looking for a detective, he told me you were defending an individual that perhaps was at the wrong place at the wrong time. Quite honestly Ms. Howell I don't generally have much interest in defense work, since my investigative skill was retained by mostly prosecutors. But

Matthew Winters and Pete Sutherland were adamant about me chatting with you before I refused the interview based solely on the side you were representing. I think that's only fair to both of us."

"Thank you for your candor Detective. Let me share the basic scenario with you, and we'll go from there." To prevent any conflict of interest – or sharing any proprietary information, Heather related the story based only on the data that had been made public. "So Detective, you see that my need for your services are great. As for my representation of the accused, I believe justice is best served when excellent detective work is done on both sides of the law. Based on what you now know, what do you think?"

"Ms. Howell, if I may, I'd like to ask you a question or two."

"Feel free."

"What kind of person do you see your client as, and how does he see himself?"

"Interesting question - I see the client as an upstanding citizen – no arrests, no complaints from anyone including his employer – and a guy who wouldn't squash a bug. As for how he sees himself, I'm guessing of course, but he carries himself well and I think most of all, he respects himself and is thankful for his accomplishments. I also believe he knows he's fighting for his life here."

"Thanks. I am interested in pursuing this, and have prepared a brief outline of my fees for service. Please look that over, consider what your thoughts are about me being the person you need, and then give me a call." Bascom stood up and stuck his hand out to Heather.

Shaking hands, Heather said no more and walked Bascom to the reception area.

Shirley waited only a moment before saying, "And?"

"He's qualified and an interesting character. I'll have to think on this for a bit. I'll most likely need another chat with the boys in Gainesville too. But time is of the essence, and he's my best bet. I need depositions done as soon as possible, and I need a witness list in order to subpoena those. Tick tock as they say."

CHAPTER TWENTY-FIVE

Darrell Dunn, FHP

It was somewhat unusual for Darrell Dunn to have two consecutive days away from his duties as a Florida Highway Patrol officer. Even when he got that time, he typically spent it working with some of the newer officers or swapped shifts with one of his co-workers.

Having teenagers was not easy in this day and time. They were so sure they were ready for the world, and Darrell knew better. By the very nature of their age, his two boys "worked" their mother, often forcing their father to override her decisions. Boys had a way with their mothers.

Darrell tried to be fair with the kids. He had seen so much on the streets, and he knew how easily temptation became reality. His parenting style came from the position of avoiding situations where temptation was greatest. Both Darrell and his wife agreed on keeping a tight rein on the boys. They had seen some of their friends' kids get into drugs and alcohol, and wanted to put a preemptive strike on that for their own children.

It was spring break in Pinellas County, and Darrell's kids were excited about the fishing trip their dad had arranged. They would leave early in the morning for a day of charter boat fishing, about fifteen miles off-shore from Clearwater.

That also gave Darrell's wife the rare opportunity of having a day on her own. She not only needed that, but deserved it even more. Being the wife of a cop was tough enough; mother to two teenage boys was just the cherry on top.

A couple of years back, they discussed having another child, but Darrell was adamant that the years of baby making were over. He reasoned that throughout their married life, there had been children. Once these two boys were out of the house, he and his wife could travel, or at least have some quality time to alone.

As Darrell approached their modest home near Clearwater, he thought about his family. He had done everything in his power to keep everyone safe and as happy as he could make them. He hoped it would stay that way.

CHAPTER TWENTY-SIX

Daniel Blair, FHP

Stomping around FHP headquarters, Daniel Blair appeared to be agitated with the world. A couple of other FHP officers asked him where his foul mood came from, but he guffawed and gave them a less than nice hand gesture.

Blair was not a happy guy. He had spent ten years working for FHP and didn't feel he had been treated fairly. While he knew his harassment accusations had a lot to do with that, he did not agree that a simple allegation or two (or even three) should have hindered his career.

He had to have a rookie ride with him today, and that added to his distress. When he was a rookie, he was treated badly and he had followed suit with any rookie unlucky enough to ride with him. But today was different. The rookie who was riding with him was a female officer named Corey King.

What that meant to Blair was that he had to watch his language, his gestures even more so, and that he be mannerly; all this for a female officer. He resented the differences, but had learned through previous accusations that he had to suck it up and be a gentleman.

###

Corey King, age thirty, graduated from the FHP Training Program with honors. Prior to the FHP training, Corey had worked as an assistant in forensics for the Tampa Police Department. She was an attractive, athletically fit woman who came from a family of police officers. She was eager to ride with Daniel Blair, knowing that he was a ten year veteran and had responded to just about every criminal activity. She knew she would learn from this officer and was ready for the challenge.

When Corey was introduced, Blair simply said, "Welcome aboard, let's roll." Thinking that was strange, Corey simply followed him to the cruiser saying, "Yes, sir".

Blair went over the territory they would be monitoring as well as the usual 'hot spots' within that area. Those 'hot spots' included areas where speeders were prevalent, petty crime neighborhoods and areas known to be infested with drug manufacturing and sales.

Corey was a Florida native and knew the areas of their patrol. She shared that information with her senior officer, but got no response.

After minutes of silence, save the police radio, Corey said, "Officer Blair, do you have a problem with me shadowing you?"

Blair simply responded by saying, "No, I'm just not crazy about training rookies. It's nothing personal."

"When I was asked what I expected and wanted out of a senior officer, I told the chief that I wanted to learn from one of the best on the force. I'd say that they must think very highly of you, sir."

Blair couldn't help himself. He laughed.

About that time, a call came ordering them to respond to a non-fatality accident on Interstate 275 just south of Gandy Boulevard.

Corey took the radio and responded "10-4, we're en route".

Base responded "copy that; EMT's and ambulance en route as well."

The travel time was less than 10 minutes, but traffic had snarled on both the north and south bound lanes. Those who weren't directly impeded by the accident were backed up trying to get a view of the wreck.

Blair had in the travel time explained what he wanted King to handle and how it should be done.

King responded, "yes, sir."

King would handle the re-route of traffic, and assist the emergency vehicles in getting into position. Blair would make contact with the drivers and assess the damage, reporting that to King via radio.

Fortunately, there were only minor injuries at the scene of the crash, with only one person requiring transport to the hospital.

Corey King took command of the situation and did an excellent job in sorting out the traffic and routing them around the accident scene. With ease, she assisted the EMT's and ambulance vehicle to the wreck site, and radioed base for two wreckers.

When all was said and done, Blair had to admit this rookie did as good a job as anyone he had ever worked with. He actually complemented her when they were back in the cruiser.

"Thank you, sir" said Corey, "I appreciate hearing that."

CHAPTER TWENTY-SEVEN

Heather Howell's Office
Tampa, Florida

Although Heather had other clients that required her time and attention, this morning she had to concentrate on Tim Tyler's case. That would begin with a phone call to Pete Sutherland about Bascom.

"Pete? It's Heather. Can we chat about Bascom?"

"So you met with him?"

"Yes – and what a character. What's your gut feeling about him as a detective who doesn't want to work for defense but is willing to do so because of *my* take on the client? I can't risk any bias here."

"Look Heather, in the past he has seen a lot of attorneys who were pure, unadulterated ambulance chasers. His experience has shown these types to be unethical or at least shady. Meeting you has no doubt cleared that aspect up for him. He also knows that Matt and I would never recommend him to anyone of less than stellar character. As for a bias, I cannot fathom the man taking an assignment where that would be a problem. He's an ace detective; he's just more of a Colombo than a Sutherland."

"I'm assuming Matt agrees with you?"

"Yes. Neither of us would steer you in the wrong direction Heather. We're depending on you to make us famous!"

"You keep up that dependency Sutherland. It might inspire me. Thank you my friend. I'll let you know my decision. And say hi to Matt."

Heather gave the phone call five more minutes of thought, and then plowed back into the research for Tim's case.

Shirley had found about ten companies that had, used, or leased the EU 4-axle dump truck and she needed to talk with each of them. As she perused the list, she opted to begin with the Pinellas County companies first, since the truck was used in that county.

Her first call turned up nothing. The company had owned two of the behemoth vehicles but had recently sold them at auction.

The second and third calls generated more follow-up as those companies only leased their EU 4-axle trucks. The owners cooperated by sharing the leasing information with Heather. However, neither of the trucks had been leased during the February 20 time period.

The fourth telephone interview was promising. The company that owned the EU 4-axle was *Big Haul* out of Tampa. They specialized in heavy duty equipment rental and leased most of their equipment to builders in the Tampa Bay Area.

Big Haul had leased one of their EU 4-axle trucks to a company called Site Select out of Clearwater. Heather Howell could hardly contain her excitement as she called information for the number.

###

"Good Afternoon, Site Select".

"Good Afternoon. This is Heather Howell calling from Tampa. Could I speak with someone who might have information about an EU 4-axle truck that was leased from Big Haul in Tampa?"

"Just one moment please Ms. Howell."

"Hello. This is Robert Barnes. May I help you?"

"Mr. Barnes, my name is Heather Howell. I am an attorney in Tampa and I am trying to find out some information about the EU 4-axle truck leased from Big Haul. I understand that your company leased one in February, is that correct?"

"Well, Ms. Howell, I would have to look in the files to see if we leased a truck from them in February. I know we have leased from them in the past. May I ask what this is regarding?"

"Of course, Mr. Barnes, I represent a client who was run off the road by an EU 4-axle, and I am trying to determine if this is the vehicle in question."

"I'm not sure that I can readily help you Ms. Howell. But I can assure you that none of my drivers would be involved in a near miss and not report it to me."

"I see. I can get a subpoena for your records if that would be easiest for you."

"Perhaps you could come to our offices and meet with me. Bring your subpoena and we will cooperate, of course. We have nothing to hide."

"Thank you sir, I will be back in touch with you. Good Day."

Robert Barnes had not been uncooperative, and he was within his legal right to request that his records be subpoenaed. She would immediately file a motion with the court.

Heather then re-contacted Big Haul and asked to speak to the owner. She made an appointment for the next day, and intended to get confirmation that they had leased the EU 4-axle to Site Select and the actual dates the vehicle was leased.

Later that afternoon Shirley buzzed Heather to say that the subpoena had been issued for the records at Site Select.

CHAPTER TWENTY-EIGHT

Tim Tyler

Thankfully, Tim was busy at work. The Humane Society spring campaign was named "Give a Chip". All donations given to the center for a two month period would go toward "chipping" each animal that was adopted out of their shelter. The actual cost to chip and register a dog or cat was about seventy-five dollars, but every fifty dollar donation would purchase one chip during the promotion. It was a tax deductible donation, and was a great incentive for those considering adoption that their animal would be readily identifiable if lost or stolen.

Grateful to be busy, Tim spent a lot of time working to keep from worrying about what was happening with his pending court case. He had confidence in Heather Howell, but was discouraged that things weren't progressing quickly enough to suit him.

Now with all the mechanics in place on the Information Technology side of the spring promotion, Tim could actually work more normal hours. He was confident that Tattoo would approve.

###

Tattoo was definitely his man's best friend. Tim was devoted to him and Tattoo's love for Tim was unconditional.

No matter how distracted Tim became, Tattoo brought him back to the here and now. Walks became runs. Blocks became miles, and both boys benefited from this added exercise.

Tim and Tattoo arrived home tired and hungry, but Tim found himself emotionally charged and feeling better about life in general. He hoped he could maintain that air of confidence as the days unfolded.

Several of Tim's friends had called. His closest friends took him out to the Philadelphia Phillies' spring training games held in Clearwater. That was an escape of about three hours, but Tim appreciated the distraction.

Tim knew he was blessed with good buddies and Tattoo. At the same time, he didn't want to be carted off to prison for something he had no part in. His prayer every night was that the real killer be revealed.

Now he had to believe that the truth would prevail and trust that Heather Howell was his best bet in being exonerated.

CHAPTER TWENTY-NINE

Heather Howell's Office
Tampa, Florida
April 2000

Taking a quick look at her calendar, Heather knew she needed to make a decision about Bascom. Listening to her gut instincts, she picked up the phone and called him to offer him the position.

They came to terms on a start date and fee schedule. Bascom would start the following Monday and would bill the firm on a weekly basis.

Bascom and Heather would meet early on Monday for a pickup on the case.

CHAPTER THIRTY

Site Select
Clearwater, Florida

Heather Howell arrived at Site Select's office first thing in the morning. She asked for Robert Barnes, and was told he would be right out.

Heather's stomach was churning even though she had tried to quiet it with yogurt and fruit. She was less nervous than apprehensive. When Robert Barnes appeared, she was a bit surprised that the face did not match the voice. Barnes was a big man who stood about six foot two. His attire was Khaki slacks and a button-down shirt with the sleeves rolled up.

"Ms. Howell? I'm Robert Barnes. Won't you come in?"

Entering Barnes office, Heather immediately reached into her briefcase for the subpoena. She politely handed it to Barnes, who took it and asked her to have a seat. He sat across the large wooden desk from her and perused the subpoena. When he had reviewed it, he used the intercom and asked his assistant to bring in the files on leased vehicles.

"While we wait, would you care for coffee?" Robert asked.

"No thank you. If you don't mind me asking, what does Site Select do?"

"We do what our name implies – help investors, developers, and builders find sites. Beyond that, we offer initial preparation of the chosen site, readying the site for development. "

"So that's why you would have occasion to lease a dump truck?" Heather asked.

"Indeed; it is more cost efficient to lease equipment rather than own and maintain the equipment. We lease probably ninety percent of our equipment."

There was a quick knock on the door, it opened and Robert's assistant handed him the large file.

"Thanks. I'll buzz if we need anything else."

Without opening it, Robert Barnes handed the file to Heather.

"I hope you find what you're looking for, although as I said on the telephone, I will be shocked if any of our operators or drivers would withhold information from me." Barnes said. "I'll show you to an office where you can have privacy going through the files."

"Thank you, that would be much appreciated."

"If you need anything or have any questions, I'll be here. Just let me know."

With that, Robert Barnes led Heather to an adjacent office and closed the door behind him as he returned to his own office.

Heather took a deep breath before wading into this huge stack of lease agreements. The time period on the folder was October 1999 to now. Obviously Site Select operated on a fiscal year of October to September.

After about an hour and a half, Heather hit pay dirt. There was a lease agreement from Big Haul in Tampa for three pieces of equipment; 1 Case backhoe, 1 Ford US 4-axle with lift axle dump truck, and 1 Caterpillar EU 4-axle dump truck. The lease agreement included the serial numbers for each piece of equipment and it ran from February 5 – February 25, 2000.

Heather immediately went to the assistant and asked her to make two copies of the document; one for her use and one for their files as she would deliver the subpoenaed original to the court. She complied and the copies were made.

Heather tapped on the door of Mr. Barnes office, and after hearing a 'come in' opened the door.

"Any luck?" Barnes asked.

"Yes" said Heather, "I found the lease agreement and the length of the lease encompasses the date in question. While that doesn't prove this was the vehicle involved, it warrants further scrutiny."

"I see" said Barnes, "what now?"

"We will have to locate the vehicle by its serial number and then inspect it for evidence. Once that is done, we will proceed as the evidence dictates. I do have a couple of questions of you, if you don't mind."

"Sure, whatever I can do to help."

"Do you keep records of the drivers/operators who handle your equipment?"

"Of course; give me a date and a piece of equipment, I'll tell you who operated it."

"February 20, 2000; the Caterpillar EU 4-axle; and also the Ford US 4-axle – same date." Heather said.

"Just a moment; I'll get that for you."

For what seemed like an eternity Heather paced the floor in Robert Barnes office. When he returned, he handed her a file folder that included the operator's name, address, telephone number, CDL (Commercial Driver's License) number and date of birth for both drivers.

"May I have a copy of this please?"

"That file is your copy. That's what took me so long; I'm not adept at copy machines."

"Thank you. You have been a great help, and I appreciate it very much."

"Ms. Howell, will you keep me updated on this please? If one of contractors caused a problem, I need to know about it. I will temporarily put their services to Site Select on hold, pending this investigation, but I need to know the outcome."

"I promise I will keep you informed. One favor I'd ask, though I have no right to do so..."

"What would that be?"

"That you refrain from sharing this information with anyone until they can be found and questioned? I don't want to lose them before I find him..."

"Done."

Thank you Mr. Barnes, good day."

###

Heather's drive back to her office in Tampa was quick and pleasant. She was impressed that Robert Barnes ran the kind of business he did, and that apparently his record keeping was outstanding. She was actually impressed with the man as well, but now was not the time to go there.

Getting to the office, Heather checked her messages, got a pick-up from Shirley on what had transpired while she was out, and headed for her office.

Once settled, Heather took out the file folder Robert Barnes had given her and noted that in addition to the contractor's CDL license, there was a copy of Martinez's driver's license, issued from the state of New York. Heather shuttered to think she could be looking at the face of the killer of Amelia Ann Blake.

Heather buzzed Shirley and asked if she could come into her office. Within mere moments Shirley appeared notepad in hand.

"I had a very productive meeting at Site Select. They indeed leased a vehicle that matches Tim's description. Additionally, we have the serial number, the name of the contract laborer hired to operate it, and a photo of his driver's licenses – both New York State and CDL. Please make a copy of everything in this folder and let's get started on trying to find the person and the truck. The priority should be Martinez, since he was the AU 4-axle driver."

"Excellent, I'll get the copies and you can let me know what part of the research you want me to handle."

When Shirley returned, Heather opted to dig into the driver's whereabouts, leaving Shirley with finding the truck.

"I'd contact Big Haul – here's the number; they leased the truck to Site Select. We'll need to get a court order to have the vehicle impounded, pending further investigation. Can you facilitate that first?"

"Sure. I'm on it."

The driver's license was issued to an Anthony Martinez, 656 Carlisle Street, Apartment 6B, Syracuse, NY. Date of birth: January 31, 1970. Anthony was listed as 6 feet 1 inch; 200 pounds. The second driver's name was Kenneth Craig of Plant City, FL.

Heather followed her private investigator routine which had proven to be the most thorough and expedient way to find out just about anything – on anyone. And once again, within a matter of hours, Heather was documenting her findings. She had enough information now to pursue a subpoena for deposition, file a motion with the court that would prevent Mr. Martinez from fleeing jurisdiction, and she had added him as a possible suspect in the murder of Amelia Ann Blake.

Heather had retrieved and/or requested: criminal records, arrest records, warrants, police records, jail records and driving records for Anthony Martinez from both New York State and Florida. She had done the same for Craig.

Calling the Prosecuting Attorney was the last thing on her list. She would relish the moment when she would give him another suspect in this gruesome crime. Luckily, he was still in his office.

###

"Good afternoon, Kevin Morrison's office," said the receptionist.

"Good afternoon, this is Heather Howell. May I please speak to Kevin? It is regarding the Tim Tyler case."

"One moment Ms. Howell," as the receptionist placed the call on hold

After a couple of minutes of elevator music, Kevin Morrison answered. "Ms. Howell, what can I do for you?"

"I wanted to let you know that we are filing a motion to have Anthony Martinez of Syracuse, New York subpoenaed for deposition regarding the death of Amelia Blake. The paperwork is in motion as we speak. I'm just giving you a heads up."

"I see. And what can you tell me about Martinez?"

"He was the driver of the dump truck that struck the black bag on the night of February 20, and ultimately ran my client off the road."

"I appreciate the heads up, but this seems a bit farfetched since we know your client struck the black bag that evening – even admitted that to the police."

"I won't waste time mincing words with you Mr. Morrison. You have now been duly advised. The required notice is being delivered to you via messenger. Thanks and have a nice day."

He could do his own research; Heather wasn't about to give him anything more than what she was legally obligated to do.

CHAPTER THIRTY-ONE

Kevin Morrison, Prosecuting Attorney
St. Petersburg/Pinellas County, Florida

Kevin Morrison had an excellent reputation, numerous convictions for the city and county, and held a degree from Stetson Law. By all accounts he was diligent, thorough and left no stone unturned in his preparation for trial.

He was a family man, with a wife and one child, and they resided in the comfortable, upscale neighborhood of Old Northeast in St. Petersburg. One could say that he was a busy attorney who was handsomely paid and well-respected.

Morrison had begun his career as a defense attorney at another firm. He was wooed away by his father-in-law and brought into that firm just in time to take it over.

Kevin Morrison was involved in civic affairs, sat on several boards and championed the relocation and cleanup of St. Petersburg's homeless population.

He was the first prosecutor in Pinellas County to retain a jury consultant; one who noted the psychographic behaviors and actions of potential jurors. He heavily relied on that information in the jury selection process. All in all, this had paid dividends in that he had never experienced a hung jury, or one that failed to return an indictment/guilty decision in favor of his client.

All in all, he was as ethical and honest a prosecutor as one could find. He was confident in his abilities and loved a good battle in court.

While he had no occasion to have experienced Heather Howell's court demeanor, her reputation was stellar. This would make his job even more challenging, and he was looking forward to the opportunity to oppose her in court.

Shirley contacted Big Haul and spoke with the office manager. After explaining the situation, the manager said he would have to call the owner of the company. Shirley informed him that a court ordered injunction was forthcoming, and at that time the truck would be impounded as evidence. She suggested that the owner of Big Haul contact her office at the first opportunity.

The call came a short while later. Surprisingly, a woman named Sophia Newton introduced herself as owner of Big Haul in Tampa. After speaking briefly with Shirley, she asked to speak with Heather Howell.

"This is Heather Howell...how may I help you?"

Sophia Newton introduced herself as owner of Big Haul in Tampa, and explained that she was contacted by the attorney's Paralegal. She then asked for additional information.

"Ms. Newton, the piece of equipment in question has been identified as one belonging to you, and it is a key piece of evidence in an upcoming trial. We will need to impound the truck pending further investigation."

"And you will have my equipment how long, Ms. Howell?"

"That's difficult to say. It will all depend on how in-depth the review of that truck is, and I cannot venture to say how long that might take. It could be days, weeks or longer."

"What that means to me Ms. Howell, is money out of my pocket. Equipment I cannot lease out is detrimental to my business. And specific equipment such as this is normally in high demand. I'm sure you understand."

"While I appreciate your business concerns Ms. Newton, this equipment may have been involved in a homicide. And in addition to impounding the truck, we will be subpoenaing all maintenance and repair credentials you have for the EU 4-axle in question; from purchase to the date of the subpoena."

"Did you say *homicide*?   Of course we will comply with your court order."

When the call ended Heather had the gut feeling that Ms. Sophia Newton had something to hide – whether or not it involved the incident on February 20, 2000 would subsequently show itself.

CHAPTER THIRTY-TWO

Sophia Newton
Owner - Big Haul,
Tampa, FL

Ms. Newton had her own 'gut feeling' as she hung up from the telephone call with Heather Howell. Sophia did not like what was happening, yet she had no control over court orders. This piece of equipment had been more of a nuisance than an integral part of the fleet.

She picked up the telephone to call her 'friend', but hesitated thinking she should not discuss it with him until she knew more.

Sophia Newton's Friend

They met in November of last year and Sophia was instantly attracted to him. She liked everything about him, at least superficially. Tall, dark and handsome – that he was, and he had this mystique about him that she found charming.

Over time, she saw him more and more frequently. He had this way of running into her – on purpose, or so she thought.

He would show up at the bar where she regularly went for cocktails at happy hour. They would always make polite conversation, but nothing more. Eventually he had asked for her telephone number and she had eagerly complied. Then, it took three weeks before he phoned her.

In the meantime, there were no chance meetings, and Sophia regretted giving him her phone number. She knew she should have waited; not appeared too interested.

When the telephone call came, he explained that he had been very tied up with work and even had to make a trip out of town. After his apology, he promised he would make it up to her by taking her to Bern's Steak House in Tampa.

Sophia was on cloud nine; this hunk of a man – and Bern's? What woman could want more?

The evening was perfect. The two of them chatted for hours. Sophia was convinced he was more than mildly interested, and invited him over for a drink after dinner. He left about half past five the next morning.

Sophia was in love – the kind of love that you don't easily get over or ever come all the way back from.

CHAPTER THIRTY-THREE

Tim Tyler
May 2000

As a trial grew closer and little information had surfaced, it became harder each day to maintain a sense of optimism. Although no one mentioned it, or asked Tim questions, he knew the staff at the Humane Society recognized the date was approaching.

When he had last heard from Heather Howell, he was encouraged. He learned that she had found the type of dump truck that he had identified from photos, had the serial number on the vehicle and not only the driver's name, but also his licenses and address.

Tim had never heard the name Anthony Martinez before, and he didn't recall knowing anyone from Syracuse, but Heather Howell was confident he was the driver of the hauler that was facing Tim that February evening.

Whenever the scene came to his mind, it was as if he was reliving it in slow motion. The trucks, the black bag in the road in front of him seemed to be in real time, but that bag hitting the side fender on his car was all slow-mo. Tim could almost hear the thud. When he thought about the contents, it made him sick to his stomach. There was no way he could have avoided contact, and he reminded himself of that constantly, but he could not shake that horrific feeling from his insides.

Heather had urged Tim to avoid conversation about that night, so he honored that by only discussing it internally – which he couldn't seem to stop – or with Tattoo, his best buddy.

None of Tim's co-workers at the Humane Society could wrap their heads around how this could have happened to such a great guy. They respected Tim and he had told them he was not at liberty to discuss it. Sure they chatted about it when he wasn't around, but only to the point of saying it was "awful" that he had to go through this ordeal. Not one of his coworkers could imagine that he was guilty of any wrongdoing.

Tim had asked around the office and among his friends, to see if anyone knew Amelia Blake. Not one of his associates had ever known anyone by that name. It seemed Tim was at a loss as to how he could help himself.

He had found it easier to wrap himself up in work, take long runs with Tattoo, or stay at home. The news media seemed to always be nearby, and Tim had managed to keep his distance from them.

On more than one occasion, Tim spotted a news van or a dark sedan lurking around his neighborhood. He had shared this information with Heather. Now he was wondering if paranoia had taken over.

That evening, Tim and Tattoo enjoyed their run together, and then had dinner in front of the television. Flipping channels until he found sports to watch Tim lay back on the couch and promptly fell asleep.

He was awakened by a vivid dream. Tim's parents, who had both died a few years before, appeared in the dream. They each had one arm around the other with their free arms extended to Tim. In his dream he ran to them and virtually felt their warm embrace. When he awakened, Tattoo was at his side, looking intently into his face.

"Wow, that was a good dream Tattoo," muttered Tim. "I need more of those dreams and less of the others. Let's go to bed my friend."

Tim opted to get on his knees at his bedside and pray. "Father, you know my heart and my innocence. Please help resolve this situation as your will dictates, and help me to handle this as you would have me do. Amen."

He had fretted, worried and realized he had done everything he could do. He had hired the best investigative attorney, told the truth, and now opted to turn all of it over to his higher power. That night Tim had his best sleep in months.

CHAPTER THIRTY-FOUR

Heather Howell's Office
Tampa, Florida

All the paperwork on Kenneth Craig of Plant City, Florida, a driver of one of the haulers meeting Tim's car on the roadway on February 20, had arrived. As predicted, Craig's licenses were up to date and his driving records were clean. Initially, Heather had presumed that Craig might be as innocent as her client; simply being in the wrong place at the wrong time. She had telephoned Craig, who readily agreed to meet with her and help in any way he could. That meeting was scheduled for later in the week.

Heather had reviewed everything that Kevin Morrison had made her privy to, and she was ninety-nine point nine percent sure that the judge would rule that the preponderance of evidence was such that the case would go to trial.

Typically in the preliminary hearing, the prosecutor will give just enough evidence to the judge to get the trial on the docket, without giving away key information to the defense. In this situation, the defense is required to establish *reasonable doubt* in order to secure a not-guilty verdict. This predicted outcome would essentially mean that the Howell team would have to find the real killer, solving the murder to insure Tim Tyler's freedom. In essence, the beginning of a legal chess match between the prosecution and the defense would begin in earnest.

While the preliminary hearing was the prosecution's "stage", Heather hoped that Kevin Morrison would give the defense something. That was a long shot, knowing he held things close to the vest, but she hoped to get lucky. At the very least, Heather might get a peek at what was to come and an opportunity to raise questions about what witnesses the prosecution plans to call, and what evidence might be presented.

She knew Morrison would bring up the fact that her client, had admitted to hitting the black bag. She also knew he would inform the judge of the autopsy report showing that the victim died from blunt force trauma. Morrison would likely leave out pertinent details that surrounded those "facts", but that was part of the dance.

Heather and Shirley met an hour or so later and went over everything they had in-work for their client. After going over all pleadings, motions and discovery, everything seemed to be in order on the defense side. Shirley was asked to review all documents from Kevin Morrison's office that had been received and check for any obvious omissions. Neither of them wanted any surprises in court.

Recognizing Shirley's workload and the short time frame, Heather decided they needed additional personnel to deal with all the tasks at hand. She made a call to Stetson College of Law to see what future star needed a job. As usual, luck was on her side and a colleague of hers named George Lewis knew of the perfect candidate. He committed to chat with the student and see if there was an interest level in pursuing the position.

"Great," said Heather, "but I need someone sharp, as well as yesterday."

"I'll call you as soon as I speak with him," committed George.

The next day, George called Heather to let her know he was sending a third year law student over to be interviewed.

"His name is Michael Trimmer and I've set up the interview for this afternoon at three. Shirley cleared that for me, and honestly I'm not sure who's happiest about this, Michael or Shirley. She's got a lot on her plate Heather."

"Thank you George. I look forward to meeting with Michael, and I'll be sure and thank Shirley for helping us both out here. Thanks again for everything."

The following day, Michael Trimmer arrived fifteen minutes early for his interview. Knowing Heather wouldn't mind, Shirley took that opportunity to ask a few questions of her own.

The interview with Heather went well and after consulting with Shirley, Michael was offered the law clerk position. He eagerly accepted and committed to an immediate start.

An email was sent to the newly expanded staff scheduling a staff meeting on Monday morning at 10 a.m. in the conference room. Now that everyone was on board, Heather wanted everyone rowing in the same direction. In preparation for that, Heather began documenting pertinent information on the most pressing case, summarizing the rest of the cases, and prioritizing assignments.

CHAPTER THIRTY-FIVE

Amelia Ann Blake
Pertinent Facts

Heather reviewed Amelia Blake's bank records, finding nothing obvious or particularly odd. She made note of the OB/GYN that Amelia had seen and asked Shirley and Michael to subpoena those records. Hopefully the physician's records would indicate who the father of Amelia's baby was. That individual was obviously a person of interest.

Amelia appeared to be a typical working woman with a modest income, living a modest lifestyle. She seemed to be in good health, seeing both a physician and a dentist on a regular schedule, and appeared to be conscientious about her mode of living.

Amelia's credit card history and credit report turned up nothing extraordinary; she only owed about a thousand dollars at her death, and her payment history was good.

Amelia was an excellent employee, managed her money well and had no outstanding warrants, no previous arrests and no record of any reports of violence, abuse or sexual harassment.

###

The Covington police department informed Beverly Blake about her daughter's death. The report reflected that Mrs. Blake showed no emotion, other than anger over the fact that an autopsy had been preformed.

Subsequently, Mrs. Blake had quietly made funeral arrangements and hired a cleaning crew to handle Amelia's personal effects. The only thing that Beverly Blake wanted from her daughter's belongings was a letter from her late husband and Amelia's father. That item was not found.

Heather had learned that mother and daughter were estranged and had been at odds for years. She wondered why a seemingly normal young woman lived mere miles from her mother, yet had had no apparent contact with her. And, in digging into Beverly Blake's history, Heather discovered the obvious animosity between mother and daughter centered on William Blake; husband and father.

Heather had to question whether this animosity was significant enough to cause a mother to kill her daughter, or *have* her daughter killed.

Thus far in the investigation there was no apparent link between Beverly Blake and Anthony Martinez, who drove the larger truck. There was no apparent connection between Martinez and anyone other than his employer, Robert Barnes, and Sophia Newton who owned Big Haul.

Heather Howell's list of possible suspects was growing, but no clear-cut connections were available – yet.

Anthony Martinez; Syracuse, NY – operator/driver of EU 4-axle
Kenneth Craig; Plant City, FL - operator/driver of Ford 4-axle
Toy Town Employee/Manager Edwin Miller; St. Petersburg, FL – formerly of Ohio
Sophia Newton; Tampa, FL – owner of Big Haul

Robert Barnes, Clearwater, FL – Rented equipment for Site Select from Big Haul
Beverly Blake; Covington, KY – estranged mother of Amelia Blake
John Doe; Anywhere – father of Amelia Blake's unborn child

Others on scene:
FHP Officers: Daniel Blair/Darrell Dunn
Tim Tyler; Client

As Heather reviewed her list she could not help but wish she could remove Robert Barnes from the suspect list. He was cooperative to a fault and she did not get any vibe that made her suspicious. He had to be included since he hired the driver/operator of the EU 4-axle. She could not leave any stone unturned.

That thinking led her back to the Toy Town Manager - Miller. She would review her notes on him to see if there were other connections to Ohio and therefore anyone on her list. She pulled the file on her interviews at Toy Town and the subsequent reports she had extracted from personnel.

A couple of hours later, a fatigued Heather Howell pulled out a poster board and started making a diagram of the suspects. There had to be a connection that she hadn't realized, and putting it on paper might help.

Creating a diagram of a crime scene was a practice Heather started early in her career. It was particularly useful in investigative matters, but often helpful in pulling seemingly obscure details out in the open. Sometimes those minute details provide the most meaningful leads.

Edwin Miller, the middle-manager from Toy Town, had worked in Ohio. Looking again at his resume Heather noted that he worked at a plant near Cincinnati. He had been employed at Toy Town since 1998, and was specifically responsible for procedures writing and adherence.

Digging deeper into Miller's resume, Heather found it interesting that one of his professional references was Daniel Blair of the Florida Highway Patrol. While she thought that a bit odd, it seemed unremarkable, but this was a connection that had to be explored.

As she sifted through the other applications and resumes from Toy Town, there was nothing that seemed to connect with Ohio, Cincinnati or Northern Kentucky. So how and where did FHP officer Daniel Blair and Edwin Miller connect? That was the next mission, and thankfully she could check this from both sides. This would be a natural first assignment for Bascom.

Kenneth Craig was yet another piece of the puzzle and Heather would depose him once all the paperwork was in order. Her one chat with him left her with the impression that he was not involved, but this was not the time to assume anything.

Heather left these notes for the staff meeting:

- Set depositions for: Edwin Miller, Toy Town and Kenneth Craig, Hauler/Driver, and;

- Anthony Martinez – has not responded to subpoena and may require extradition.

- Look into the background of FHP Officer Daniel Blair; may have a connection to Ohio and/or Edwin Miller.

- Investigate Sophia Newton's background; admittedly just a hunch/gut feeling that she may have something to hide.

- Ditto background on Beverly Blake – depose?

- Review deposition schedules for everyone.

CHAPTER THIRTY-SIX

Just Us Bar & Bistro
Tampa, Florida
June 2000

Heather stopped in for a post happy hour cocktail and some bar food. Even though it was 7 o'clock, there was Bob Zee seated on his usual stool at the bar. They waved to one another and Heather sauntered over taking a seat next to him.

"Why Ms. Howell, it appears that you need sustenance," Bob said while turning to the bartender with a wave of his hand.

"Gee Bob you're a quick study. Does it show?"

"Yeah, you look pretty tired. All work and no play makes Heather a dull gal."

"True – and heard a time or two before. I'm happy to see you Bob and I'll try not to let all that flattery go to my head. I am ready for a martini though. Who's bartending?"

"Mel's here. She'll be over in a minute."

"Order for me please? I suddenly feel the need to go freshen up. Dirty martini made with Tito's please."

When Heather reached the ladies room she had to agree with Bob. She looked tired and took the opportunity to refresh her hair and lipstick, and adding a bit of bronzer to her cheeks. By the time she reached the bar, her drink was waiting for her.

"Hi Ms. Howell" said Mel. "Hope your drink is ok."

"Please call me Heather – and the drink looks wonderful. Thanks."

As she sipped the shaken not stirred concoction of vodka and olive juice, Bob shared the content of his day.

Bob Zee had recently retired from a long stent as an engineer in a plant that supplied equipment to the military. While he had never said so, Heather knew that this company supplied more than 'standard' operating equipment to our armed forces. His secrets were his; hers were hers. They had made great friends.

Bob Zee was a regular at Just Us, as were his two drinking buddies, Allen and Jimmy. The three of them always sat together at the bar, rehashing 'the war' - the state of the world at any given moment and discreetly evaluating the females who frequented the place. By the end of happy hour, the three would disperse, often leaving only Bob Zee to defend their territory until the next day.

Heather realized she had drifted away from Bob's conversation without meaning to do so, and she couldn't blame the two sips of vodka for that.

"I'm sorry Bob say that again? It's been a long day and I'm trying to stop focusing on work. I just drifted back there without meaning to."

"Heather Howell, you have to separate work and play. You work harder than most everyone I know, but you don't play as hard as you work. Take my word for it – and I have a couple of years on you – you have to balance the two."

"You are absolutely right my friend. I've been on fire for my career ever since I landed in Tampa Bay. And as soon as this case is resolved, I'm going to take some time off."

"Another drink Mr. Zee - Heather?"

"Yes for both" said Bob.

"And I'll need some munchies please" Heather asked.

"Here's our bar menu Heather. I'll be right back." Mel said.

Mel returned with the drinks and asked for Heather's food order.

"Crab-stuffed mushrooms please, and a side salad."

"Are you dating anyone Heather?" Bob asked.

"What – me - no" said a sputtering Heather.

"You should" said Bob. "It would be good for you."

"Really – and did you have someone in mind for me?"

"Well, no not exactly, but you're a great gal and I'm sure you meet a lot of men who would make suitable suitors for you."

"Suitable suitors...I won't try to say that three times in a row."

The two of them laughed clinking their glasses.

When Heather's food arrived she offered something to Bob, but he declined.

"Everything ok with your food Heather?"

"Excellent, thanks."

"We made great appetizers at Mike Fink's. I haven't tried these, but they look yummy."

"Mike Fink's?"

"Yes, it's where I worked before I moved to Tampa. It's in Covington, Kentucky – on the River just across from Cincinnati."

Heather nearly choked.

"Are you okay Heather?"

"Yes, I'm so sorry. I'm fine – just eating too quickly. Excuse me for a minute please."

Heather made her way again to the ladies room. She made a notation on her cell phone – interview Melanie about Amelia. When she returned to the bar, she took another sip of her martini and asked for her check.

"Heather, you sure you're ok?" asked Bob

"I'm good Bob thanks for the company! I'll see you again soon."

"Here you go Melanie" said Heather "and if you don't mind me asking, what's your last name?"

"Of course – it's Sergeant, like an officer" she said smiling. "I'll be right back."

A thousand thoughts were running through Heather's mind as she waited to sign her credit card slip. When Mel arrived with it, Heather quickly signed it telling Mel she would see her again soon.

Saying so long again to Bob, Heather tried not to show her enthusiasm over this find. As soon as she arrived at her home, she made notes in her computer about the encounter. She would ask Bascom to check out Melanie Sergeant – formerly of Cincinnati and determine whether or not she and Amelia Ann Blake had indeed worked at the same restaurant. For Heather, Monday couldn't come soon enough.

Heather tried to relax and unwind but to no avail. She tried everything from television to the great book on her nightstand, but the only thing she could think about was the possible connection between Amelia and Melanie. She pulled her laptop from the floor to her bed and opted to look for Melanie on some of the social media sites.

There she found Mike Fink's restaurant with some photos of Mel working the bar and a few candid shots of Mel with others. Heather did not see any photos that appeared to include Amelia.

Switching to the restaurant's website, she found no employee photos, just the typical menu, hours of operation and marketing information.

Heather then did a search on Amelia. She had an account on one of the social sites, but it offered very little information. Heather felt a positive vibe for that because it meant that Amelia wasn't the type of young woman who posted her activities for the world to view. She feared that many young people were divulging too much information that predators could easily take advantage of.

Realizing how quickly time had passed while she was surfing the internet, Heather opted to turn off the computer and try to sleep. And, while it took her some time to quiet her mind, she did so by saying her prayers – a typical bedtime ritual for Heather.

CHAPTER THIRTY-SEVEN

Daniel Blair, FHP
Tampa, Florida

Daniel finally had a couple of consecutive days off and decided spending them alone wasn't what he really wanted to do. While he didn't have a steady girlfriend, he did have a casual relationship or two.

After his divorce – which he deemed as unfair and ugly – Dan vowed not to allow any future relationship to get serious. Besides, his fitness and good looks afforded him many opportunities to meet and ask out any number of women.

Since moving to Tampa, the only woman he had 'dated' for any length of time was a *friend with benefits* kind of relationship. Daniel was quite happy with that arrangement – no strings, no pressure – and she seemed to understand his position on their interactions.

The two had met at a local bar during happy hour. Daniel liked her looks – she was a professional and ran her own company. They had easy conversations about their common interests. He liked the fact that she listened to him when he talked. Daniel decided early on that this woman was more likely his intellectual equal than the other women he had met, and that was a plus in his mind.

Sophia was a bit forward with Daniel, but that only fed his ego. She was not the first or the last woman who had come on to him.

Enjoying the 'game', Daniel backed off a bit when Sophia became a little too attentive. He made it a habit to run into her occasionally at the bar where they originally met, but not so often that he became predictable.

Daniel Blair was anything but predictable. While enjoying being in control, he loved the hunt and avoided too much contact with any one woman. He was an 'all things on my terms' kind of guy, and if a woman didn't like that, he would find one who did.

After playing cat and mouse with Sophia for a few months, Daniel found her at happy hour, bought her a few drinks and asked for her phone number. She eagerly provided work, cell and home phone numbers.

It was about that time that Daniel got a phone call from an out-of-town friend who needed his help. As he thought back on it now, that was a turning point in his life – a disruption he didn't need.

After returning from the trip, Daniel phoned Sophia. He sensed her hesitation and opted to appease her with a night on the town. That took care of any inkling of dissatisfaction she had with their relationship. They went out, had a great evening and he spent the night with her in her condo.

Deciding that had been a while back, Daniel chose to call her.

Sophia answered and again sounded less than enthusiastic about his call.

"Hey – do you have plans tonight?" Dan asked.

"Well – I'm surprised to hear from you. It's been a while."

"You know my line of work – it's been nuts lately. I finally get a couple of days off and call you, and you're ticked with me?"

"No Daniel, I'm not ticked at you – I've just missed you. I actually thought of calling you a couple of weeks ago, but decided I'd wait and see what happened."

"Are you interested in a bite to eat and a movie?" he asked.

"Sure, we can do that."

"Great; meet me at CDB's at 6:30 pm. You can leave your car there and I'll drive us to the movie."

"OK; see you there."

After he hung up the phone, Daniel shook his head. He was aggravated by her attitude. *'Women'* he said aloud.

CHAPTER THIRTY-EIGHT

Howell Legal Services & Investigations
Tampa, Florida

The staff meeting began with Shirley ushering everyone into the conference room. Getting together for the first time, Heather asked everyone to introduce themselves and briefly talk about their area of expertise. She began, setting the tone and pace for the rest to follow.

Shirley introduced herself as Paralegal and Office Administrator, Michael as a Law Clerk and third year law student at Stetson, and Bascom as a Private Investigator. Although not present or on staff per se, Heather briefed the group on both Peter Sutherland and Matthew Winters, who were retained colleagues and advisors on the firms' largest case.

Shirley described the firm's new computer calendar that encompassed all deadlines by case. In order to more accurately track and bill for time, the firm asked that all progress notes and billable hours be updated at least daily on that calendar.

Heather welcomed everyone and thanked them for their interest in the firm. She announced that there would be regular morning staff meetings on subsequent Mondays to assure that all deadlines were being met and a general pick up on each case would be shared.

Thoroughly but succinctly Heather described each case and gave an update on where the case stood. As she reviewed the status of each, she gave specific assignments to the staff along with their deadlines. The bulk of the updates and assignments were regarding Tim Tyler's case. Heather gave the staff a brief summary of the particulars in the case, reminding everyone that confidentiality was paramount.

Heather then announced that she would be looking to hire an experienced Legal Accountant and asked the staff for any recommendations they might have. "If you know of a good accountant, have them send a resume to me as soon as possible. Shirley will continue to work on billing and general office administration until an accountant is secured, and I would like to find someone as soon as possible. A special thanks to you Shirley, for wearing so many hats around here."

Turning back to the group, Heather said "If there are no questions, we'll be adjourned. Let's make it a great day."

Steven Bascom stayed behind to speak one-on-one with Heather. The two of them moved to Heather's office where they went over the particulars on Timothy Tyler's case.

Mentioning the possible connection between bartender and the deceased, Amelia Blake, Heather requested that Bascom dig further. She related how she knew of Melanie, and that there was a good chance the two women worked together at Mike Fink's Restaurant in Cincinnati.

"So you didn't question Ms. Sergeant at all?" Bascom asked. When Heather told him she did not, he was pleased. "You did the right thing. Now that I'm on board it is better that I handle this potential witness." Heather nodded in agreement.

"I'll proceed immediately with her background" Bascom said, "and will meet with her as soon as possible. Perhaps she will know more about the dead woman's relationship with her mother too. I believe we need to check her out as well."

Heather, while in total agreement with this plan of action, was compelled to offer Bascom her compiled list of information on each person of interest. "I believe you will find this helpful, and once you've reviewed it you will no doubt have a clear direction on next steps. I'm not a micro-manager, Mr. Bascom, and I hired you because you know what you're doing and how to do it. I simply want you to be privy to what we have garnered to date." She pushed the dossiers across the desk.

"Thank you Ms. Howell."

"Heather, please."

"As you wish, Heather, Bascom is fine for me."

Taking all the information on the Tyler case, Bascom made his way to his office. It was certainly nicer than he had expected, though he didn't plan on spending a lot of time in it. He was more of an explorer. His job would take him wherever it led, but this was a nice base to work from.

Steven Bascom spent most of the rest of the morning digesting the information Heather had given him. She was nothing if not thorough – and just as Matt and Pete had told him. That made him happy because it meant he didn't need to start from scratch or redo what she had already done. He decided that Winters and Sutherland had attached him to a winner, and no one liked winning more than Bascom.

Bascom jotted his own notes in the margins of the pages of material. One of his notes was a suggestion that he *and* Heather return to question Edwin Miller at Toy Town, and that they should give that a priority only second to Melanie Sergeant. He would attempt to talk with her today.

Having worked for the Bureau out of the Tampa Bay offices, Bascom was more than mildly familiar with Just Us Bar & Bistro where Melanie worked. He decided to drop in around lunchtime to get a bite to eat and create an opportunity to meet Melanie.

With Heather's description fresh on his mind, Bascom immediately recognized Melanie Sergeant. He hesitated for a moment, and a greeter asked if he wanted a table for lunch. He opted for the bar, and she said he had his choice of seats there.

Timing was everything in this business, and Bascom did not intend to question the bartender about anything. He just wanted to get a fix on what kind of person she appeared to be, and he would form his plan beyond that.

Melanie immediately made her way to Bascom and while wiping down the bar in front of him asked what he would like to drink. He ordered a club soda with a lime. She placed a luncheon menu in front of him – pointing out the day's special and said she would be right back with his drink.

She seemed to fit the description planted in his mind by his boss, but he'd give it the lunch hour. Besides, he needed to be back to the office for the afternoon's depositions.

CHAPTER THIRTY-NINE

A Deposition Primer

A deposition is a process whereby witnesses provide sworn evidence, and are used to gather pre-trial information. Typically, a deposition will provide insight into what the witness may know as well as to preserve that testimony for later use in court.

The person being deposed (the deponent) is under oath and must answer all questions posed by the deposing attorney. In any deposition, counsel is present – though not required - along with a court reporter that provides a verbatim transcript of everything asked and answered.

Deposition questions vary on a case by case basis, but most attorneys have a "go-to" list of standard introductory questions, basic background questions and preparation questions.

Heather Howell's top 10 deposition questions are:
1) Have you ever been arrested?
    If yes – Have you ever been convicted?
2) Have you ever been deposed before?
    If the answer is yes – Howell follows up later with prior deposition particulars; (Have you ever testified in court? Have you ever been a plaintiff or a defendant in another lawsuit?)
3) Have you ever seen my client before the events that relate to this lawsuit?'
4) Did you meet with (opposing counsel) prior to this?'
    If so, she asks the number of meetings, where they were held and the length of those meetings.

5) Have you signed any written statements, made any recorded statements or spoken to anyone else – including the press about this lawsuit?
6) Did you read any witness statements or listen to any recorded statement, view any diagrams or photos, or were you read any statements prior to this deposition?
7) Please tell me everything you did to prepare for this deposition.
8) Was there anyone else present when you met with your lawyer?
9) How did you find/hire your attorney?
10) Do you have your driver's license with you, and may I see it?

Once these questions are completed, Ms. Howell proceeds with introductory questions which serve two purposes. Primarily they are designed to put the witness at ease and secondly, the responses help keep the witness honest at trial.

Introductory Questions

The deponent is instructed to give a verbal response for each question so that the answer becomes a part of the transcript, and are then asked to answer yes, no or I do not know. Once that distinction is made and understood, the following questions ensue.

1) Do you understand that during this deposition you are under oath, and that being under oath means you are sworn to tell the truth?
2) Have you ever had your deposition taken in the past?
3) Do you understand that your responses here have the same force as in a courtroom with a judge and jury?
4) Are you prepared to answer my questions today?

5) Is there anything that will prevent you from giving me your full attention?"
6) Are you taking any medications that will prevent your answering my questions?
7) And you agree to let me know if you don't understand one of my questions?
8) If you need to take a break at any time, just tell me and we will take a break.

Basic Background Questions

Once preliminary responses are recorded, Ms. Howell moves on to specific questions concerning personal information and the deponent's historical background.

Identification

- What is your full name? (Basic question that is necessary to get on the record and distinguish this witness from others with similar names.)
- Have you ever used or been known by any other names? Maiden name?
- Do you have any nicknames, and if so what are they?
- What is your date of birth?
- Where were you born?
- What is your age?
- What is your social security number?
- Is there any mental or physical reason why you would not be able to give accurate and truthful answers to my questions today? (This counters any question of impairment that may be raised in the future.)

Residential History

- What is your current address?
- How long have you lived there?
- Where have you lived previously?
- How long were you at those addresses?
- Why did you move?
- Did anyone live with you? Who? For what length of time?

Marital History

- Have you ever been married?
- What is your spouse's name?
- What is your spouse's occupation?
- Where does your spouse work?
- Do you have children?
- Are they employed? If so where?
-

Educational History

- Where do/did you attend school?
- What level of education do you have?
- What schools or colleges have you attended?
- Did you complete that school? Why not?
- What degrees do you hold?

Legal History

- Have you ever been arrested? When? Why?
- Have you ever been convicted of a crime? (This speaks to the witness's credibility to a jury. Felony convictions and any convictions for fraud, dishonesty or moral turpitude are generally admissible for impeachment.)
- What crime did you commit?
- What was the penalty for your crime?

- Have you ever been deposed before? If yes, have you ever testified in court? Have you even been a plaintiff or a defendant in another lawsuit? (Prior testimony and lawsuits can be a great source of information about the witness as well as potential grounds for impeachment.)
- Have you ever been involved in any other legal claims or lawsuits? When? Where?

Deposition Preparation Questions

The deposing attorney is allowed to question the witness as to how they prepared for the deposition. Ms. Howell's common questions in this vein are:
- How did you prepare for this deposition?
- Are you a party to this suit?
- Have you spoken to anyone other than your counsel about this case? Who? (If another person was present during the meeting, the witness may have waived their attorney-client privilege.)
- What, specifically was discussed?
- What documents including but not limited to drawings, maps, photographs, pertaining to the case have you reviewed?
- Have you ever seen the {plaintiff/defendant/employee/lawyer} before the circumstances related to this lawsuit? (The information uncovered by this question could reveal connections between a supposedly independent witness and the other party in the case.)
- Did you meet with counsel for the other side prior to this deposition?
- Have you spoken with or signed any agreements with reporters regarding the cause in question?
- What social networks do you use? What are your profile URLs? (For witnesses who are heavy social media users,

delving into their person online accounts can offer more information than any other single source.)
- Tell me everything you did to prepare for this deposition?

"Why"?

Most attorneys were taught not to ask this simple question, but Ms. Howell sees "why" as essential at the deposition stage for more information on a specific topic. Answers to "why" often provide a litigator key information that can be used to your client's benefit. It may help identify potential leading questions to use at trial or even get to an insight into opposing counsel's strategy. If the explanation is not helpful, then it's likely that the opposing party will present the "why" during their case. This also provides an excellent opportunity to impeach the witness if he or she changes the story at trial. The exception to this rule is that you should not ask "why" in depositions that will be used in lieu of live testimony at trial.

"Is that all?"

Asking this question prevents witnesses from adding information to their answers later without facing impeachment of their deposed testimony. Ms. Howell asks this question anytime she wants to cap the explanation as stated in the deposition; i.e., the witness gives an answer that is specifically helpful to her case. The risk in asking the question is that the witness may clarify the answer to your client's detriment.

CHAPTER FORTY

Deposition Schedules
Offices of Howell Legal Services & Investigations
June 2000

Scheduled for deposition today was Kenneth Craig, a thirty-five year old who drove haulers for a living and was reportedly on scene at the time of the Tyler incident. Craig was a local operator/driver and well-known by leasing companies who provided both driver and truck on a job by job basis. Basically Craig was a hauler for hire.

Kenneth Craig was driving the lesser sized vehicle on February 20, 2000, and would be deposed today to garner information about the events that he witnessed and/or took part in.

Time permitting, the second person to be deposed today was Edwin Miller, from Toy Town. He was tentatively scheduled for 2:00 pm.

The third deposition would be that of Anthony Martinez; a thirty year old who had to be extradited from Syracuse, NY. Martinez drove the larger truck that allegedly was driving in the path of the oncoming Tyler vehicle, forcing Tyler off the road. Martinez's deposition would be held within the next week, dependent solely on his arrival in Tampa.

Subsequent depositions were scheduled for Florida State Police officers Daniel Blair and Darrell Dunn, Sophia Newton, Owner of Big Haul in Tampa, and CEO Robert Barnes, of Site Select in Clearwater.

CHAPTER FORTY-ONE

Deposition of Kenneth Craig
Offices of Howell Legal Services & Investigations

Kenneth Craig was sworn in. Heather Howell used her "go-to" list of questions, learning that Kenneth Craig was thirty-five years of age, single with no children and had never been deposed prior to this date. He was represented by Cliff Young, Esquire, the company retained attorney for his employer, Florida Haulers of Plant City, Florida.

Mr. Craig's preparation for the deposition had been with his counsel only and he testified that he had reviewed a map showing the location of the incident and that his counsel had read the State Police report to him. He further stated he had not seen Timothy Tyler previously.

Mr. Craig stated that he was a resident of Plant City, Florida and lived for a short time in Lakeland, Florida. He attended University of South Florida and earned a two year Associates degree. He stated that he had attended a trade school where he learned to drive semis and subsequently trained for heavy equipment and haulers. Mr. Craig had gotten his CDL license in 1985. He further stated his record was clear – no arrests or charges had ever been filed against him, and he had never testified in court.

Kenneth Craig stated that he used one social network – Facebook – and his profile was under his own name.

"Mr. Craig, have you ever met or seen Timothy Tyler prior to the circumstances related to this lawsuit? If so, please tell me when and where."

"I've never met him.."

"Do you recall where you were on February 20, 2000?"

"Yes, I was sent on a hauling job in Clearwater, Florida."

"And did that hauling job place you at any time on Florida 28th Street North?"

"Yes."

"Would you explain why you were on that particular road?"

"Yes, I had dropped off the contents of my hauler at Toy Town. I left Toy Town at 5:45 pm according to my sign-out sheet. It may have been 5:50 pm or even 6:00 pm when I entered that roadway."

"And where were you going after leaving Toy Town?"

"I went South on 28th Street North to get on Gandy Boulevard and was headed to Interstate 275, then I-4 east to Plant City."

"Thank you. And did anything unusual happen that night on 28th Street North?"

"Yes. I noticed a big hauler in my rearview mirror barreling down on me. He pulled to the left and was overtaking my truck when I saw a car headed north in the lane of the big hauler. I slowed as much as I could, and moved over as far to the right as possible and said a prayer."

"So the big hauler you mention was larger than your truck?"

"Yes. They're called Cat Four's because they're Caterpillar 4 axle trucks. They're bigger and heavier than the hauler I was driving."

"Did you notice anything in the roadway that evening?"

"No ma'am, but it's not unusual for there to be trash of some kind all along that roadway. I didn't notice anything out of the ordinary."

"And was the Cat Four in the same lane as the car headed northbound?"

"Yes, when he was trying to pass me."

"So, let me be clear Mr. Craig. Did you see a car, driving in the northbound lane – the same lane – as the Cat Four?"

"Yes."

"And was there a head-on collision between the two vehicles?"

"No, ma'am. The Cat Four cut back in front of me when I moved to the right."

"And did you see anything that happened after you moved your hauler as far to the right as you could?"

"I didn't see anything in particular, but I did hear something."

"And what did you hear?"

"I heard two distinct thuds."

"Like a crashing sound?"

"No, it wasn't a metal on metal sound. It was two hollow-sounding thuds."

"Did you stop your vehicle to see what had happened?"

"No ma'am, I did not."

"And why didn't you stop Mr. Craig?"

"I knew the Cat Four didn't hit the car, or I would have heard a crash. In hindsight, I should have stopped. I guess I really didn't want to get involved."

"I see. And as you proceeded toward Gandy Boulevard, did you encounter a police vehicle?"

"I did. I hadn't gone a quarter of a mile when a State Trooper was headed north on 28th Street."

"How did you know it was a trooper's car, Mr. Craig?"

"His lights were flashing and his siren was on. He swept by me like a bat out of hell."

"And that was approximately a quarter of a mile from where you heard the two 'thuds'?"

"Yes, ma'am."

"And about how many minutes would that have taken you?"

"I'd say five minutes or so – no more than five minutes."

"You stated earlier that your attorney, Cliff Young, read the Florida State Police report to you, correct?"

"Yes – I didn't see it. He read it to me."

"And did Mr. Young say that he was reading the entire report to you, or simply parts of the report?"

"He did not say how much of the report he was sharing with me."

"Can you recall whether the reading of the police report included the date and time of the incident?"

"Not that I recall."

"Would you say the reading did or did not include those details about the accident?"

"I would have to say it did *not* include the date or time of the incident."

"Thank you Mr. Craig. This concludes your deposition. We appreciate your cooperation in this matter, and you will be advised of any further steps we will be taking. If you are needed in court you will be so advised."

###

Walking back to her office, Heather Howell thought back through the deposition she had just taken. It had gone as expected with no surprises. Mr. Craig seemed to be genuine, honest and forthright with nothing to hide. He had been contrite about not stopping at the scene and Heather felt he would be a good witness for trial.

As she entered her office Bascom was right behind her. He had witnessed the deposition of Kenneth Craig.

"Come on in Bascom. Give me your take on the testimony you heard."

"It appeared that Craig was telling the truth. He didn't fidget or seem to be nervous. I noticed that he dropped his head – as if to say he was ashamed – when you asked why he didn't stop. That told me a lot about the guy."

"I agree Bascom, and I have to say I don't think he had any further involvement in this other than being in the wrong place at the wrong time. Is that your take?"

"Yes, and I think he gave us some good information on 'timing'. He pointed out the sign-out time from Toy Town. Wonder if Mr. Anthony Martinez left Toy Town immediately after Craig or if he was just 'barreling down the street' and ran up on Craig?"

"Good thought. I marked that in my notes as well. Looks like you and I think alike on those things. Good work Bascom."

"Thanks, I'm just trying to fill in the gaps."

"Bascom, remember Craig said it could not have been five minutes between the encounter with the Cat Four and seeing the FHP en route with sirens and lights?"

"Yeah and my first thought was that FHP must have had a 'vision' about an accident. There would have been no time to call the police between when the event occurred and when the police arrived on scene."

"And the official report from FHP said the hotline received a call at 6:05 pm from an 'unidentified source'."

"Sounds fishy to me" Bascom said. "Who's next, Miller?"

"Yes. We're set for 2:00 pm."

"Great. That gives me a chance to grab a bite to eat. You want something?"

"No, but thanks for asking. I have lots of notes to review and I'll have something at my desk."

Shirley had placed the firm's file on Edwin Miller on Heather's desk. She had also ordered in a salad and some iced tea for the boss.

Edwin Miller was being deposed in the Tyler case because Heather had found an Ohio connection between Miller and Amelia Blake. It was a stretch, and Heather knew it, but any link was worth looking into. She predicted no complications with the upcoming deposition, but reviewed Miller's resume and her notes from their previous conversation at Toy Town.

Being a visual person, Heather was sketching out a diagram of sorts with possible connections. While she had done this earlier, she was now honing in on 'probabilities' rather than just coincidence or possibilities.

Edwin Miller was linked, albeit loosely with FHP officer Daniel Blair, who had provided Toy Town with a positive character reference on Miller. Miller *could have* a connection to Amelia Blake or her mother, Barbara Blake, as they all had been living in the greater Cincinnati area during the same periods of time.

The deposition questions to Mr. Miller were designed to flush out those associations and clarify any links between those individuals.

Miller had a secure position at Toy Town, and had worked there since 1998. So far, he was the only staff person from Toy Town to be subpoenaed for deposition.

Bascom tapped lightly on Heather's office door. "Got a minute?"

"Sure" said Heather, "come on in."

"I just want to let you know that I discovered a connection between two of our upcoming deponents: Daniel Blair and Sophia Newton. They have been seeing each other for a few months now."

"Interesting - Sophia owns Big Haul."

"Yes, and she and Daniel started dating around the end of 1999."

"Thanks Bascom, you've just earned your pay. We'll talk again after this deposition. Is there any further info on Miller and his connection to Blair?"

"Just that when Miller left Cincinnati, he was actually 'let go' by his former employer. It appears that he reached out to Blair because he was a highly respected FHP Officer, and Miller thought that would ease him into Toy Town. It obviously worked."

"And Miller has been at Toy Town for a couple of years now."

"Yes, with an unblemished record."

"I'm sure you are planning to dig deeper into the link between Miller and Blair" said Heather, "but I'd also like to know more about the relationship between Ms. Sophia Newton and Patrolman Blair."

"Next on my list – oh and we also need to talk strategy on Melanie Sergeant and her connection to Amelia."

"Next on my list – now let's go depose Edwin Miller and see what other gems we find."

CHAPTER FORTY-TWO

The Deposition of Edwin Miller
Offices of Howell Legal Services & Investigations

Edwin Miller was sworn to tell the whole truth, and nothing but the truth.

He appeared at the deposition wearing a suit and tie. After Heather explained how the deposition would work, she began by asking "Have you ever been arrested, and if so, have you ever been convicted?"

Edwin Miller squirmed a bit in his chair, looked over at his counsel who simply nodded, and then replied "I have been arrested twice and was convicted once."

"Please state for the record the reason(s) you were arrested and elaborate on which crime resulted in a conviction."

"I was arrested and convicted for driving under the influence. I spent one month in jail and received counseling. The other arrest was bogus."

"For the record Mr. Miller, we need to know the nature of the arrest."

Miller again sought his attorney's advice. His counsel again nodded, indicating he should answer the question. "I was arrested and charged with laundering money."

"And what was the resolution on the money laundering charge?"

"The charge was dismissed before the case went to court."

"Is that all there is in relation to that charge?"

"Yes."

"Have you ever been deposed before?"

"No."

"Please tell me everything you did to prepare for this deposition."

"I met with Mr. Carlson – he is the attorney who represents Toy Town. He simply went over the basics of how a deposition works, and instructed me to answer truthfully and succinctly."

"Fine, let's move on. If at any time you need to take a break, just let me know. Please state your full name for the record."

Coming out of the deposition answers, Miller was forty years old, born in Ohio and lived in the greater Cincinnati area most of his life. He had been married once, but had no children. Miller said the marriage lasted only five years. He had attained a college education, majoring in business administration from Ohio State.

"How did you come to work for Toy Town Mr. Miller?"

"I lost my job in Cincinnati in a cut-back. While I wanted to stay in the Cincy area, there were no jobs there that met my qualifications or pay grade. I applied for many positions including the job at Toy Town."

"And exactly what duties do you perform at Toy Town?"

"I am in charge of procedure creation and compliance."

"Can you give us an example of what your duties entail, please?"

"Of course," said Miller. "Most every large company has a set of procedures they expect their employees to follow. I write those procedures, they are approved or revised by management, and once approved they are enacted. It is also my responsibility to see that our enacted procedures are followed. If and/or when they are not, I must report the infraction and the employee(s) who are responsible. They are then dealt with by management."

"And have you always operated in this capacity at Toy Town?"

"Yes, I was hired specifically for my expertise."

"When procedures are established, are they reviewed by top-level management, a team of executives or by whom?"

"Since we are a site that accepts waste materials, our procedures are examined and approved by local and federal government, OSHA and various EPA representatives. We must follow their respective guidelines for safety purposes."

"When you applied to Toy Town, were you required to provide professional and personal references?"

"Yes, three to five of each."

"And was one of your professional references your former employer in Cincinnati?"

"No."

"May I ask, why not?"

"My former employer did not give references after the downsizing of the plant."

"And what about personal references, Mr. Miller?"

"I provided Toy Town management with the names of people I was closest to who also knew of my professional abilities."

"And was one of those an individual named Daniel Blair?"

"Why yes, Daniel was a reference for me."

"Great. And tell me how you and he know one another."

"Daniel used to visit me in Cincinnati when I was married. My wife and I met him at a Cincinnati Reds baseball game and became friends. After my divorce, Daniel would often stay with me when he came to town. We've known each other for years. When I mentioned Toy Town he told me he knew exactly where the plant was. I asked if I could use him as a reference and he agreed."

"How often did Mr. Blair visit you in Ohio, and what was his business there?"

"He had friends there – a girlfriend or two – and one of his male friends had complimentary access to Riverfront Stadium's Guest Boxes."

"Do you recognize the name of Amelia Blake?"

"No. I don't know that name."

"Do you know a woman named Barbara Blake?"

"No, I do not."

"And have you had occasion to visit with Mr. Blair since you came to St. Petersburg in 1998?"

"Sure – we go out occasionally for drinks or dinner."

"And I must ask you if you know that Daniel Blair is a Florida Highway Patrolman?"

"Yes."

"And did he tell you that he was the reporting officer on the night of February 20, 2000 in regards to this case?"

"No ma'am. I am not aware of that. He never told me."

"And did you ever mention to Daniel Blair the fact that you were being deposed in regards to this case?"

"Absolutely not."

"Mr. Miller, for the record and I am reminding you that you are under oath, have you read any statements, viewed any diagrams, maps or photos or been given any information about this case prior to this deposition?"

"No."

"Last question: have you and Daniel Blair ever discussed anything about this case?"

"Mr. Miller – I need a response from you."

"The only thing Daniel said was that this was a slam dunk."

"Thank you Mr. Miller. If we require anything further, we will be in touch. If you are called to testify in court, you will be regarded as a hostile witness because of your association with Daniel Blair. Thank you for your time."

Heather Howell was not impressed with Edwin Miller or his corporate counsel. There were several areas in the deposition where she expected an objection from him, but got none. Either he was incompetent or he didn't care, but she was happy to have garnered some insight into the link between Miller and Blair.

Bascom was pacing outside her office when Heather approached.

"Wow" said Bascom. "We've got some work to do."

"Yes – like who were Blair's other 'friends', particularly the 'couple of girlfriends' that Miller alluded to. That's the end of today's depositions. Rest up my friend, we're on tomorrow for a couple more. Would you mind closing my door? I need some time to process all of today's revelations."

"Sure boss, I'm out of here. See you tomorrow."

CHAPTER FORTY-THREE

Toy Town
St Petersburg, Florida

Edwin Miller wasn't happy with his deposition. He returned to his cubicle at the site to find several messages waiting for him. He reviewed them, returning the internal call backs and then sat staring at the telephone. He knew that once Daniel Blair got word of his testimony he was in for the tongue-lashing of a lifetime – maybe worse.

Prior to the deposition, the attorney from Toy Town had told Miller that if he chose to lie or withhold information, he would be discovered for doing so and faces charges. Background research – even poorly done – would show his previous charges, as well as his association with Blair. Rather than face perjury charges, he had complied.

That didn't change his situation now. He opted to sleep on things and take some action tomorrow. Blair of all people knew that one couldn't lie when giving a sworn statement, and he had been subpoenaed for the deposition. He would figure something out – he had to – and he knew he needed to be proactive with Blair.

On the ride home Miller thought about Blair, but also about his former employer and not having been forthright with Toy Town about how that job ended. The site's attorney now knew about it and Miller was sure he would share that information with Toy Town's upper-level management. This situation was spiraling out of control.

Edwin Miller parked in his garage that evening, left the car running and lowered the garage door. His lifeless body was found the next morning when a neighbor heard the engine running and called the local police.

CHAPTER FORTY-FOUR

Heather Howell's Office

Bascom was the first to report Miller's untimely death. Heather appeared to be unmoved by the news.

"You know Bascom; he seemed to be the type that couldn't handle the truth."

"I've seen it many times Heather, and even so, I look at suicide as a most selfish act."

Heather nodded in agreement. "I think we should plan on entering his deposition as testimony at trial. The contents are important enough to share with the jury, and Miller's link to Blair is clear. The elephant in the room will be Miller's statements about 'girlfriends'. I don't know where we can go with that."

"We don't know *yet*, but I assure you if there is a way to find out who Blair was seeing, I'll find it." Bascom said.

"Thanks Bascom – I'm counting on your expertise."

"Now, can we chat about Melanie Sergeant? I would like to meet with her one-on-one and get a better handle on what and whom she knows. Depending on what I learn, I may ask you to join us for a subsequent chat. Does that work for you?"

"Of course – that's fine with me. We'll need to decide whether or not to depose her, and our time is transitory."

CHAPTER FORTY-FIVE

Deposition of Robert Barnes
Offices of Howell Legal Services & Investigations
June 2000

Heather Howell stood to greet Robert Barnes as he entered the conference room where his deposition would be taken. She told him she appreciated his time and cooperation, and asked him to be seated. After Barnes was sworn in, Heather began as always by explaining what a deposition was and how it would be administered.

As Howell had suspected, the preliminary questions were unremarkable. Barnes had been deposed prior to this case, but only in the realm of Chief Executive Officer of his business, Site Select in Clearwater, Florida.

Of his own choosing, Mr. Barnes was not accompanied by counsel. He stated he had met with no one prior to the deposition and that he was not acquainted with Ms. Howell's client.

Robert Barnes stated that he was forty-five years of age and had been CEO of Site Select for nearly ten years. He earned his Master's Degree in Business Administration at the University of South Florida, was widowed and had two adult children; a son who worked for Site Select and a daughter who lived in Tampa and worked for BB & T Bank. Both children were unmarried.

Mr. Barnes stated that he had never been charged with a crime or arrested for any reason.

"For the record Mr. Barnes, would you tell us what Site Select does?"

"We search for sites that might be of interest to investors, builders and developers. We then assist them in land preparation; clearing, leveling and prepping the land for its intended use."

"Mr. Barnes, is it true that your company hires CDL licensed drivers or operators of large scale hauling trucks?"

"Yes, we do."

"And for the record could you share with us how that hiring process works?"

"We have chosen to lease equipment on an as-needed basis rather than invest in the equipment itself and find that to be most cost effective. We have a group of equipment companies that we work with on a regular basis, and those companies are chosen based on the specific need(s) for readying the site."

"Mr. Barnes, do you lease only the equipment per se or do you also have your equipment supplier also provide drivers and/or operators?"

"Most of the time the driver or operator has a contract with the equipment company. In so doing, the leasing companies take responsibility for up-to-date CDL licensing and permit to operate."

"Thank you. When Site Select leases equipment such as a backhoe and a dump truck, your company chooses the size or style of equipment, is that correct?"

"Yes."

"And when the equipment is leased, is there a written contract between Site Select and the equipment rental company?"

"Yes."

"Does that rental agreement include make, model, serial number and condition of the equipment?"

"Yes absolutely."

"Mr. Barnes does Site Select use an equipment company named Big Haul of Tampa, Florida?"

"Yes, we use them regularly."

"Is the name Sophia Newton familiar to you?"

"Yes, Ms. Newton is the owner of Big Haul."

"Am I correct in saying that a subpoena was issued for your records from January 1, 2000 to February 28, 2000 for all heavy equipment leased from Big Haul?"

"Yes, that is correct."

"And in reviewing those records is it also true that Site Select entered into a lease agreement with Big Haul in Tampa for three pieces of equipment specifically; 1 Case backhoe, 1 Ford US 4-axle with lift axle dump truck, and 1 Caterpillar EU 4-axle dump truck?"

"That is also correct."

"Mr. Barnes, those lease agreements included the serial numbers for each piece of equipment and it ran from February 5 through February 25, 2000, correct?"

"Yes, that is correct."

"Was Site Select made privy to the driver or operator's name by each piece of equipment? "

"Yes, along with their CDL license numbers and/or certifications for operation."

"Do you happen to recall the driver's name of the Caterpillar EU 4-axle dump truck?"

"Yes, his name is Anthony Martinez."

"Thank you. And is it also true that my office requested that this Caterpillar EU 4-axle be inspected for damage before it was returned to Big Haul?"

"Yes. I received an order from the Pinellas County Court that required me to have the dump truck thoroughly inspected for damage."

"And what were the findings, if any, of that inspection?"

"There was damage to the front grill."

"Can you be more specific?"

"The grill covers the front of the truck and showed evidence of damage to the center portion of the grill cover and some denting on the front of the hood. The center of the grill was broken."

"Mr. Barnes, was this damage evident when you leased this vehicle?"

"No, there was no damage when we leased the vehicle. We take photographs of all rental equipment; much like a car rental facility does – to show any existing damage."

"Are you in possession of those photographs?"

"I am."

"And did you discuss the damage to the vehicle with Big Haul?"

"We did. Big Haul assumed responsibility for the damage, releasing us from all liability."

"Thank you Mr. Barnes. If we need additional information from you, we will be in touch."

Kevin Morrison, Prosecuting Attorney for Pinellas County had been among those present for the deposition of Robert Barnes. His office was represented at every deposition, but Morrison had taken a keen interest in attending this in person.

Heather Howell made it a point to personally thank Barnes as he was leaving the conference room.

"You have been extremely cooperative and my office appreciates your time Mr. Barnes."

"I am happy to help in any way I can. I'm the kind of guy that likes to see justice prevail, regardless of whose shoulder it falls on. And please, call me Robert."

"Thanks Robert."

"I don't want to sound indelicate, but perhaps when all of this is over, we could have lunch or dinner sometime?"

"Perhaps" Heather said with a smile.

Another deposition complete presented Heather with an optimistic attitude. Through the deposition process, she had uncovered some new information and substantiated her belief in the innocence of her client, Tim Tyler. She made a mental note to contact him at the end of today's sessions.

Glancing over her shoulder as she left the conference room, she saw Robert Barnes leaving her office. On a purely personal note she had learned that he was 'available', but forced herself to eliminate those thoughts at this time. Heather had too much integrity to cross the line with a deponent, least of all with this case. She knew her win or loss of the Tim Tyler case could make or break her new career in Tampa Bay.

As usual, Bascom was waiting near her office for her return. She nodded politely at him and invited him in.

"Bascom, talk to me."

"The CEO was definitely a plus for our side. If I didn't know better I would swear that you two rehearsed his deposition. You two had some chemistry going in there that was obvious."

"So much for chemistry – where's the value in his testimony?"

"He named Sophia Newton, had her dead to rites on the damage to the front of the hauler, and by adding that they would underwrite the repairs of same made her look bad. Thankfully the guy's company keeps good records."

"It's thanks to Robert Barnes that we have the name of the truck driver."

"And it will appear obvious to anyone who hears that testimony that Anthony Martinez caused damage to that vehicle."

"Agreed, but I'm not sure Martinez will dispute causing that damage. Obviously he was 'the' driver who sustained damage. The pertinent detail we need to find and prove is that a) he hit the bag first; and b) he purposely pushed that bag into the path of an oncoming car; i.e., our client."

"That's a horse of a different color."

"Indeed and I am trying to figure out 'who' was behind the whole incident. Our client, as well as Kenneth Craig was on the wrong road at the exact wrong time; on that we agree, but 'who' instigated the bag being struck in the first place? How did the bag get there? Was Amelia alive or dead when she was placed in the bag? Was she targeted or a victim of circumstance?"

Heather was pacing now.

"We have to find a connection between Anthony Martinez and *someone else*. I don't think its Sophia Newton, although he's done a lot of work for Big Haul. And unless she convinces me otherwise via her testimony, I don't think Sophia Newton would cook up this scheme on her own," said Heather.

"From what I've learned about Anthony Martinez, it appears he would be incapable of pulling off the perfect crime, much less orchestrate it. We will know much more after his deposition." Bascom stated.

"And so we move toward next week. Martinez is in the custody of the Pinellas County Sheriff and will be brought over first thing Monday morning. My gut tells me this won't be the quickest or easiest deposition I've ever done. If you think of anything between now and then that should be explored in his testimony, please let me know. We don't have much to go on with this guy."

"Will do. I'm having Michael check into his social media accounts as we speak. I'll see how that's progressing and either Michael or I will let you know. We might get lucky."

"I'll take lucky, thanks."

Michael Trimmer was hard at work with two computer screens open. He didn't even notice that Bascom was standing at his cubicle.

"Michael – how's the research on Anthony Martinez coming along? His deposition is scheduled for Monday morning and the boss needs a briefing."

"He's an Interesting character Mr. Bascom. He has a Facebook page, a page on LinkedIn and an Instagram account. I found an account on Craig's list as well, but he hasn't accessed that for a while. He tends to be on Facebook most often. I'm summarizing what I've been able to find out about him and should have that done within the hour."

"Excellent, please share that with Heather as soon as possible."

"Oh and Michael – please print out Martinez's friends list from Facebook. That may provide a link we've been searching for."

"Yes, sir I will."

Michael went back to his computers and started printing out the contacts lists from Facebook, LinkedIn and Instagram. There were two-hundred fifty on Facebook, roughly one hundred on LinkedIn and another fifty or so on Instagram.

Michael cross-referenced the contacts lists, placing them in alphabetical order. He then cross-referenced the messages associated with those contacts and printed them.

Going to Martinez's home page on each site, Michael printed out the information that Martinez had opted to share. They were markedly different.

On Facebook, Martinez listed his birthplace as New Jersey and his current residence in New York. On LinkedIn his place of birth was Rhode Island, and on Instagram his birthplace was said to be New York.

Martinez's postings were markedly different as well. Virtually all of his LinkedIn postings were work related – seeking work, touting his unblemished record etc. His Instagram account was filled with photos and off-color jokes. Facebook was opened daily and its content was milder and more family acceptable. There were a few photos of Martinez and his 'big rigs' as he called them.

Calling up his account on Craig's list generated several "dating/personal ads". His given name, Anthony Martinez, was not mentioned on the site. The photographs he had uploaded bordered on pornographic and the type of dating Martinez was offering was less than conventional. He referred to himself in these ads as "Thor" and listed his attributes as an "experienced no-holds-barred partner".

As a third year law student at Stetson, Michael Trimmer had been exposed to all sorts of personality types, but in his estimation, this guy took the prize.

Michael had been as thorough as possible in reviewing the social media accounts and was as politically correct as possible in reporting what he had found. He hoped what he had uncovered about Martinez would be helpful to Ms. Howell and that she was prepared to review the summary.

Walking down the hall to the boss' office, Michael took a deep breath before knocking on her door.

"Michael, please come in."

"Ms. Howell, this is the report on Anthony Martinez's social media activity. I cross-referenced his contacts and friends from three accounts: Facebook, LinkedIn and Instagram. I found another account on Craig's list that denied me access to his user list, but I took the liberty of printing out his latest ads on that site. They are rather risqué, and I just wanted to make you aware of that before you review the detail. "

"Thank you Michael. I appreciate the report and the head's up. Before I review it, would you mind giving me your take on this guy?"

"As I said to Bascom, this guy is a piece of work. He's obviously living more than one lifestyle – perhaps showing signs of multiple personalities. He is inconsistent in his 'facts' – like his birthplace which you will see is either New York, New Jersey or Rhode Island – or perhaps his real place of birth is somewhere totally different. His postings indicate that he is narcissistic across all of his lifestyles, and my gut tells me that if the guy were ticked off, he could be lethal."

"And other than that Mrs. Lincoln, how did you enjoy the play?" Heather laughed.

Michael smiled and blushed. "My apologies Ms. Howell, my second interest beyond law is psychology."

"No apology necessary. I appreciate your input and I'm sure it will prove helpful. Every good attorney that I know excels in 'reading' people. Some attorneys are so adept at it; they avoid having to hire profilers. So think of your interest as a talent to be honed, and be proud of your innate ability to read between the lines. Thank you Michael."

"If you have any questions, I'm available. Thanks Ms. Howell."

CHAPTER FORTY-SIX

Just Us Bar & Bistro
Tampa, Florida

It was too late to call it lunch and too early to call it dinner, so Bascom opted for happy hour. He walked to the bar and noted that Melanie Sergeant was working.

"I'll have Club Soda on the rocks with a lime, please."

"Here you are Mr. Bascom, and here's a menu in case you want something."

Melanie calling him by name took Bascom by surprise. When she came back to see if he wanted food he asked how she knew his name.

"I try to remember people by their drink and name. The last time you were here you had club soda with lime and paid by credit card. I just remembered it because it is unique and it has a certain 'club' feel to it – club soda – Bascom." She smiled.

"I often make word associations to remember names too. In my line of work, I need to call on all sorts of people, and need to keep their names straight."

"If you don't mind me asking Mr. Bascom, what type of work do you do?"

"I'm an investigator by trade and curious by nature."

"Wow, what kind of investigations do you do?"

"At the moment, I work for Heather Howell. I believe you may know her?"

"I do. She's a nice person. She comes in fairly often."

"Yes, she's a friend of Bob Zee."

"Yes, Mr. Zee is a regular and a peach of a guy."

Noting that he had made a bond with Melanie rather than frightening her, Bascom opted to forge ahead.

"Ms. Howell and I are working on a case that you may be able to help us with if you could spare some time to chat with us. We wouldn't want to interrupt your work, but would gladly meet you any other time you might have available. Would you be willing to do that?"

"I can't imagine how I could help you two, but if you and Ms. Howell need to speak privately with me, I'd be happy to oblige. When would you want to meet?"

"The sooner the better" said Bascom. "When are you free?"

"Let me look at the schedule in back and I'll know when I'm off work."

Bascom hoped he had not frightened Melanie, and that when she came back she would have a window of opportunity to meet.

Melanie was gone for a few minutes, and Bascom was getting nervous. About that time his cell phone rang; it was Heather. He answered, but never got a word beyond 'hello'.

"Melanie Sergeant just phoned me to make sure you were working with me and that we would like to jointly meet with her. I assured her you were legit. Book it anytime other than during depositions - got to go, bye."

Melanie approached Bascom rather sheepishly.

"Forgive me if this offends you, but I had to call Ms. Howell to make sure you were working with her. Not that you would ever do something untoward, but in this line of work, you cannot be too cautious."

"I am not offended in the least, and I think you are very smart in checking out the invitation. Ms. Howell is eager to chat with you, and so am I."

"Actually, I'm off Monday at 5:00 pm – or as soon as my relief bartender shows up. Is that too late?"

"I'll double check with Ms. Howell, but I believe 5:30 pm or so should work out well. We can meet in Ms. Howell's office. If there's a conflict, we will let you know. Does Heather have your telephone number?"

"I gave my number to her just now, but if there's a conflict about Monday, you can reach me here before 5:00 pm. "

"Great" said Bascom as he put a $20 bill on the bar. "See you then."

"Thank you Mr. Bascom!"

CHAPTER FORTY-SEVEN

Deposition of Anthony Martinez
Offices of Howell Legal Services & Investigations
Monday Morning
June 2000

Meeting with Melanie Sergeant was scheduled and Heather was eager to talk with her, but between now and then she would have to conduct the deposition of Anthony Martinez and she suspected he would be a handful.

Reviewing Michael's report had at least prepared her for the 'type' guy Martinez appeared to be, and forewarned is as they say forearmed.

As Heather entertained that thought, her intercom rang with Shirley letting her know that Martinez – along with a deputy – had arrived for the deposition.

"What about an attorney?" Heather asked.

"No, he professes that he doesn't need one." Shirley replied.

"We'll see, won't we? Thanks Shirley. I'll be right in."

As Heather entered the conference room she could feel the icy stare of Martinez, and noted that the deputy that accompanied Martinez was seated at the table next to the deponent who was handcuffed to the chair.

Precluding anything else Heather went on record by asking Martinez about his attorney, stating that it was appropriate for deponents to be accompanied by their legal counsel.

"I am more than willing to allow you the time to have an attorney present, and with any legal proceeding, an attorney will be appointed to you if you cannot afford one. Do you understand Mr. Martinez?'

"I don't need an attorney," was his curt reply.

"Very well; let the record show that Mr. Martinez has waived his right to have counsel present at this deposition."

Preliminary questions were tedious. When asked about his place of birth, Martinez went with New York - specifically Syracuse, where he was currently residing.

"Isn't it true that you have also given your state of birth as Delaware and New Jersey Mr. Martinez?"

"I may have put that on an application or something at some point in time, but I am from New York" Martinez answered.

"And why would you have not provided your correct place of birth on an application, sir?"

"I don't know; I guess I just thought it would look better being from Delaware or even New Jersey. I don't really remember why I would have done it. Are you sure that I did do that?"

"Moving on Mr. Martinez, is it correct to say that you have, in the past been employed by Sophia Newton of Big Haul in Tampa, Florida?"

"Yeah, I was working there, but recently I've been working out of state."

"And could you tell us where you have been working recently?"

"A day-labor contract job in Syracuse."

"Could you explain what you mean by day-labor, and exactly for whom in Syracuse?"

"Day-labor is just that – you're hired for a day to do a job. The calls are from various contractors that need temporary help. We meet at a convenience store in north Syracuse and they pick who they want from those of us who are there."

"So, is it correct to say that you are not currently employed on a full-time basis Mr. Martinez?"

"I guess so. It's kind of hard to find a full-time job when you've been arrested for something you had nothing to do with."

"And what charges are you facing, Mr. Martinez?"

"The ones you cooked up in your mind, Ms. Howell; suspicion of committing a murder that I *didn't* do and I have nothing else to say about it."

Martinez's anger was apparent, and Heather moved forward. "Have you been gainfully employed since leaving Big Haul in Tampa?"

"I told you – just day labor."

"In north Syracuse, New York?"

"Yes."

Moving on to credentials and family ties, Heather learned that Martinez had only a high school education, plus trade school to learn how to operate heavy equipment and haulers. He provided a CDL license that was current.

Martinez said he was divorced and had no children. He also stated that he occasionally spent the night with 'girlfriends' but had no legal or permanent attachment.

"Mr. Martinez, is there any physical or emotional reason that you cannot answer the questions in this deposition honestly and truthfully?"

"Hell no – what kind of question is that?"

"Sir, I remind you that you are under oath and sworn to tell the truth. I am asking if there is any impairment that you might have that would preclude you from telling the truth in this matter."

"There's nothing wrong with me except that this is a waste of my time."

"Have you ever been arrested?"

"A couple of times, but it has nothing to do with this."

"And would you state for the record what you were charged   with?"

"Aggravated assault – but it was bogus."

"And were you convicted of that charge?"

"Yes, but…"

"Thank you Mr. Martinez. Could you tell us when that conviction occurred and whether or not you spent any time incarcerated?"

"It was a couple of years ago, and I spent two months in jail. I was released for good behavior and the rest of my sentence was spent doing community service."

"And the other time that you mentioned being arrested, when was that?"

"When I was twenty-five; I got into a fight in a bar over a woman."

"And were you convicted on that charge?"

"I was released on bail and it never went to court. The bastard that hit me couldn't prove that I started it, so it just went away. Hey – I need a break here. I have to go to the head."

"Let the record reflect that the deponent has asked for a break. We will reconvene in fifteen minutes."

As the deputy and Martinez walked out of the conference room, Heather glanced over at Bascom who looked as though he was a million miles away.

Walking over to him, she suggested they meet in the hallway.

"This guy is a ticking time bomb Heather. I know you're cautious and smart, but I would suggest that you don't poke the bear, if you know what I mean."

"I hear you Bascom, and I agree. I just need enough of his 'guff' on record to show his disrespect and belligerent attitude. When we restart I'm moving to the night of February 20. It should be pretty straightforward questioning."

When the deposition resumed, Heather's first question was in regard to whether or not the name Amelia Ann Blake meant anything to Martinez. He stated that he had never heard of her.

He was then asked to relate for the record his recollection of the incident near Toy Town on the night of February 20, 2000.

"Yeah, I was working a job for Big Haul in Tampa. I had to go to the recycling station and drop off a load from a job site in Clearwater. "

"And do you know what time that drop off occurred Mr. Martinez?"

"Around six, I guess."

"And what were the contents of that 'load'?"

"It was garbage – just garbage."

"And was that garbage bagged?"

"Some of it was bagged, some wasn't. It was trash, you know?"

"What time did you sign out of Toy Town?"

"Hell, I don't know – six-ish – six-thirty-ish."

"Did Toy Town give you a sign out slip?"

"I guess, I don't know."

"And in your own words, can you relate what direction you went when you left Toy Town, and what happened after you left there?"

"I was headed back to Tampa – to Big Haul, so I turned right onto the access road headed for Gandy Boulevard. From there I took the Interstate 275 to Tampa."

"And can you share with us what happened as you left Toy Town?"

"Nothing."

"Nothing, Mr. Martinez? Did you or did you not strike a black garbage bag with your hauler after you left Toy Town?"

"Oh – yeah, I guess."

"And what lane were you in when your hauler struck that bag?"

"Southbound lane – had to be."

"Do you remember encountering another hauler also headed south?"

"Oh yeah – a real slow poke. I passed him."

"And when you passed him, is that when your vehicle struck the black garbage bag?"

"Yeah, I guess."

"Do you remember any other vehicle(s) being on that roadway at that time?"

"Yeah – a four-wheeler."

"By four-wheeler, do you mean an automobile – a car?"

"Yeah, that's right."

"What do you remember about the car you were approaching?"

"He swerved like hell to get out of my way, that's about all."

"And what do you recall about the black bag?"

"There's always trash on that road. My guess is it falls off trucks and nobody cleans it up. When I hit it, all I know is that it went flying up in the air."

"And did you know that the black bag struck the approaching automobile?"

"No – I don't think so. I don't remember."

"Why were you driving in the left lane?"

"I was passing this other hauler."

"Did you recognize there was oncoming traffic when you opted to pass the other hauler?"

"I saw a four-wheeler, hit my brakes but then realized I had time to get around the slow poke, so I sped up again to pass him. "

"Once again, did you see the black bag in the roadway?"

"Well, I guess – maybe. Like I said, there's always stuff in that roadway."

"And you remember striking that bag with your vehicle?"

"Yeah, I guess so."

"Mr. Martinez, for the record – and I am reminding you that you are under oath – do you know anything about that garbage bag you admittedly struck with your vehicle that you have not told us about?"

"Not that I remember."

"One last question for you Mr. Martinez, did you deliver that black bag to Toy Town, or did you leave Toy Town with that black bag?"

"How the hell would I know that?" Martinez smirked. "I don't inspect the bags that I haul."

"Thank you Mr. Martinez, that will be all for now."

The silence in the room was palpable. Bascom nodded to Heather and motioned for them to meet outside the conference room.

"He's lying like a cheap rug Heather."

"I know. I also know he is no dummy. He avoided all the right questions, and gave me the 'I guess' and 'I don't know' answers that couldn't be challenged in a deposition."

"He's withholding information – information that is critical and pertinent, and I think he's protecting someone besides himself."

"I agree Bascom, and I'm wondering who."

"I'm on it boss."

"Let's put our heads together to review his deposition. I'd also like to include Michael Trimmer since he did such an exemplary job of preparing me for this character. Can you arrange that while I put a rush on the transcript?"

"Sure – consider it done."

Heather was perplexed but then there was a multitude of thoughts and scenarios going through her head right now. She also recognized that she and Bascom had a scheduled meeting with Melanie Sergeant that she needed to prepare for. She also wanted to call Matthew Winters and Pete Sutherland to update them on the latest information. But first – above everything else – she wanted to have a few precious minutes alone in her office, uninterrupted and undisturbed.

Walking toward her office, she stopped by to ask Shirley to arrange those precious minutes for her. Shirley gladly agreed and offered to bring her some tea. Welcoming that thought, Heather thanked her.

Heather closed the blinds, walked to the couch she rarely used and sat down. As soon as Shirley brought the tea, Heather propped up her feet and closed her eyes. She stilled her thoughts and forced the calmness that was typically hers to return. She maintained that stillness for about five minutes. When she opened her eyes, she felt transformed, refreshed and more than ready to tackle her 'to-do' list.

Allowing the light to again filter in the room, Heather buzzed Shirley and said simply, "thanks – I'm open for business".

In less than five minutes Shirley delivered a rough transcript of Martinez's deposition. She thoughtfully provided three copies; one for Bascom, one for Trimmer and one for Heather.

A tap on the door resulted in Bascom and Trimmer, ready to review what had transpired in the deposition earlier that day.

"Gentlemen, come in – take a seat and a copy of Anthony Martinez's deposition. Let's review it together, and as tedious as it sounds, let's go line by line please."

Almost an hour later, the three completed reviewing the Martinez deposition. They were all in agreement and had independently and collectively noted the red flags in the document.

Bascom was the first to say that the bulk of Martinez's 'don't know/don't remember' answers had to do with the black bag.

Michael Trimmer hypothesized that Martinez may have purposely planted the bag in the roadway.

Bascom challenged that by asking why then he (Martinez) would then hit it?

Heather said "because there's always garbage on that roadway" – isn't that what Martinez kept saying?

And Bascom replied – "to make sure the contents of that bag wasn't alive."

And Michael interjected – "and that he wasn't the only one who struck the bag."

"Plausible guys, but how would he have placed the bag in the roadway without being seen?"

"He could have had the bag on the hood of his hauler. If he did and he stopped the truck suddenly, the bag would most likely slide onto the roadway. That way he'd never have to touch it." Michael said.

Both Heather and Bascom looked at Michael, then at one another.

"You may just have something there Mr. Trimmer" said Bascom. "Remember Martinez said he was going to pass the other hauler – saw a car – hit his brakes suddenly and then realized he had time to pass? That could have been the moment the bag made it onto the road."

"It's a bit of a stretch" said Heather, "but I would suggest that the three of us give this more thought tonight. We can reconvene on the subject tomorrow. In the meantime, remember that while Martinez may have had the opportunity to do this, he's not linked in any way to Amelia – or Ohio for that matter. If he did this, someone else was involved – someone hired him to do this. We need to figure out who that was."

CHAPTER FORTY-EIGHT

Melanie Sergeant
Heather Howell's Office
5:30 pm

Melanie Sergeant was on time for her meeting with Detective Bascom and Heather Howell. Bascom greeted her at the door and they made their way to Heather's office together.

Heather stood to greet her and suggested they sit away from the desk area, on the sofa and two chairs that flanked it. In anticipation of the meeting, Shirley had supplied them with coffee, tea and water.

Speaking first, Heather said "Melanie, Mr. Bascom and I appreciate your agreeing to meet with us. I'm sure you have no doubt wondered what this is about, so let me first fill you in on that. We represent a client who has been accused of a homicide. We also believe he is innocent. What brought us to you is that we understand that you know the victim – Amelia Ann Blake."

"Amelia is dead? I had no idea." Sergeant said.

"And we're sorry to have to be the ones to tell you that. We know that you and Amelia worked together at Mike Fink's in Cincinnati." Heather said.

"I'm sorry – this is such a shock. Was she killed in Cincinnati?"

Bascom spoke up. "We're not at all sure where the incident took place Melanie. It could have happened there or here; we just don't know."

"We really want to chat with you about Amelia. We'd like to know what kind of person she was – who her friends were and who she may have been closest to." Heather paused before continuing. "You see Amelia was pregnant when she died, and we have no idea who the father might be."

"Wow" said Melanie. "I haven't seen Amelia in a long time - but when we were last working together, she wasn't seeing anyone that I knew about. I'm not even sure she was dating."

Bascom said, "Would you talk to us about what Amelia was like? It would help us to know more about her, and that could assist us in trying to figure out who might have done this horrible thing."

"Amelia was the best person I think I've ever known. She was sweet and helpful to everyone at work. She was always on time, always willing to work extra shifts or fill in for someone who had to be out. She actually filled in at the bar one day when I had to take my daughter Lily to the doctor. I could always count on Amelia for help."

"And when would you and Amelia have last worked together, Melanie?" Heather asked.

"I left Cincinnati right after Thanksgiving, and she was still working at Mike Fink's then. She was the hostess – why she could have run that place, she knew it so well."

Heather asked, "And how did she get along with her boss at the restaurant?"

"They were good friends and had worked together for a long time."

"And do you think they were perhaps more than friends – outside of working together?"

"No, Ms. Howell – Sam, the manager, was married and Amelia would have never had a relationship with a married man. She is, well *was*, a devout Catholic and would never have even thought about Sam."

Bascom asked – "Can you give us Sam's last name – I'd like to talk with him about Amelia."

"Sure, it's Coburn – C o b u r n."

Heather resumed the conversation by asking Melanie if anyone she knew of would have wanted to hurt Amelia.

"Only her mother" said Melanie quickly, "and I hate to have to say that, but Mrs. Blake is a piece of work. She and Amelia parted ways when Amelia's father died. Amelia told me that her mother wanted her out of the family home, and that she had moved out the day after the will was read. I know that Amelia was really upset by all of it, and that she didn't want anything to do with her mother after that."

"Do you know any particulars about that?" Heather asked.

"Just that Amelia was a daddy's girl, and both of us thought her mother was jealous of all the attention Mr. Blake paid to Amelia."

Bascom told Melanie he was curious about Amelia's social life; was she a social person who went out to different events, or more reclusive?

"The one thing Amelia loved was going to watch the Red's play. Mike Fink's is just across the river from the stadium, and I'd see Amelia glancing over in that direction all the time. She and her father used to go to a lot of the games. It was their little outing together. She even bought him a baseball cap for Father's Day one year and when she moved out, she took his cap with her. It was a bittersweet reminder of Mr. Blake I guess."

"Melanie, other than watching baseball, did Amelia go out to concerts, plays or any other place where she might have met someone special?" Heather asked.

"Amelia worked all the time. She went to Mass on Sundays or Holy Days went to baseball games, home and back to work. She may have met someone at Mike Fink's, I don't know. She was hostess, and as such she met a lot of people. She just never told me there was anyone special. Well – wait a minute, she told me that a guy who she met at a baseball game had come into the restaurant several times to see her. I don't know his name; just that he was an out-of-towner that came to Cincinnati several times for baseball. I think he had friends with box seats or a private suite or something – anyway, she was impressed with him."

"Do you know of anyone who Amelia would have confided in about her relationship with him – or perhaps about her pregnancy?"

"The only person I can think of would be her priest or maybe the nun that she liked so well in college – her name was Sister Mary Agnes. She's at Mount St. Joseph College in Cincinnati."

Heather stood, reaching a hand out to Melanie. "Thank you so much for your time today. You have been very forthcoming and helpful. Mr. Bascom and I apologize for having to tell you about Amelia's death; I hope you understand our motives are sound."

"I appreciate that you two are looking into this. I can't imagine that anyone would purposely hurt Amelia. I hope you find out who did this and that they are punished." Melanie said. "If there's anything else I can do, please let me know."

"Thanks" said Bascom, "I'll walk you out."

Heather heard the front door close and saw Bascom headed her way.

"Long day Heather Howell," said Bascom.

"Yes, very long. I'm heading home."

"See you tomorrow, boss."

Tomorrow would come before either of them was ready for it. Heather opted to go straight home, picking up Chinese food take-out on the way there.

Bascom stopped by Just Us for a drink and some good old greasy food. He knew he wouldn't encounter Melanie, since she had gone home to her rescue her daughter from the babysitter.

Bob Zee was there – in his normal place at the bar. He asked about Heather and Bascom just stated that it had been a long day for both of them.

Bascom ordered a draft beer, a burger and fries. That should knock him out.

CHAPTER FORTY-NINE

Sophia Newton, Owner
Big Haul, Tampa, Florida

Looking at her calendar, Sophia realized that her deposition was the day after tomorrow. She was admittedly aggravated that she had to be deposed and was at the same time eager to put it behind her.

Remembering that her driver, Anthony Martinez had been arrested, arraigned and remanded to Tampa for his deposition, she couldn't help but wonder how that had turned out. Poor Anthony – he just wasn't good at much. Sure, he could handle heavy equipment and was a decent CDL driver with no registered complaints, but he could be a loose cannon.

He had contacted Sophia as soon as he received the subpoena from Howell's office. Try as she might, Sophia couldn't convince him that he had no choice but to comply. When he ignored the summons, he was held in contempt of court and jailed up in Syracuse. Sophia had 'vouched' for him and hired an attorney to get him out on bail. That was where it ended as far as she was concerned.

Martinez had damaged her most expensive hauler in that February incident near Toy Town. The truck was impounded for a good month before she could add it back to the active fleet, and the damage from whatever he hit was extensive and costly.

She would make sure and review all the information she had been given about the damage to the hauler, believing this would encompass the bulk of the questioning directed to her in the deposition. She had already soothed her client, Richard

Barnes of Site Select, by absorbing the cost of the repair to the hauler.

Sophia did not plan to hire Anthony Martinez again. There were lots of qualified drivers/operators locally, and she would hire from that contract pool. No need to ever have to think of Martinez again after her deposition was over.

Now assured that this was concluding, she was happy that she had chosen not to involve her friend. Their relationship had been strained to say the least, and Sophia didn't want to infringe on his time for something she was able to handle on her own.

What Sophia didn't realize was that her friend *was* involved; and in a way that she couldn't possibly imagine.

CHAPTER FIFTY

Tim Tyler
June 2000

Tim had not spoken with Heather Howell for a few days. He made a mental note to call her the following day. He was aware that depositions were taking place and had even been invited to sit in, but Tim's preference was to maintain his presence at work.

Work had always had a calming effect on Tim. He enjoyed what he did and loved working in St. Pete. His parents had always urged him to follow his dream; to work at something he loved which would translate to never working a day in his life. The Humane Society brought him challenges and making things work for them made him happy.

Tattoo was in rare form tonight when Tim arrived home. After giving him the coded command, he ran to Tim and rolled over for a belly rub. It was trust and love all rolled into a gorgeous, brave German shepherd.

Tim Tyler had developed a deep trust in Heather Howell's ability to prove his innocence. She was methodical, fair and diligent. He recognized and admired those traits in her as his parents had instilled the same values in him.

Tim had some moments of angst when his faith was tested. Driving home from work each night brought on its own challenge. He had opted to no longer take that shortcut from Interstate 275, deciding it was safer to sit in snarled traffic than traverse 28th Street North.

He relived those moments more often than he would have chosen, and for some reason today the moments became frequent. Something was nagging at him about that night and he couldn't place what that might be.

After taking Tattoo for a run, Tim opted to eat dinner in front of the television. The only sports airing on the tube was tennis, which Tim liked and Tattoo disliked because of the constant thuds of the ball being hit.

As soon as Tim figured out what was bothering Tattoo, he muted the sound and finished his meal.

Just before heading to bed, Tim took Tattoo out for his evening walk. As they were turning the street corner to go home, Tattoo's ears perked up and he pulled on his leash trying to go in the opposite direction. Tim urged him to heal and follow, and with some reluctance the shepherd obeyed. Within a minute Tim heard the sound of screeching tires and a "thud" which sounded like two cars had collided.

It was a couple of streets over, but Tattoo had either sensed a threat or was suspicious enough to want to go there. When Tim obliged, he and Tattoo came upon a car that had been struck while parked on the street. A young woman was trapped in the car and there was no one around. Tim immediately called 911 on his cell phone for emergency assistance.

When the paramedics arrived, they used an instrument called the "Jaws of Life" to open the driver's side door and extract the young woman. She was unconscious and was immediately transported to the nearest hospital.

The Clearwater Police had arrived on the scene prior to her extraction from the vehicle and were questioning Tim Tyler.

Tim relayed all the information he had which was very little. He did not know the young woman, had not seen but only heard what he assumed was the crash and was unable to assist in providing additional information.

Tim left all his personal information with the police officer and he and Tattoo walked home.

Feeling anxious about all that had transpired yet realizing the time, Tim opted for sleep. Sleep came, but it was restless. Tim kept seeing the face of that young woman trapped in the car. He realized he had no way of learning the outcome of her injuries and said an audible prayer for her complete recovery.

The next morning Tim turned on a local news channel as he readied himself for work. He was listening for any information that might be reported about the woman he and Tattoo had assisted last night. Unfortunately, it was not one of the news stories.

CHAPTER FIFTY-ONE

Heather Howell's Office
Tampa, Florida

Checking her calendar, Heather knew her first priority today was her client, Tim Tyler. It had been a few days since they had spoken, and there was a lot to brief him on.

"Tim, good morning – it's Heather Howell."

"Ms. Howell, you must have read my mind or my 'to do' list. I was just going to ring you. Do you have information for me?"

"I do – actually I have a lot of info to share with you and was wondering if we might get together to review where we are? My schedule is good today, with another deposition in your case scheduled for tomorrow. Would today be possible for you?"

"I'll make it possible. How about this afternoon – say four or four-thirty? If that works, I'll go straight home from your office."

"Then let's say four-thirty. See you then, and thank you."

###

Heather made a list of all the information she wanted to share with Tim. She would brief him on the depositions that had been taken, review the things of interest in the autopsy report, and review the progress the firm had made in analyzing the 'players' in this legal entanglement.

If his schedule permitted, she would ask Bascom to be present so that he could demonstrate his knowledge and skills.

She wanted Tim Tyler to see that his case was their number one priority.

Next on the agenda was to prepare for Sophia Newton's deposition tomorrow. Heather's telephone conversation with Sophia had been their only interaction so far. She would do a little sleuthing on her own to find out who Sophia Newton was – beyond owner of Big Haul.

Because Michael Trimmer had done such a good job looking into the background of Anthony Martinez, Heather was now asking him to research Barbara Blake – mother of Amelia.

Initially, Heather had not included her as a person of interest, but having spoken to Melanie Sergeant, she was compelled to find out more about the elusive and perhaps indifferent mother of the deceased.

Heather sent an inter-office email to Michael with all information she had on Barbara Blake of Covington, Kentucky. She asked Michael for a detailed report on her background and any pertinent information he could find about her character. Michael quickly responded that he would start that project immediately.

"Tim Tyler is here to see you," said Shirley.

"Please send him in."

Heather met Tim at the door to her office, shaking his hand. "Tim I'd like you to meet Steven Oliver Bascom, a private detective."

Bascom shook hands with Tim and they sat down across the desk from Heather.

"We have made significant progress on your case Tim even though there is still much to do from here until trial. Bascom and I have conducted several depositions and from those we have been able to clarify some things that were not so clear cut before."

"Great, I'm all ears," said Tim.

Heather began. "Let's start by letting you know we have deposed both of the truck drivers that were on scene on February 20. It was obvious from their respective testimonies that the truck driver who forced you off the road was negligent. Without being too specific, we believe the driver of the first truck was simply at the wrong place at the wrong time and had no direct connection to the second truck or its driver."

Bascom referred next to the autopsy report. "Heather and I have reviewed the official ruling of the Coroner which reflects that Amelia's death was indeed a homicide. The clearly stated report concludes the primary cause of death was blunt force trauma, occurring between six o'clock am on the 19th of February and six o'clock pm on the 20th of February. This helps us in several ways: the blunt force trauma left an imprint on the scull of the victim which is clearly defined and was used on the victim within that time frame." Bascom paused briefly.

"Heather and I know your car was the second to hit the black bag. Based on the observations of the Medical Examiner, the victim was struck by vehicle one (the hauler) and vehicle two (your car) *subsequent* to her demise."

Tim asked, "How can the Coroner or ME be certain that she was dead before I hit her?"

"In simplest terms Tim, dead bodies don't bleed."

"OK, but I don't quite follow."

"The Coroner noted the contusions on the torso of the victim's body which *had she been alive,* would have produced bleeding – commonly known as bruising. If the capillaries under the skin are not receiving blood flow, there's no bruising. When one dies, the blood no longer flows." Heather stated.

"Dead bodies don't bleed," repeated Tim. "I am so relieved to hear that. While I did hit the bag, I didn't cause her death."

"No," said Bascom "but we're not out of the woods *yet.*"

"In order to have you exonerated, we need to produce the person or persons who actually took the life of Amelia Blake. That's what we're trying to do now, but it's a tedious process. We have a suspects 'list' that we're working off of, and Bascom is the best at finding out things that other people would prefer remain hidden."

"I appreciate all you and the rest of the firm are doing on my behalf."

"We have some theories and we have some things that we are keeping close to the vest Tim. We're following the leads and fully intend to see justice done. While there are no guarantees in this world, it has been my experience, and that of Heather's, that the guilty always show their hand. We just need to be there to see it."

"Thank you Mr. Bascom."

"Please – just call me Bascom."

CHAPTER FIFTY-TWO

Barbara Blake
Covington, Kentucky

Barbara Blake made Amelia Ann's burial arrangements with the funeral director's that handled her husband's death. They were trusted friends and would take great care in handling what was left of her only child.

Mrs. Blake had bombarded the Covington Police department demanding information leading to the death of Amelia. All the police could provide was that Amelia Ann was the victim of a homicide and had been discovered in a black garbage bag near St. Petersburg, Florida.

Try as they might to convince her they were not withholding any information from her, whoever had the misfortune to answer her call got an earful. Suddenly Mrs. Blake was the hovering mother who wanted all her questions answered, whether factual or fictional.

After several telephone calls to St. Petersburg Police Chief, he referred her to the Florida Highway Police in Tampa, explaining that they were the official responders to the discovery of her daughter's body and might be able to answer some of her questions.

The FHP referred her to the Prosecuting Attorney, and the seemingly endless circle of avoidance was complete. Kevin Morrison's office had been given a head's up about Mrs. Blake's incessant questioning, but even that was not enough to prepare them for the onslaught of phone calls they received.

In an effort to dissuade her, Kevin Morrison personally contacted Mrs. Blake stating that she would be informed of all activity on her daughter's case, and assured her that she would be kept in the loop.

"Until the positive identification of the body was available from the Coroner, our office and the police had no way of knowing this was your daughter, Mrs. Blake," said Kevin Morrison. "We searched national missing person's reports, but found no one had reported Amelia's disappearance. We have a person of interest in the case and will be pursuing it through the justice system. Now that we know who you are and where you can be reached, we will be in touch with you as the case warrants. I'm sure you understand that we are working as diligently as possible to bring the perpetrator to justice."

In the meantime, Amelia Ann's remains were returned to Covington for a private ceremony and burial adjacent to her father.

CHAPTER FIFTY-THREE

Michael Trimmer's Research
On Barbara Blake

Publicly, Barbara Blake was considered an upstanding citizen. She had taught school for years and appeared to have no harmful marks on her record. Her employment was spotless and she had rarely missed a day of work. The only times she required a substitute teacher take her classes was the day of her husband William's funeral.

A devout Catholic, Barbara Blake had only been married once, although by the rules of the church, she could remarry after William's death if she chose to do so.

Now retired from teaching, she appeared to lead a quiet sedentary life, belonging only to a book club that met monthly and attending Mass on weekends. She lived in the house left to her by her husband, maintained a healthy bank account and had never been arrested.

Appearing to be so unblemished, Michael opted to dig deeper. Searching all the social media he found that Barbara Blake was active on an 'over fifty' matchmaking service. Her screen name was listed as BarB.

Looking into her profile, Michael saw that her stated preference skewed toward younger men who were intellectual and strong in character. She favored contact from professionals involved in one of the service industries: physician, policemen, firemen or the military; strictly noting no politicians need apply.

He noted several 'hits' on her site and made note of the screen names they left. He would check those out and see if there was any correlation between his list of names and Barbara Blake.

Looking into the sites that she 'liked' he noted that she had researched several plastic surgeons in the Cincinnati area as well as other metropolitan areas within a couple of hundred miles of Covington.

Her profile indicated that Barbara was a widow with no children, and there was no profile picture on the site. The email address she left was simply her user name in care of the matchmaking service.

Trimmer also found the newspaper account of William's death and a short blurb on the discovery of Amelia's body in Florida.

To be a woman who cared so much about appearances, Barbara Blake was, in Michael Trimmer's mind, a closet diva. He based that assumption on what he had unearthed about her private life which was incongruent with her public one.

Reviewing the Covington Police contact report, Barbara had openly expressed indignation about her daughter's death rather than remorse.

Again, she appeared to care more about what the reflection would be on her rather than the fact her daughter had been murdered.

Having called in a favor from a friend who worked with the St. Petersburg Police department, Trimmer learned that Barbara Blake had 'burned up the telephone lines' to the chief to have her daughter's remains returned to Kentucky. Ms. Blake had threatened a civil lawsuit – which everyone suspected would still happen – and was insistent that the autopsy of her daughter was an unmitigated travesty.

In all his research activities, there had been no mention of Amelia's pregnancy. The Covington police had not shared that information with Barbara Blake, nor did she ask to see and read the autopsy report. Again, Trimmer suspected that *if* Barbara knew her daughter was pregnant at the time of her death, she would bury that fact along with her daughter to 'save face'.

CHAPTER FIFTY-FOUR

Steven Oliver Bascom
Tampa, Florida

Two names on Bascom's list would keep him on his toes today. He would look into Sophia Newton's background and also take a cursory look at Sam Coburn of Mike Fink's Restaurant in Cincinnati. He expected the former to take significantly longer than the latter, and his hunch proved to be on target.

Having had experience in several 'three letter' governmental agencies, he could run a thorough background check on Coburn that would be delivered to his computer within minutes. And, as he suspected, Coburn was as clean as a whistle.

Samuel Coburn, age 35, married for ten years to Kimberly Coburn; two children aged seven and five. Restaurant manager, no arrests, warrants or liens; filed taxes every year – no audits. Coburn had a continuous employment history, and a good credit rating with no debt other than his home and cars.

Coburn was somewhat active on a Facebook account, with the majority of his postings relating to his family and the Mike Fink's restaurant.

Sophia Newton, age 36, never married and owner/operator of Big Haul in Tampa, Florida. Newton purchased Big Haul in 1995 from the former owner who was preparing to file for chapter thirteen (reorganization) and/or bankruptcy. Funding for Ms. Newton had come from Bank of America who held a promissory note and a lien on the equipment. Her payments had been made on time for the past four years.

Newton had never been arrested. In 1996, she was accused of stalking a man she had previously been involved with romantically. She was court ordered to cease any/all contact with this individual and a restraining order had been issued by the Hillsborough County Court. There were no infractions noted once the restraining order was served on Ms. Newton.

Sophia Newton maintained social media accounts on LinkedIn, Craig's List and Facebook. She was also a member of a dating/matchmaking website called "Plenty of Fish".

"Plenty of Fish" showed her preferences in dating partners to be professionals aged thirty to fifty, preferably with no children and at least a college education. She stated that she was looking for a companion, friend and someone who enjoyed travel, good food and adventure.

Knowing Heather was prepping for the deposition of Sophia Newton, Bascom buzzed her on the intercom to let her know he had prepared a report for her review.

"You my friend have saved me precious time today by taking the lead on getting this background information," Heather told him. "I have Michael working on gathering info about Barbara Blake, and didn't want to give him too much at once."

"You're welcome Heather, and I was just about to suggest that we take a look at Mrs. Blake. I guess we think alike, huh?"

"Scary thought, isn't it?"

"I'll drop the report off to you in a couple of minutes if that's okay?"

"Sure, anytime."

As he had promised Bascom delivered the information on Sophia Newton. He surprised Heather with the background on Samuel Coburn.

"Wow, the boys in North Florida were right about you Bascom. They said you were the best."

"But did they say 'the best what'?"

The two laughed at the exchange and then went back to their respective tasks.

Bascom stuck his head back in Heather's office door saying, "And I'll bet it was Matthew that called me the best, not Pete. He thinks *he's* the best."

Smiling and grateful to have two things off her list, Heather dove right in to the information.

CHAPTER FIFTY-FIVE

Sophia Newton's Deposition
Offices of Howell Legal Services & Investigations

Arriving at Heather Howell's office, Sophia Newton was accompanied by the attorney representing Big Haul of Tampa, as well as her personal attorney.

Ms. Newton was sworn in. Heather asked Ms. Newton about her marital status and noting that she was unmarried, Heather asked if she was currently seeing or was involved with anyone.

"I don't see that as pertinent Ms. Howell and would prefer not to divulge my personal relationships." Newton responded.

Heather turned to Newton's counsel and without uttering a word, Ms. Newton's personal attorney stood and asked for a moment with his client.

That was granted, and Sophia Newton and her attorney adjourned to a private office outside of the conference room where the depositions were being taken.

Returning shortly, Ms. Howell asked that they go back on record. The stenographer stated "after a brief recess requested by the deponent, we are now on record in the deposition of Sophia Newton."

Heather again asked the same question of the Sophia Newton.

"I am currently dating Daniel Blair."

"And is this the same Daniel Blair who works for the Florida Highway Patrol?"

"Yes, it is."

"Are you aware Ms. Newton, that Officer Blair was the FHP Officer who was the first on scene and arresting officer of my client, Timothy Tyler?"

"I am."

"I must ask you then if there is any reason that you cannot or will not be one- hundred- percent truthful in your responses to these deposition questions."

"I understand that I am under oath."

"And returning to my previous question is there any reason that you cannot or will not be truthful in your responses to the deposition questions."

"I will be one-hundred-percent truthful in answering your questions Ms. Howell," Newton curtly replied.

"Thank you. Now we can continue. How did you become aware of the incident involving Timothy Tyler?"

"I was informed by Robert Barnes, that a piece of equipment my company had under lease to Site Select had been involved in an accident."

"And Mr. Barnes is with Site Select?"

"Yes."

"And did Mr. Barnes mention the name of Timothy Tyler to you?"

"No, he did not."

"When you were contacted by this office, were you given the name of Timothy Tyler?"

"No, not that I recall."

"Did Daniel Blair provide my client's name to you?"

"I suppose he could have. I really don't remember."

"Is it your recollection that the piece of equipment – specifically an EU 4-axle hauler/dump truck – was impounded for inspection?"

"Yes. "

"And that vehicle was a part of your fleet, correct?"

"Yes."

"For the record, can you describe for the damage that was found on that particular piece of equipment subsequent to the incident on 28th Street North on February 20, 2000?"

"The EU 4-axle had scratches on the hood, and a cracked grill."

"Isn't it also true that the EU 4-axle was found to have an oil leak?"

"Yes."

"Please state the name of the driver/operator of that EU 4-axle."

"Anthony Martinez."

"And is Mr. Martinez an employee of yours?"

"He is a contract employee for Big Haul."

"Do you know that Mr. Martinez is a resident of the state of New York?"

"I do."

"And is it standard operating procedure for Big Haul to hire out-of-state contract employees?"

"No. Big Haul hires the best available driver or operator for the specific equipment we are leasing regardless of their place of residence."

"Thank you. And did your client Site Select request Mr. Martinez to be the driver of the EU 4-axle?"

"No, Mr. Barnes merely asked for the equipment and a driver/operator."

"Does Mr. Martinez have an up-to-date and current license to operate this piece of equipment?"

"Yes."

"Has Mr. Martinez ever been involved in an accident or situation that resulted in damage to the equipment he was operating or driving?"

There was a lull in the activity; an obvious silence.

"Ms. Newton? Do I need to repeat the question?"

"I don't know."

"Ms. Newton, it is impossible to tell which question you are responding to with 'I don't know'. Please clarify for the record."

"I do not know if Martinez has ever been involved in damaging another piece of equipment."

"Very well, thank you for your clarification."

Heather paused before continuing.

"How are your employees screened or interviewed?"

There was an objection by the Big Haul attorney - "Objection to form."

Heather agreed to rephrase the question.

"When a driver or operator applies for a position with Big Haul, what procedures take place?"

Newton looked at the company attorney who nodded his head.

"Our company's personnel department reviews all credentials and applicable licensing to assure the candidate is competent to perform the duties required."

"Does that personnel review include prior jobs or positions that applicant has had?"

"Yes, of course."

"Then how would Big Haul not be aware of previous accidents or damages sustained on equipment from prior jobs?

"I stated that I *personally* was not aware – *not* the company. I am confident that research was done prior to hiring Mr. Martinez, and that he would not have been approved for hire otherwise."

"Does Big Haul require personal or professional references?"

"Yes we do."

"And those references are followed up on how?"

"Usually by telephone."

"Very well Ms. Newton."

"Did you hire Mr. Martinez?"

"I approved his hire."

"And roughly what would be the value of an EU 4-axle hauler/dump truck?"

"Purchased new, it could be as high as $125,000; used but in good condition, about half of that."

"And how many of these EU 4-axle haulers are currently in your fleet – meaning Big Haul's fleet?"

"One."

"Has anyone other than Anthony Martinez driven/operated this particular piece of equipment for Big Haul?"

"Not to my knowledge."

"And how long have you had the AU 4-axle as part of your fleet?"

"About a year."

"How long have you known Anthony Martinez?"

"We hired him about a year ago."

"How long have you known him, ma'am?"

"I met Mr. Martinez when he came to Tampa to apply for a position with my company."

"And when was that?"

"About a year ago."

"Do you recall any of Anthony Martinez's references?"

"No."

"But if asked in court to present the names of those references you could produce them?"

"Yes."

"Thank you. Ms. Newton, would you under the current situation and as Owner of Big Haul use Anthony Martinez as a driver or operator of equipment in your fleet?"

"I do not plan to employee Mr. Martinez in the future."

"Do you know or have you ever met Amelia Ann Blake?"

"I do not know who that is."

"Do you know or have you ever met Barbara Blake?"

"Not that I recall."

"Have you ever been arrested or charged with a crime or a misdemeanor?"

Looking at her personal attorney, Sophia Newton paused. He nodded.

"I have never been arrested or charged with a crime. I was accused of a misdemeanor."

"What was the misdemeanor?"

"Stalking."

"Can you state for the record how that stalking charge was handled by the courts?"

"I received a restraining order and honored it."

"Is it correct that you were accused of stalking an ex-boyfriend?"

"Yes."

"Have you ever had any interaction or contact on Craig's List with another member?"

"I have."

"And on any occasion did you interact with a member whose screen name was 'Thor'?"

"It may have been I can't be sure."

Heather was looking at the stenographer and said, "Please mark the record showing that Thor – that's spelled T H O R – is a screen name that used by Anthony Martinez of Syracuse, New York."

An audible gasp was heard coming from Sophia Newton. Her lawyer quickly objected to form and evidence, and then sat back in his chair.

"Ms. Newton, what information if any, about this case has been given to you by FHP Officer Blair?"

"None."

"So for the record you are saying the two of you have never discussed it?"

"That's correct."

"Do you personally have any connection to the greater Cincinnati, Ohio area?"

"No."

"Do you have any professional connection to the greater Cincinnati, Ohio area?"

"No."

"Have you ever traveled to the greater Cincinnati, Ohio area?"

"Once."

"And when did that occur?"

"In December of 1999."

"And what was the purpose of your visit in December of '99?"

"I went on a shopping trip."

"And did you travel alone or with someone else?"

"I traveled alone."

"Where, and for how long did you stay in Cincinnati?"

"I stayed at a hotel in downtown Cincinnati –The Loewe's Hotel – for three nights."

"Did you drive, fly, or travel by train to Cincinnati?"

"I drove my personal vehicle."

"Lastly Ms. Newton, did you happen to eat at a restaurant called Mike Fink's during that visit?"

"I did. It was quite nice."

"Thank you to everyone. That concludes my questions."

Sophia Newton and her two attorneys quietly walked out of the conference room. Heather Howell gathered her paperwork and left behind them. Heather was relieved to have that deposition behind her.

She had purposely deposed Sophia Newton a few days after the deposition of Anthony Martinez. It was obvious to her now that the two had not spoken. The only item that had not come to light was the triangular connection between FHP Officer Blair, Newton and Martinez.

Behind her desk now, Heather added another 'link' to her flowchart. She was also confident that one of the 'references' for Martinez would be Daniel Blair, FHP.

Bascom appeared in the doorway saying, "Great work in there counselor." Heather smiled and nodded in appreciation.

"Bascom, how about a drink?" Heather asked.

Without any hesitation Bascom said "I'll drive."

On the drive neither of them spoke about the case or the deposition that had just concluded. Heather appreciated the silence and wished at the same time she could silence her thoughts. While Bascom undoubtedly had his own thoughts, he was mindful of the weight of Heather's burden in finding out who killed Amelia Ann Blake.

As the two arrived at **Just Us,** Bascom broke the silence. "I've checked it out thoroughly Heather, they make a great burger and fries here – just what the PI ordered!"

Heather laughed aloud. "You've been around Bob Zee too long, and you obviously know me too well."

CHAPTER FIFTY-SIX

Sophia Newton

There was no time to figure out why she had been drilled during the deposition, much less how this attorney knew so much about her activities. Sophia had to figure out how to proceed from this point forward.

Obviously it looked suspicious that Daniel and she had become an item since equipment she owned was involved in an accident that he had made an arrest for, but what was the implication?

The most nagging question in her mind was 'professional or personal references' for Martinez. To satisfy her curiosity she pulled the company's personnel file for Martinez and saw that Daniel Blair had highly recommended him for a job at Big Haul.

As for Martinez aka Thor – she had no idea they were one and the same when she corresponded with *Thor* on Craig's list. The photo he had sent to her was him sitting at a computer, but his face was only partially visible. The rest of his body was naked, and while not totally exposed, his well developed muscles indicated that he was well endowed. She had to get rid of that photo and all correspondence she had with Thor.

Sophia felt stupid and used. Now she only had more questions about Daniel Blair and *his* relationship with Martinez. What she knew was that she could not ask Daniel about this.

Each time she had asked him something personal, he clammed up, got angry or both.

Recalling the time she simply asked where he had gone when he was out of town, he not-so-politely told her it was none of her business.

His reaction to her question, made her all the more determined to find out where he had been. When he spent the night with her she riffled through his pockets and discovered a matchbook from Mike Fink's. Finding the home of the restaurant was easy – she simply searched on Google and found it to be near Cincinnati, Ohio. Why he was there was still a mystery.

Everything seemed to improve in their relationship after Daniel's trip, and now Sophia questioned even that.

Trying to put everything she now knew in perspective, Sophia decided it best that she avoid contact with Daniel Blair, and purge her personal computer of all things Thor.

CHAPTER FIFTY-SEVEN

Timothy Tyler

Since leaving his attorney's office Tim had experienced some relief. Howell and Bascom had provided information from the medical examiner's office that at last pointed toward Tim's innocence.

He had learned that the young woman trapped in the auto accident near his home was alive and well, which gave him another boost of positive news.

Tim had read a report in the local newspaper and had seen coverage on televised reports about the hit and run in his neighborhood.

The woman was Natalie Graham. According to media sources she was a single mother who worked as a dental technician in Clearwater. Tim remembered seeing an infant seat in the car when the EMT's broke into Ms. Graham's car that night. He was relieved then to see that there was not a child on scene.

The report stated that Ms. Graham's car was struck by the hit and run driver as she was returning home from work. The hit and run driver had been arrested with charges pending.

Ms. Graham had been admitted to a local hospital for treatment of her injuries, and was now – according to the reports – being released to recuperate at home.

Tim looked at Tattoo (who was the only reason they were able to get almost immediate help for Ms. Graham) and said "maybe we'll take a stroll by her house in a few days."

CHAPTER FIFTY-EIGHT

Melanie Sergeant

Having met with Heather Howell and Bascom, Melanie was experiencing loss over her friend Amelia. They had been close friends – at least in Mel's estimation, and she was thinking back about the good times they had shared together in Cincinnati.

After feeding Lily her dinner, reading a story and getting her to sleep, Mel brought out her old boxes of photos and memorabilia. She poured herself a glass of wine, turned on some music and sat down to leisurely go through the photos.

There were lots of pictures of Amelia and Mel, arms wrapped around each other's waist as they posed for friends at Mike Fink's. The funny shots were just that and made Mel smile.

As she made her way through the boxes, she found a note from Amelia; a thank you that said: 'Mel, thanks for being there each and every time I've needed a friend. You are that and more. You are the sister I wanted but never had. I love you! - Amelia.'

Tears were easy now. Amelia's life had been cut short – and she had a baby on the way as well. Mel dried her eyes and walked quietly to the bedroom where her own daughter slept. She bent over lightly kissing her on the forehead and then went back to the living room.

Going through the contents again Mel found a few photos of the crew at Fink's restaurant, the manager Sam, and a few of the regulars at the bar. She could not help but wonder who the father of Amelia's baby was and if Amelia had met him through Mike Fink's.

Mel decided she would keep out a couple of photos of Amelia to show Ms. Howell and Bascom. She slid them into an envelope and placed it in her purse. Shaking her head, in a whisper she said, *'I wish she had told me about the baby...'*

CHAPTER FIFTY-NINE

Heather Howell's Office
July 2000

"Ms. Howell, line one is Matt Winters," Shirley said.

"Thanks – just who I needed to talk to," replied Heather.

"Hi Matthew!"

"Good morning Heather – I'm calling to get a pick up from you about Tyler's case."

"Wow, you must have ESP. I was just thinking of calling you. Here's the latest..." Heather proceeded to share the revelations that the latest round of depositions had provided.

"Great work. It seems that you and Bascom have things under control. When are you deposing the FHP Officers?"

"We're deposing them next week. And I've also added the mother of the deceased as a person of interest."

"Are you planning to depose her as well?" Matt asked.

"That depends on what I discover from the FHP Officers."

"Do you think one or both of them is involved in this?"

"I hate to admit this, but I am more than a bit interested in one of them in particular. There are too many connections to ignore, so I'm relying on my gut feeling and my father's sage advice about eating a bear...one bite at a time."

"Is there anything Pete or I can do from here?"

"Yes, as a matter of fact. Can you look into the professional backgrounds of Darrell Dunn as well as Daniel Blair? Since you are physically closer to FHP Headquarters, you may be able to shed some light on these two."

"Consider Pete and me to be earning our retainer. I'll let you know what we find as soon as possible. Have a great day Heather."

CHAPTER SIXTY

Office of Matthew Winters
Gainesville, Florida

Matthew and Pete were looking into the career history of Daniel Blair, as an assist to Heather Howell. They were meeting this afternoon to compare notes.

Pete Sutherland had a longstanding inside track to the Florida Highway Patrol. Many of his cop friends worked there and more than a few of them were in the management ranks of the FHP Headquarters in Tallahassee. A simple telephone call from Pete resulted in a bevy of reports transmitted back to him at the law firm.

When Pete walked in for their meeting, Matt's secretary had compiled, copied and coordinated the reports in chronological order.

Taking a cursory look at the write ups on Blair, the worst and most apparent offenses were the accusations of sexual harassment from female counterparts – both subordinates and equal rank being represented in that group. And while this might not be front page news, it did indicate a 'character' imperfection that could break his career as a police officer.

Matthew was reviewing the same reports. Based solely on those, Matt's take was that Blair was most likely a ladies' man until the lady demanded to be treated fairly and equally, and he was a narcissistic. Narcissists were vain, egocentric and self-absorbed. They were typically selfish with their time and possessions and didn't like to be questioned or challenged on issues. And unfortunately, there were some attributes associated with the narcissist that made them perfect for the job of a police officer.

"What do you get from these Pete?"

"Blair is probably tall, dark and handsome – and he knows it and uses it to get what he wants. I see he was married and divorced not too long afterwards and the cause was an 'irretrievably broken' marriage; translation: he slept with someone else. He seems to keep his nose clean on the job, save the harassment complaints, and he's probably decent at his job."

"Your turn Matt..."

"I get the same impressions, but because I see him as a narcissistic guy, he's probably ill-tempered when or if he's backed into a corner. He's not someone who appreciates being challenged or given an ultimatum. I could see him blowing away a guy who resisted arrest; easy without a second thought. A woman telling him 'no' might cause an inappropriate reaction on his part. He appears to be a guy who wants what he wants – when he wants it."

"The men in blue at the state don't particularly like Blair, but he has been with FHP for a decade and has never done anything that demanded suspension or separation from duty. He was warned however, that if another harassment charge came about, he was most likely headed for anger management class as well as weekly sessions with an appointed shrink. That would mean a suspension with pay, loss of his weapon and his cruiser."

Matthew asked if Pete had reviewed the most recent report on Blair.

"Is that the one where he was assigned a rookie named Corey King?"

"Yes, that's the one."

"I believe that was a set-up. The Corey King that I know of is in forensics – a sharp cookie by all accounts. If she is the Corey King that road with Blair, she is a good looking white woman, confident and secure in her abilities. Maybe the Tampa FHP Post wanted to see if he would harass her?"

"Do you think we could find out?"

"Sure – here partner, dial this number for me..."

"FHP – how may I direct your call?"

"Chief Joe please – it's Pete Sutherland."

"One moment..."

"Pete – what the hell do you want now?" asked Joe.

"Uh, Joe – you're on speaker with my partner Matthew Winters, so let's mind our manners, shall we? And I'm checking out Daniel Blair down in Tampa. Did you guys set him up with a good looking rookie in hopes he'd make an egregious error in judgment and harass her?"

"Why Pete, you know we would never do anything that could undermine our brothers in blue. Blair is one of our fine officers who tends to dislike having rookies ride with him. He just needed to have a little push. The report I got from that ride was that our rookie handled the situation with great success. Anything else Pete, I'm sort of busy here."

"Just one question chief – would you be happy if Blair transferred here?"

"I'd say that would never happen, but then again, who knows?"

"See you Joe – and thanks!"

Pete looked across the desk at Matt and said, "Well, what do you think?"

"I think Joe did everything but indict Blair." Pete smiled.

Matthew continued – "For Heather's purposes, she needs to know that her gut feeling about Daniel Blair warrants digging deeper."

"Yeah, I'm just wondering if she thinks he's in on the murder of Amelia Blake."

"It appears that she's getting there. Look, I know we haven't really sunk our teeth into this case, but it has always seemed too convenient for an FHP Officer to reach the scene of an accident within two to five minutes of that accident occurring – unless he was expecting the accident to happen. Next, Heather says that Blair was probably a reference for the truck driver who first hit the garbage bag, and he was definitely a reference for the middle manager at Toy Town. That guy is now dead – committing suicide the day after his deposition, and lastly, Blair is dating the woman who owns the dump truck that hit the bag. Coincidence?"

"I think not partner. And our/Heather's client was set up to hit that garbage bag."

"Not personally, but yes. He was driving toward Toy Town – the truck that struck the bag first was driving away from the facility, and that put Tim in the wrong place at the wrong time."

"So our advice to Heather – if you agree – would be to look for any connection between Blair and Amelia – if there is one of course."

"Yes. I think we need to make a trip to Tampa and meet with Heather and Bascom. We could share our thoughts and ideas and have a chance to get a better pickup on all the workings in the case."

"I agree," said Pete "and wouldn't it be great if our visit just happened to be in time for Blair's deposition?"

"Let's call and get Heather's opinion before we go further." Matt immediately initiated the call.

After sharing their collective information about Daniel Blair, Matthew proposed their trip to Tampa. Heather did not hesitate with her answer – it was affirmative. She gave Matt and Pete the deposition date for Daniel Blair and said she would have Shirley forward info to them on hotels near the office and they could have their staff make the reservations.

"So the gang (plus one) gets together again," said Pete enthusiastically.

"I'm looking forward to assisting Heather on this case – it's appears to get more involved all the time."

"I agree Matt – see you tomorrow. Let me know when its wheels up."

"'Night Pete, thanks."

SIXTY-ONE

Heather Howell's Office
July 2000

There was no escaping the fact that Heather was grateful for the help she was being offered by Matthew Winters and Pete Sutherland. They were not only her friends, but mentors as well. She had learned a lot from working with them on the Carmine Lorenzo case, and trusted them implicitly. Being in town for the deposition of Daniel Blair had its plusses and minuses, but she would happily accept their input.

She had asked them to send her their notes on Blair, and would make sure to share those with Bascom.

Heather sent a note via inter-office email to Bascom, advising them of Matt and Pete's impending visit, and assuring him she would share their research as soon as she received it.

By the time she finished her email to Bascom, the ping of her computer showed that she had an email from Matthew. She opened it, read the contents and immediately forwarded it to Bascom.

As she perused the report she couldn't help but shudder to think that an officer of the law might be involved in something so sinister. And if Blair were involved, why and how he was involved were questions that needed answers.

The logical thought led her to a crime of passion. Crimes of passion can be premeditated or committed without premeditation by rage. Blair fit the stereotype – high strung, disliked being challenged or controlled etc. But why Amelia

Blake who had no apparent connection to him, unless…a chill ran up her spine…what if Amelia Blake's baby belonged to Daniel Blair?

Heather pushed her chair away from her desk and walked to the window, as if to clear her head.

She then pulled out the autopsy report for Amelia. Pushing through the pages, there was no indication that the Coroner typed the DNA of the fetus, but by this time tomorrow, Heather would know if DNA had been extracted or preserved from Amelia's unborn child.

Secondly, she noted that further explanation was needed from the Coroner on the tissue scrapings found under Amelia's fingernails.

Reviewing the autopsy once more, she backed up the Coroner's timeline of fifteen weeks of pregnancy, which would have Amelia conceiving her child in early to mid-November of 1999. She would confirm that timeline with the Coroner's office as well.

Heather knew she had to leave, have dinner and get some sleep, but tomorrow couldn't come soon enough. She had something to sink her teeth into here – another couple of big bites of the bear.

CHAPTER SIXTY-TWO

Sister Mary Agnes
Mount St. Joseph University
Cincinnati, Ohio

Sister Mary Agnes was now one of the oldest Catholic nuns in residence at Mount St. Joseph. She had taught at the university for many years, and was also part of the convent that had been established prior to the development of the school.

She was devout, serious about her duties and an integral part of the order. She had spent her life teaching, comforting and advising students at Mount St. Joseph and Amelia Ann Blake had been one of her most cherished.

The news of Amelia's death was devastatingly painful for Sister Mary Agnes, and she had just learned of her passing by seeing a small obituary in the local newspaper. The obit gave virtually no information and while nothing was stopping her other than her own good judgment, she wanted to contact Barbara Blake to learn more.

Sister Mary Agnes opted to pray about what she should do, and had sought counsel with the priest. He had urged her to continue her prayer vigil and then to sit quietly to hear God speak His will to her.

"You will make the correct and appropriate choice Sister. Of that I am sure," said the priest. "God always answers our prayers."

Two weeks later, Sister Mary Agnes decided to pay Mrs. Blake a visit. She telephoned Barbara Blake, who wasn't eager to talk with her, but ultimately agreed they could meet. The get together was scheduled for the following week.

CHAPTER SIXTY-THREE

Heather Howell's Office
Tampa, Florida
July 2000

Heather arrived early, her eyes revealing her lack of sleep. Shirley was in the office before anyone else and had coffee brewing in the break room. Relieved to be greeted with the aroma of caffeine, Heather stuck her head in the door of the break room startling Shirley.

"Oh my" said Shirley, "I didn't hear anyone come in."

"Sorry Shirley, I didn't mean to startle you. I followed the aroma of the coffee."

"You're in early – something happening?"

"Perhaps so" said Heather, "I've had some revelations and need to talk with the Coroner who did Amelia's autopsy. I have some questions that only he can answer."

"Just let me know when you're ready to talk with him and I'll get him on the line for you."

"Thanks Shirley – you're the best."

"Here's your coffee...enjoy it."

Signing on to her computer Heather found an encrypted email from Matthew Winter's office with an itinerary for his trip to Tampa, accompanied of course by Peter Sutherland. They would arrive on Sunday evening, 2 days prior to the deposition of Daniel Blair, and would be staying at the Radisson Hotel. The trip was open-ended.

Heather added notations to her calendar and forwarded the information to Bascom's email as well as to Shirley.

Buzzing Shirley immediately thereafter, Heather said she was ready to talk with the Coroner.

Within a short time, Shirley had the Coroner on the phone for Heather.

"Good Morning, Dr. Moray, this is Heather Howell. How are you this morning?""

"Fine thanks, what can I do for you Ms. Howell?"

"I'm phoning you in regards to your report on Amelia Ann Blake. I just have a couple of questions if you would indulge me."

"I will certainly try to oblige you counselor; what are your questions?"

"First of all, the autopsy report mentions 'scrapings under the fingernails' referring to those as 'tissue'. My question is two-fold, was the tissue identified; and was the tissue sample kept?"

"I'm looking at the report as we speak Ms. Howell. The tissue was identified as human skin – nothing beyond that, and all samples taken during the autopsy are preserved in the event further descriptions or identification is necessary. Both questions answered as yes."

"Thank you Dr. Moray. Lastly – at least for now, did you run any DNA testing on Amelia or on the fetus?"

"In the state of Florida, DNA testing has become an integral part of autopsies where we have a viable fetus whose existence is terminated as a result of the host's – the mother's demise. So yes, DNA testing was done on the fetus of Amelia Ann Blake. And the test sample is of course saved as a part of the autopsy bi-products."

"Thank you again Doctor for your time and cooperation. Have a nice day, goodbye."

Heather gave an audible sigh of relief. The "tissue" was human skin – most likely that skin belonged to the killer. Once the killer was named, the sample could be tested against the killer's DNA as confirmation. That was the first success for today.

Had the DNA typing not been done as part of the autopsy, the body of Amelia would have to be exhumed. That would have been costly for her client and time-consuming since getting an order to exhume is a difficult process. Score the second success for today – and it was early.

Hearing Bascom in the hallway, Heather called him in for an update. When she shared all that she had learned, he was elated.

"The boys from north Florida will be arriving on Sunday," said Heather "and if I know the two of them like I think I do, they have a scenario or two in their minds that they will be sharing."

"No doubt – don't we all?"

"Yes. I have some ideas myself but I can't quite cross all the 'T's' yet. While we're talking about that, why would a woman from Tampa drive to Cincinnati – where she allegedly knows no one - to go shopping? It's a good 15 hour drive, and if you wanted to shop in Cincinnati, wouldn't you fly up there? It just doesn't compute."

"Sophia Newton is a liar – and not a good one. Her deposition was full of holes; in part because you rattled her from the get go asking her who she was dating. She had no idea that we knew about her relationship with Blair."

"Do you think she knows Amelia or Barbara Blake?"

"I'm not sure yet, Heather. I think she was on a mission to find out why Blair went to Cincinnati. My guess is that something she learned led her there, and specifically to Mike Fink's. And by the way, what made you question her about the restaurant?"

"It was a hunch that paid off, but if anyone else asks, it was because I am a darn good PI, as well as an attorney. Actually my logic says that something or someone brought Amelia Blake to Florida. Who or why isn't totally clear yet, but I had to ask Sophia Newton if she had ever been to Fink's in order to know if she had an occasion to meet Amelia, whom she said she didn't know."

"Okay, what about Barbara Blake?"

"My initial answer is that I think she's involved somehow. Here's this cold, detached mother who hasn't spent any time with her daughter for almost 15 years, and suddenly after her death plays hover mom? That doesn't compute either. Plus she was and is so indignant about the autopsy; it's almost as if she has something to hide."

"I think there is a connection between Barbara Blake and Sophia Newton," Bascom stated. "I can't pinpoint how or why but there's a commonality there that bugs me."

"Let's play devil's advocate. Can we draw a line connecting Barbara Blake with Sophia Newton?"

Bascom interjected, "Only if the connector is either Amelia Blake or Daniel Blair."

"That is precisely my thought. And my money is on Blair."

"For the moment, mine too. Hope you have sharpened your pencil for that deposition."

"I have a thing or two up my sleeve for Officer Blair. Remember that he is the linchpin for Edwin Miller, Anthony Martinez, and Sophia Newton – all with roles in this play – and perhaps we can add Barbara Blake to the program."

CHAPTER SIXTY-FOUR

Sophia Newton
Tampa, Florida

Having purged her computer of her Thor-related correspondence including the suggestive photo he had sent her, Sophia was both angered and frightened. The connection between Daniel Blair and Anthony Martinez made her nauseous. The thought that Daniel had hooked up with her and facilitated a relationship between her and Martinez literally made her ill.

Daniel Blair had been in touch after her deposition, asking about having dinner and catching up.

Sophia agreed to meet him at CDB's restaurant after work one evening. When he arrived she told him that the deposition was dreadful and that she feared her company had been negatively thrown into this litigation because of her relationship with him.

She had told him that she was directly questioned about their relationship and virtually accused of discussing the case with him, which was a bad reflection on her as well as her company.

When she mentioned Anthony Martinez, she told Blair that she had no idea he was a character reference for the guy. Blair sloughed it off saying he just owed the guy a favor – that it was no big deal.

Sophia did not make any comment to Blair about 'Thor' – still somehow hoping he wasn't aware of it. She simply told

Daniel that she would prefer they cool things until the case was settled. He had simply agreed, kissed her on the cheek and left.

At least Daniel Blair did not know that she had ever gone to Cincinnati, or met Barbara Blake. She hoped and prayed he would never find out.

CHAPTER SIXTY-FIVE

Residence of Barbara Blake
Covington, Kentucky
July 2000

Sister Mary Agnes rang the doorbell at precisely one o'clock in the afternoon. Mrs. Blake had set the time, no doubt to avoid a luncheon invitation or an afternoon tea.

"Sister Mary Agnes?" asked Barbara Blake.

"Yes, Mrs. Blake, thank you for seeing me."

"Please come in. Sit wherever you're comfortable."

"Thank you," said the humble nun, "I know it probably isn't the best time for you, but I was so troubled when I heard about Amelia, I had to contact you."

"I appreciate your concern and that you also understand these are very trying times for me." Barbara Blake answered.

"I was very attached to Amelia when she was a student at Mount St. Helen's; I was her counselor and helped her choose her coursework. She was a beautiful girl with a tender heart."

"Yes, indeed. Everyone loved Amelia. She was just never the same after her father passed away. It was like she had lost her way in the world..." said Barbara.

"The article in the newspaper didn't give much information. Was Amelia ill?" asked the nun.

"No Sister Mary Agnes, my daughter was killed in Florida."

"Oh no – I am so very sorry for your loss. What a tragedy. Have they found out who did this?"

"No, not yet; the investigation is ongoing."

"Mrs. Blake, I never had the opportunity to meet you, but I loved Amelia and I trust that the person who did this will be found out and brought to justice."

"Thank you Sister. I am grateful for your kind words."

"I will be praying daily for you, Mrs. Blake. May God bless you and hold you close in your grief. Thank you for your time."

Barbara Blake walked Sister Mary Agnes to the door and said goodbye.

CHAPTER SIXTY-SIX

Sister Mary Agnes
Cincinnati, Ohio

"Father I pray for your child Amelia, whom you have welcomed into heaven, and ask that she be at peace. I pray for her mother Barbara as she deals with the realization of losing her only child. I ask for your infinite wisdom and guidance to fill the hearts of those who are seeking the person who committed this act of violence against Amelia. And I would ask for your favor in righting the wrong that has been done. Through the blessings and grace of the Virgin Mary, I ask all these things. Amen."

Leaving the sanctuary, she encountered the priest. He asked if she had resolved the conflict she had been struggling with.

"I visited the mother of the young woman I told you about just today, Father. I learned that Amelia had been murdered in Florida. Her mother did not provide any details. All I know is that the matter is being investigated by the police."

"I am sorry for your loss, Sister."

"Thank you Father. I just said a prayer that the perpetrator would be found, and expressing my thanks that Amelia is now in the arms of God."

"I will pray as well."

"Thank you. I will take my leave now."

CHAPTER SIXTY-SEVEN

Daniel Blair
Tampa, Florida

Things had been going well for Daniel, other than the hindrances caused by the women in his life. He was looking toward this year's baseball season and getting back to Cincinnati to see the Reds play. He had been able to take in some of their Spring Training sessions held in Tampa and felt that they had a real chance this year to win the League Championship.

He had the deposition in Tim Tyler's case coming up and he had not decided how he was going to handle that.

Blair was smart enough to know that Tyler's attorney had run a background check, and while he wasn't overly concerned about that, Edwin Miller may have thrown him under the bus during his deposition. While Blair wasn't privy to exactly what was said, he knew there was something that pushed Miller over the edge.

Blair also knew Sophia Newton had been deposed, and while she really knew nothing of importance about him or anything else, she was not the sharpest pencil in the holder. She had flatly refused to talk with him about her deposition and that made him suspicious.

She had told him they should cool things until this case was resolved, that her company was being unduly scrutinized because of their relationship. Daniel didn't see a 'relationship' so it was all the same to him.

Blair knew that he could stick to the facts and to his initial report to get through the deposition. He had reviewed that report as well as the one filed by his counterpart, Darrell Dunn. They weren't vastly disparate.

As for Timothy Tyler, he was in the wrong place at the wrong time. That wasn't Blair's fault.

Daniel Blair had been through numerous depositions in his ten plus year career. He convinced himself this would be just one more.

CHAPTER SIXTY-EIGHT

Radisson Hotel
Tampa, Florida
July 2000

Matthew and Pete checked into their adjoining rooms late Sunday afternoon and promptly telephoned Heather.

"The cavalry has landed" said Matt.

"Great," answered Heather "are you two up for dinner?"

"Of course, we miss a lot but never a meal. Where and when?"

"I'll come to the hotel and pick up two up in about an hour."

"Great, we'll be ready."

Heather thought about phoning Bascom, but opted to spend some quality time alone with Matt and Pete to catch up.

After meeting them in the lobby, Heather took them to south Tampa's famous Bern's Steak House.

Both Matthew and Pete were impressed by the ambiance and equally shocked at the size of the menu which rivaled a New York City Telephone Directory. All three of them had cocktails then ordered steak, salad and potato. Heather ordered a bottle of red wine with dinner.

The three of them reminisced about the Lorenzo case they solved. They had made quite a team, and were responsible for Heather's career change.

Heather told them she wanted to postpone talking about Tim Tyler's case until the following day when Bascom could be present. They agreed that was best.

After a most pleasant evening and too much food, Heather delivered the boys back to the hotel. She provided her office address and asked them to be there at nine sharp.

CHAPTER SIXTY-NINE

Heather Howell's Office

By nine that morning all was present and accounted for. Heather held a brief staff meeting to introduce Matthew and Peter and to get an overall status check on the firm's accounts. Immediately following that meeting, Heather, Matt, Pete and Bascom took over the conference room to meet on the Tyler case.

Heather and Bascom took the lead and brought Matt and Pete up to speed on not only the factual information but also their own thoughts on who, why, where. Matt and Pete took copious notes and then shared their own thoughts. The four of them were basically on the same page.

Probable suspects in the murder of Amelia Blake were: Daniel Blair, Sophia Newton, and/or Barbara Blake. Suspects implicated in her murder were: Anthony Martinez and Edwin Miller, deceased.

All of them were eager to get a sworn deposition from Officer Daniel Blair. They spent most of the rest of the day going over the intellectual information they collectively had on Blair, and assisting Heather in her preparation.

Heather had arranged for Tim Tyler to come by the office around eleven-thirty so that he could meet Matthew and Peter. Shirley had lunch brought in for the group so that they could be with Tim in a more relaxed environment. That meeting went well and Tim was grateful to have the opportunity to personally know all the people working on his defense.

Both Matt and Pete felt after meeting Tim that he was just as Heather said a victim of circumstance.

"He appears to be a great guy," Matt said when Tim left the office.

"Yeah, and anyone who meets him – or hears his testimony – will agree," said Pete. "I'd love to meet Tattoo!"

"I think Tattoo has kept Tim's spirit up during all of this." Heather said. "This guy has never had more than a speeding ticket in his life!"

Getting back to work, the group outlined their strategies in pursuing Tim's case – dependent on the deposition of Officer Blair.

The four of them left Heather's office around five-thirty agreeing to meet for dinner at seven. Once again, Heather offered to pick everyone up at the Radisson Hotel.

Harbor Island was adjacent to the Radisson and offered several eateries. The group opted for casual seafood. Heather made sure it was an early evening since she needed to be on top of her game the following day.

All of the conversation during dinner was light and more social than business. Everyone had worked hard to make Heather feel confident and she appreciated that. She also knew that she was ready.

After dropping off the guys, Heather made the short trek home. She was tired and felt that tonight she would get a good night's sleep.

Heather slept until her alarm awakened her.

CHAPTER SEVENTY

Deposition of FHP Officer Daniel Blair
Offices of Howell Legal Services & Investigations

Daniel Blair was sworn in by the clerk. He was accompanied by Kevin Morrison, Prosecuting Attorney for Pinellas County. Also present: Steven Oliver Bascom, Matthew Winters, Peter Sutherland, Heather Howell and the stenographer.

"Officer Blair, had you ever seen my client before the events that relate to this lawsuit?"

"No."

"Prior to this deposition, have you signed any written statements or spoken with anyone else – including the press about this lawsuit?"

"I signed the written report I authored and submitted on the incident on February 20, 2000."

"And that would be the official police report, am I correct?"

"Yes."

"And have you spoken with anyone else about this lawsuit?"

"I have spoken with the second officer on scene and the prosecuting attorney."

"And for the record sir, would you provide the names of those individuals?"

"That is Officer Darrell Dunn and Attorney Kevin Morrison."

"And what about Sophia Newton – did you ever discuss the case with her?"

"No."

"What if any documents (drawings, maps, photographs) pertaining to this case have you reviewed?"

"Other than my own sketch of the incident site and that of the forensics team, I have reviewed only the report submitted by my counterpart, Officer Dunn."

"And do you typically review the reports of your counterpart, Officer Blair?"

"Only for substantiation of the data, ma'am."

"And this is a typical action on your part?"

"Yes."

"Do you know if Officer Dunn reviews your reports as well?"

"I have no idea."

"Did you find discrepancies in the two reports?"

"Not that I recall."

"How long have you been in service with the Florida Highway Patrol?"

"Ten years, ten months."

"And do you like your job, Officer Blair?"

"I do."

"Thank you. I'd like us to talk about the night of February 20, 2000. Where were you when you received the dispatch to go to Florida 28th Street North?"

"I was on Gandy Boulevard."

"And the record shows your post received an anonymous telephone call which resulted in your dispatch, is that correct?"

"Yes."

"And what time did this occur?"

"It was 6:22 pm."

"And what time did you arrive on scene?"

"I arrived at roughly 6:25 pm."

"So you were only three minutes away from the accident scene?"

"Yes."

"Do you normally respond to anonymous phone calls that are received at your post?"

"If the dispatcher instructs an officer to respond, we do so."

"So am I correct in saying that this is at the discretion of the dispatcher?"

"Technically, yes."

"And what did you find when you arrived on scene?"

"I found a vehicle driven by Timothy Tyler on the shoulder of the road with damage to the front passenger side. Mr. Tyler was standing near the front of the vehicle."

"And did you question him about what had happened?"

"Yes."

"And his statement to you was what?"

"Mr. Tyler stated that he had been forced off the road by a large dump truck that was travelling southbound in his northbound lane."

"And did Mr. Tyler mention a garbage bag that had been struck by the dump truck, forcing it into his vehicle?"

"Yes."

"And what happened after that?"

"I radioed for backup, and then saw the garbage bag in question off the front passenger side of Mr. Tyler's car."

"So you did not approach the bag at that time?"

"No, I did not."

"Officer Blair, I'm confused as to why you were hesitant to approach the bag initially, and why you felt the need to call for backup. Could you explain that please?"

"In any police matter, the responding officer has to make a judgment call on whether or not backup is needed. Because of the location of the accident and only Mr. Tyler and myself on scene, I requested back up to inspect the contents of the bag."

"I see. Did you ask for Mr. Tyler's identification, license, and insurance?"

"Yes."

"And did you tell Mr. Tyler not to make any sudden moves – to keep his hands in sight as he retrieved these items from his glove box?"

"I may have. I don't remember."

"Did you ask Mr. Tyler to open his trunk?"

"Yes."

"And did you have a warrant to examine his vehicle or the contents of his trunk?"

"No."

"Were you expecting to find something incriminating there Officer Blair?"

"Objection to form" said Morrison.

"And what did you find during this unwarranted search?"

"Nothing."

"Did you complete the search before or after Officer Dunn arrived"

"Before."

"Thank you.   We will take a fifteen minute break – reconvening at ten fifteen."

Blair inquired about the location of the restroom, and made his way there. No one else left the room.

Upon his return, Heather nodded her head to the stenographer and said "we are back on the record in the deposition of FHP Officer Daniel Blair."

"Who opened the black bag?" Heather asked.

"Officer Dunn."

"What were the contents of that black garbage bag Officer Blair?"

"A woman's body."

"And was this woman believed to be dead?"

"Yes."

"Did you ask Mr. Tyler is he knew the woman?"

"Not at that time. We did ask him if he knew her when he was taken into custody."

"And his response was?"

"No."

"So without putting words in your mouth Officer, did you make the assumption that Tim Tyler killed the woman in the black bag?"

"When Mr. Tyler was asked, he openly stated that he had stuck the bag with his vehicle. We had no reason to believe that was not how she was killed."

"And so you arrested Timothy Tyler on a homicide charge?"

"Yes."

"Did Mr. Tyler mention that he was the *second* vehicle to strike the bag?"

"He said that, yes."

"And what if anything did you or Officer Dunn do to find the dump trucks that were travelling on that same highway at the same time as Mr. Tyler?"

"We dispatched a BOLO - a request for all units to be on the lookout for them."

"And did anything come of that BOLO?"

"Not to my knowledge."

"Officer Blair, isn't it correct to say that this office found both the trucks and the drivers who were on scene on February 20, 2000?"

"Yes."

"And have you ever had the occasion to interview the driver – Anthony Martinez - of the truck that first struck the garbage bag?"

"No. He was interrogated by Officer Dunn."

"And has he been charged with homicide?"

"Yes."

"Do you know Anthony Martinez?"

"Yes."

"Is it true that you were a professional reference for him when he applied for a contract position at Big Haul of Tampa?"

"Yes."

"How do you know Anthony Martinez?"

"He and I used to attend baseball games together."

"And what about a gentleman named Edwin Miller, do you know him?"

"Yes."

"And you were also listed as a reference for Mr. Miller, is that correct?"

"Yes."

"Mr. Miller was employed by Toy Town – were you aware of that?"

"Yes."

"Do Mr. Martinez and Mr. Miller know one another?"

"Objection to form," Morrison said.

"Did you introduce Martinez and Miller Officer Blair?"

"Yes – at a baseball game."

"And is it correct to say that you and Sophia Newton, the owner of Big Haul are or have been in an intimate relationship?"

"Yes."

"Did you ask Ms. Newton to hire Anthony Martinez?"

"No."

"Do you know or have you ever known a woman named Amelia Ann Blake?"

"Yes."

"And what was the nature of your relationship with Amelia Blake?"

"I am a friend of her mother, Barbara Blake."

"So you had no direct contact or relationship with Amelia Ann Blake?"

"That's correct."

"Isn't it true that the 'Jane Doe' found in the black bag was positively identified as Amelia Ann Blake?"

"Yes."

"And do you, Officer Blair have any information about who killed Amelia Ann Blake?"

"No."

"Would you describe your relationship with Amelia's mother Barbara?"

"We are friends."

"Did you kill Amelia Ann Blake?"

"No, I did not."

"Have you been in contact with her mother, Barbara Blake?"

"No."

"Has Mrs. Blake contacted you?"

"No."

"Do you consider yourself objective in this matter although you know or are involved with many of the persons of interest?"

"I do."

"Thank you. That concludes my questions."

Heather felt as though she had run a marathon without the proper training. She was exhausted and frustrated. Officer Daniel Blair was lying, but he was good at it. He didn't get rattled or lash out. He was cold and calculating – both characteristics of a killer with no conscience.

Now it was back to the drawing board.

"Ok gentlemen, let's pick it apart" said Heather as Bascom, Matt and Pete gathered in her office.

Bascom started by saying "He lied under oath – no doubt. But he convincingly lied to the point where a jury would probably believe him. Hell, he was cool enough to trick a lie detector with those answers."

"I so wanted to ask him if he had been intimate with Barbara Blake," Heather said, but I did not want to risk it."

Pete said, "Friends with benefits is my guess. This was most likely a crime of passion."

"Agreed, but where does that point the finger, to Barbara or to Blair?" Matt posed, "Or to Sophia Newton?"

Heather had been particularly quiet. Going to the white board in her office she drew a circle. Inside the circle she put Amelia's name. From there she added 'spokes to a wheel' that connected the names of Barbara Blake, Sophia Newton, Anthony Martinez and Daniel Dunn.

"Are there any other suspects I have omitted?" she asked.

Bascom was the first to speak. "I wouldn't even include Martinez as a suspect for murder. I think he facilitated the whole bag in the highway caper, but he may not have even known the contents of the bag. He's a thug, but most likely not a cold blooded killer. Plus he had no passion for Amelia – maybe he didn't even know her."

Matthew said, "I agree with Bascom *unless* Amelia was alive when she was placed in the bag. The Coroner's report indicates that she was already deceased, correct?"

"Correct" said Heather. "And the Coroner also took a DNA sample from Amelia's unborn child. We can and will find out who the father was. If that's Blair, then we have him dead to rights for lying under oath."

"But not dead to rights for murdering Amelia," Pete said. "Why would Blair deny knowing Amelia – or having a relationship with her? And why would he admit to a relationship with her mother? Here's my take: Blair is up to his neck in this and knowing he had to lie about something in the deposition, he opted to lie about his involvement with Amelia. He thought that was the easier option since Barbara Blake is still alive and can testify against him or at least dispute what he says."

Bascom could not be quiet any longer. "And along those lines, perhaps he has been threatened by Mrs. Blake. As we know she digs her heels in and won't stop. She gives new meaning to persistent. So, let's say their relationship was more than platonic, when she learns that Blair has also had a relationship with her daughter. What would Mrs. Blake do? Confront Blair? Confront Amelia?"

"What I don't see any evidence of is *how* Mrs. Blake found out about Amelia and Blair?" Heather posed.

Looking intently at the white board Matthew interjected a new thought. "What if Sophia Newton – who we know travelled to Cincinnati for something other than shopping – found out about Amelia and Blair? What would her first reaction be to that news?"

"From a woman's point of view she would most likely try to find out everything she could about Amelia." Heather said. "We know she went to Mike Fink's restaurant where Amelia was hostess, but that doesn't mean Sophia knew who Amelia was. She went there because of finding the matches on Blair."

"And maybe I'm reliving my younger, single years, but when a non-smoker saves matches or bar napkins, that used to mean you were interested in someone who worked there...." Matt said.

"And maybe Ms. Newton – knowing Blair's 'type' – chose Amelia?" Pete interjected.

Heather said, "Let's just assume for the moment that Sophia Newton checked out Amelia. What would she have found and how would she have found it?"

"Or most likely 'who' would she have found?" posed Bascom.

As if rehearsed they collectively said "Barbara Blake".

"Would Sophia Newton have the nerve to contact Barbara Blake?" asked Pete.

"She's a stalker – of course she would." Heather replied. "And we know that Amelia wasn't active in social media; but *BarB* was and is."

Bascom said "Let's remember that Sophia Newton used several social sites to access information about various people and groups – a cyber stalker if you will – and there she could have gotten Barbara Blake's profile. If you recall, Barbara posted a list of attributes she looked for in a man – professional – in a service industry…."

"Policeman fits that bill." Matt said.

Heather added a word of caution. "We're making a lot of assumptions here. Sophia Newton was asked if she knew Barbara Blake in the deposition. Her answer was 'not that I recall'".

"Well 'not that I recall' is not the same as a '*no*'." said Pete.

"We are making assumptions" said Bascom "and we can fill in the blanks on Mrs. Blake and Sophia Newton from a deposition of Barbara Blake."

"So the take away from this brainstorming session is that we subpoena Barbara Blake for a deposition." Heather said. "Gentlemen, it's time for a break. I will ask Shirley to secure the subpoena."

"We're going back to the Radisson as soon as we make a few telephone calls" said Matthew. "I'll call you from there to see what's in the works."

"Thanks Matt, you and Pete have been an amazing help."

"Just earning our keep, ma'am."

"Speaking of which, how long are you two planning to stay?"

"I think we'll try to get out of here tomorrow or the next day – we'll see what the flights are and let you know. We can always brainstorm by phone or Skype from here on out, unless you need something more?"

"Thanks, but I agree. While I'd like to keep you two, I know you are both busy. I would like you to meet someone before you leave however. Her name is Melanie Sergeant – she's a friend of Amelia Blake, and worked with her at Mike Fink's. Bascom and I interviewed her a while back."

"Great – let's meet her."

"I'll call and see when Melanie's available."

"Hi Melanie – it's Heather Howell."

"Hi Heather, how are you and Mr. Bascom?"

"We're good thanks. I have some associates in town that are working on Amelia's case with us and I'd like them to meet you if you're free. When would be a good time?"

"I'm off work at five tonight and I could meet you after that if I can arrange a sitter for my daughter?"

"How about you and your daughter meet us for dinner? You'll get a nice meal and not have to hire a sitter?"

"That's so nice Heather we'd love to meet you. Just tell me where and when and we'll be there."

"How about CDB's at six-thirty? I'll reserve a table in my name."

"Perfect. See you then."

Heather reserved a table for four and a half at six-thirty pm. Arriving first was Bascom who opted to drive himself and Heather arrived with Matt and Pete in tow shortly thereafter.

Melanie Sergeant arrived shortly after, alone.

The hostess seated her with the group. Heather introduced Mel to Matthew and Peter before asking where her daughter was.

"Thanks for including her. She would have been with me but I was upstaged by her new best friend forever who asked if she could spend the night. I couldn't say no."

"Daughters have a way of getting their way," said Pete. "My daughter sets our curfews now."

After ordering a round of drinks, Heather gave Mel the short story of how she knew Matt and Pete, a bit about their working together on a case and how the guys had gotten her hooked on private investigations.

Bascom said, "And these two put Heather and me together because Pete has always been envious of my PI prowess..." They all laughed at that.

"Speaking of Amelia's case, I was going through some boxes that included some old photos from Mike Fink's. I brought a few of the best ones so that you could see how beautiful Amelia was when we worked together."

Opening the envelope Melanie handed Heather three photos.

"The first one is of the two of us – we were gal pals through and through. And the second one shows a group shot of the servers, bartenders and Sam, the manager just before opening one night. The third one is just a panoramic shot of the inside of Mike Fink's. You can see the river through the back windows. That's me at the bar with some of our customers. I guess that may have been one of my last night's there."

Heather looked quickly to Bascom, pointing at the last photo and specifically to one of the people sitting at the bar. Neither said anything; they simply nodded to one another.

"Mel, it was so nice of you to bring these pictures. Do you think we could hang on to them for a while? I promise to get them back to you." Heather said.

"Sure, that's no problem."

Bascom said, "I know you haven't been in Tampa very long. When did you leave Mike Fink's?"

"I was there through December." Mel said.

Sensing what was happening without understanding it, Matthew said, "Would you guys like to order soon? I for one am starving."

"Great idea" said Heather, as she motioned for the server.

The five of them had a leisurely dinner and enjoying the Italian food. Everyone was stuffed except Pete, who had to order dessert.

Matthew opted to pick up the tab for everyone, telling Pete he had to pay for his own dessert.

"Take it out of my pay, boss."

"No wonder you all work so well together," said Melanie, "you're all alike! Thank you for dinner Mr. Winters."

"You're welcome and feel free to call me Matt or Matthew."

"I hope the photos give you a better perspective of the environment Amelia worked in. We were all like family – sort of like the four of you. I should go now. Thank you again."

Heather stood and gave Mel a hug as she left the table. "We will talk soon."

Waiting until she had gone out the door of the restaurant, Heather said "Take a look at who happens to be sitting at the bar in Mike Fink's – Mrs. Barbara Blake, sitting alongside a woman who is a dead ringer for Sophia Newton."

"Is Amelia in the same photograph?" Pete asked.

"No. The hostess stand is not in that photo. Look at the picture of Amelia and Mel taken at the hostess stand. It's in a completely separate area of the restaurant."

"So, Mamma Blake could have come in without the knowledge of her daughter and taken a seat in the bar?" Matt said.

"That's how it looks," said Heather. "And maybe Mamma Blake didn't care if she was seen by her daughter or not?"

Bascom said quietly, "I think it best to take this conversation into work tomorrow."

CHAPTER SEVENTY-ONE

The Next Day – Heather's office

Matthew and Pete had scheduled a flight back to Gainesville for two in the afternoon. They arrived at Heather's office at nine sharp and wanted to take a closer look at the photos Melanie Sergeant had provided the night before.

"My computer guru pulled up photographs of Fink's Restaurant," said Matt, referring to Pete. "It is obvious from them that because Mike Fink's is a boat for all intents and purposes, its rooms are intimate and separate. Amelia's hostess station is at the front, but the view to the bar area is obscured. If Mrs. Blake came in while Amelia was seating someone else, she could have easily made her way to the bar unnoticed."

"Perhaps Mrs. Blake was asked to meet Sophia to talk about a mutual acquaintance, or perhaps she mentioned the name of Daniel Blair?" Heather posed.

"Mrs. Blake would meet there rather than at her home." Bascom added.

"And if Newton wanted to meet in a public place she was familiar with – albeit only on one occasion – she would have suggested Mike Fink's, not the hotel she was staying in." Heather said.

"Regardless," said Matt, "we have a connection between the two women – in living color."

CHAPTER SEVENTY-TWO

Barbara Blake
Covington, Kentucky
August 2000

When the doorbell rang, Barbara was surprised. She wasn't expecting anyone today and it was too early for the mail man. When she went to the door she was looking into the face of a deputy from the sheriff's office.

"Yes sir, what can I do for you?" asked Barbara.

"Are you Barbara Blake?" the deputy asked.

"I am."

The deputy handed her a group of papers saying, "Then this is for you. Please consider yourself served. Have a nice day."

Barbara was mortified. She was being subpoenaed to appear at an attorney's office in Tampa in a mere three days. As she perused the documents she saw that she would have to give a deposition relating to the death of her daughter, Amelia.

Barbara immediately telephoned her family attorney – who was more of a friend who happened to *be* an attorney – and he told her she had to comply or she could be held in contempt of court.

Slamming the phone down on that conversation, she then telephoned a travel agent and booked a flight to Tampa in two days. She also had the agent book a room in downtown Tampa for two nights.

Once that was done she telephoned the Pinellas County Prosecutor's office. While she had asked to speak to Morrison personally, she had to settle for his assistant. After her initial rant, Barbara explained the receipt of the subpoena and gave Morrison's assistant her itinerary. Barbara was insistent that Morrison be present at the deposition to insure that she was not unlawfully questioned.

"Our office has a representative at each deposition regarding this case Mrs. Blake, and I can assure you that if Mr. Morrison is available on that date, he will make every effort to attend your deposition."

"You tell Morrison that I expect him to be there," Barbara said and promptly hung up.

She was poised to call Sophia Newton when she decided she would wait and surprise her once she got to Tampa. She also considered placing a call to Daniel but thought he might deserve a surprise of his own.

Thinking about little else, Barbara decided that either Sophia or Daniel had caused this subpoena to be issued. She was confident that each of them had given depositions; she just wasn't sure who threw her under the bus.

CHAPTER SEVENTY-THREE

Officer Daniel Blair
FHP Tampa, Florida

Blair was never 'friendly' with his fellow officers, but he was in a foul mood these days. Everyone including the janitorial staff took note of his bad disposition, and avoided contact with him for that reason.

Darrell Dunn was the first to ask him what was going on.

"Nothing is going on, I'm just busy," snapped Blair, "and don't you have better things to do than hound me?"

"Excuse me Officer Blair for giving a crap." Dunn said. "But I'll tell you that the whole post is wondering what your attitude is about. Clean it up; we're all busy around here." Dunn walked away – envisioning the gesture that had just been hurled in his direction.

Blair finished the paperwork in front of him and left the post. He stormed out, got into his cruiser and left the parking lot.

Out on the road he thought about what Dunn had said to him. As painful as it was for him, he did need to present better, particularly at work. If he did not, people would be suspicious and he did not need that.

CHAPTER SEVENTY-FOUR

Heather Howell's Office
Tampa, Florida
August 2000

Time was fleeting. The court date for Timothy Tyler was swiftly approaching and her discovery was incomplete.

Tomorrow's calendar included the deposition of the other FHP Officer on scene in February, Darrell Dunn. Heather predicted it would be straightforward and would likely produce no new discovery in the case.

Reviewing the intellectual background Bascom had provided her on Dunn, he appeared squeaky clean. In his fifteen years with FHP he had never had an infraction, no accusations and no reprimands.

Hopefully the deposition would be a couple of hours maximum.

Heather reviewed Dunn's police report – probably for the third or fourth time – and made a few notes in the margins of discrepancies from Daniel Blair's report.

Heather had been notified that the subpoena had been served on Barbara Blake, so she would move forward with the preparation for that. She had Shirley contact Kevin Morrison's office to make sure they were on notice for the deposition.

Having done that, Shirley reported that Mrs. Blake would be arriving tomorrow and had hotel reservations for two nights.

Heather then sent a quick email to Matthew Winters letting him know the deposition was set.

CHAPTER SEVENTY-FIVE

Sophia Newton
Tampa, Florida

It was almost business-as-usual, and Sophia was feeling the relief that this semblance of normalcy brought with it.

With the deposition behind her, no recent contact with either Daniel Blair or Anthony Martinez and having heard nothing new about the case of Timothy Tyler, Sophia concentrated on her company, Big Haul.

The repairs on the EU 4-axle hauler had been expensive. She decided that if she were ever approached by Anthony Martinez again, she would file a lawsuit against him in the amount of the damages.

Despite that claim on the company's insurance, the year had been in the black, her annual payment to Bank of America had been made with a bit leftover and she was beginning to think that the year 2000 would indeed be a new start for her.

When her telephone rang, the receptionist said there was a woman on the line who refused to give her name. "Want me to take a message?"

"No, I'll handle it," said Newton.

"This is Sophia Newton," she said.

"Ms. Newton, this is Barbara Blake. Remember me?"

"I do. What can I do for you?" Newton asked.

"You can start by telling me you're no longer seeing our mutual friend," Barbara said.

"Affirmative, Mrs. Blake. Now if you will excuse me, I have a company to run."

"Sure, but before you go to run your company, you might be interested to know that I am in town for a couple of days and plan to seek the advice of an attorney on filing a civil suit against your little company on behalf of my deceased daughter. Have a nice day." Barbara hung up, satisfied that she had added a little drama to Ms. Newton's otherwise dull day.

Sophia Newton was shaking. She had never thought about civil action. She knew enough to know that punitive damages in a civil suit could ruin her business. Fearful and angry at the same time, Sophia knew she had to do something. She just had no idea what that might be.

CHAPTER SEVENTY-SIX

Deposition of FHP Officer Darrell Dunn
Offices of Howell Legal Services & Investigations
August 2000

"Good Morning Officer Dunn," Heather began. "I will simply remind you that having been duly sworn in, the contents of this deposition are considered testimony and carry the same responsibility, weight and merit of testimony given in court."

"Please state for the record your full name."

"Darrell Anderson Dunn."

"And you are employed by the Florida Highway Patrol, correct?"

"Yes."

"How long have you been with FHP?"

"Fifteen years."

"How long have you worked with your fellow officer Daniel Blair?"

"Ten years."

"Is it correct to say that you are typically Officer Blair's backup?"

"Yes."

"And is it fair to say that you work together on a daily basis?"

"We provide backup for one another on the days and shifts that we have in common."

"Thank you. Were you called to the scene of Florida 28th Street North on February 20, 2000?"

"Yes."

"And you were called as backup to Officer Blair on that occasion?"

"Yes."

"And you filed a police report for that call, correct?"

"Yes."

"Can you describe what you saw at the scene on February 20, 2000?"

"I arrived on scene to find Officer Blair questioning Timothy Tyler whose automobile had struck a black garbage bag."

"And did you and Officer Blair speak privately at that time?"

"Yes."

"For the record Officer Dunn, please describe the content of that conversation."

"Officer Blair said that Mr. Tyler's vehicle had struck a garbage bag of unknown contents. He had radioed me as backup prior to examining the contents of that bag."

"Tell me Officer Dunn, is that standard procedure?"

"If an officer senses danger or feels the need to have a witness present before examining evidence, then the standard procedure is to call for backup."

"And did Officer Blair indicate that he was suspicious of the contents of that black bag?"

"Officer Blair found a sticky residue on the headlamp of Mr. Tyler's vehicle and felt that warranted having a witness present before the content was examined."

"Officer Dunn, did you examine the contents of that bag?"

"Yes."

"What was the contents sir?"

"The body of a female."

"And did you or Officer Blair continue an examination of the contents of the bag?"

"No."

"What did you and your fellow officer do at that point?"

"I called FHP's Crime Scene Investigators to the site."

"While you called for a CSI team, what action did Officer Blair take?"

"He placed Timothy Tyler under arrest and read him his Miranda Rights."

"Did Officer Blair ever look inside the black garbage bag?"

"No."

"Did you recognize the female in the black garbage bag?"

"No."

"Do you personally know Timothy Tyler?"

"No."

"Did you ever meet Timothy Tyler before the night of his arrest on February 20, 2000?"

"No."

"When you filed your accident report, did you confer with Officer Blair?"

"No."

"Did Officer Blair ever ask to see or read your account of that evening?"

"Objection to form," Kevin Morrison said.

"I will rephrase. Did Officer Blair ask to see your accident report?"

"No."

"Would another officer have ready access to your report?"

"No."

"So if there were discrepancies in the two reports, neither of you would know that?"

Morrison started to raise an objection, but opted to allow the question in its original form.

"No."

"Officer Dunn, how did FHP identify the victim that was found in that black bag?"

"An autopsy was performed and dental records were obtained."

"Did you know Amelia Ann Blake?"

"No."

"Had you ever met Amelia Ann Blake?"

"No."

"Have you ever met or do you know, Barbara Blake?

"I have never met her, but recognize that name as the mother of Amelia Ann Blake."

"Would you consider Daniel Blair to be a friend of yours?"

"No. Our relationship is strictly that of officers working for the same justice department."

"Thank you. That concludes my questions."

On his way out of the conference room Kevin Morrison moved toward Heather. "I guess you have heard that Mrs. Blake arrived in town."

"Yes, I'm aware of that. Will you be attending her deposition or have you drafted someone on your staff to preside?" Heather asked.

"Oh, I'll be here. Actually counselor I am panting with anticipation for this one. I wouldn't miss it. See you tomorrow," Morrison said as he sauntered out of the conference room.

"What was that about" Bascom asked.

"I believe in the animal kingdom it is referred to as *posturing*." Heather replied.

CHAPTER SEVENTY-SEVEN

Tim Tyler
August 2000

Tim knew that depositions were ongoing yet he had no interest in sitting in on any of them. The upcoming trial would be difficult enough; he saw no need to hear the preliminary comments.

Heather had been great in keeping him up to date on where they were in the process. He trusted her implicitly, and knew she was handling his case with the utmost care.

Tim's monthly statements from Howell's office did not reflect any hourly charges for Matthew Winters or Peter Sutherland, both of whom had spent a great deal of time in working on his case. When Tim had asked Shirley about it, she had informed him that their fees were incorporated into the staff charges that appeared on each statement.

###

Happy to think about something other than the trial, Tim had allowed his thoughts to slip back to Natalie Graham. He decided that tonight he and Tattoo would incorporate her street on their evening walk.

Tattoo seemed to take the cue from his pet parent, heading off in the direction of Natalie's street.

As luck would have it, Tim caught a glimpse of a young woman and a child as they neared Graham's home. Tattoo saw them too and started pulling on his leash. As Tim was commanding him to heal, the woman heard him.

Not wanting to frighten her, Tim put a hand in the air and waved. He stopped, making Tattoo sit, and she smiled.

Approaching ever so slowly, Tim spoke as soon as they were within earshot. "Hi, I'm Tim and this is Tattoo. We live a couple of streets over."

"You're the man who called the police and the EMT's for me, aren't you?"

"Yes. I'm glad you are up and about. When we first found you, it didn't look good."

The woman put out her hand to Tim and introduced herself as Natalie Graham. "I don't think that saying thank you is quite enough, but thank you for what you did."

Tattoo was cooing and restless. "It was Tattoo here who alerted me that something was wrong."

"Thank you Tattoo," she said. "He's a beautiful German shepherd, isn't he Mattie? This is my daughter Mattie, she's five, and she's never seen a dog she didn't like."

Squatting down to see her eye to eye, he said "Hi Mattie, my name is Tim. It's nice to meet you."

Mattie smiled and blushed, clinging to her mother's leg.

"Would you like to meet Tattoo and maybe even pet him?"

Mattie nodded.

"Tattoo, heal" said Tim. Tattoo sat down next to Tim, and then lay down on the sidewalk.

"Okay Mattie, Tattoo would love for you to pet him. He's being quiet now so that you won't be scared."

Mattie looked up at her mother who nodded her approval. Mattie walked over to Tattoo and patted his head.

"Do you believe in love at first sight?" Natalie asked.

"I do now," Tim said. "May we come see you and Mattie again sometime?"

"Of course," said Natalie "we'd like that, right Mattie?" Her daughter was hugging Tattoo and nodding her head at the same time.

CHAPTER SEVENTY-EIGHT

Deposition of Barbara Blake
Offices of Howell Legal Services & Investigations
August 2000

Barbara Blake walked into the conference room accompanied by Kevin Morrison.

Mrs. Blake was sworn in and then seated. Heather introduced herself and Steven Bascom, then proceeded to explain the procedures for the deposition. She asked Mrs. Blake if she had any questions – to which she had none – and the deposition began.

"Mrs. Blake, have you ever been arrested?"

"No."

"Have you ever been deposed before today?"

"No."

"Did you meet with Kevin Morrison or anyone else in his office before this deposition?"

"Yes, Mr. Morrison."

"Where were the meetings held?"

"In Mr. Morrison's office."

"Have you signed any written statements, made any recorded statements or spoken with anyone else about this lawsuit?"

"No."

"Do you have a personal attorney?"

"I do."

"And is that counsel present?"

"No, he is in Cincinnati, Ohio."

"Did you discuss this case or prepare for this deposition with your personal counsel?"

"Yes."

"Please tell me everything you did to prepare for this deposition."

"Since it is unclear why I was subpoenaed for a deposition, I contacted my personal attorney. He advised me to honor the court order and here I am."

"Did you view any reports or obtain information from anyone – including media sources – regarding this case?"

"No."

"Is there any reason – medical, psychological or physical – that might prevent you from answering my questions today?"

"No."

"I remind you Mrs. Blake that you are under oath and have sworn to tell the truth in answering my questions. And that this oath carries the same weight as it would in a courtroom with a judge and jury present. Do you understand that?"

"Yes."

Heather went through the identification questions quickly as well as Barbara Blake's residential history.

"Mrs. Blake, have you ever been married, and if so, to whom?"

"I was married for over twenty years to William Blake who is now deceased."

"So you have only been married once?"

"Correct."

"And do you have children?"

"One daughter, Amelia."

"And am I correct in saying that is Amelia Ann Blake – the victim in this lawsuit?"

"Yes."

"And was your daughter living at home with you?"

"No."

"Where did she live?"

"In Cincinnati."

"And when did your daughter leave your residence to live elsewhere?"

"After her father died."

"And when was that?"

"Amelia left home approximately fourteen years ago."

"And what age was she then?"

"She was eighteen."

Heather paused intentionally.

"Did Amelia depend on you for her livelihood?"

"No."

"And after Amelia moved out of your home, did she ever ask you for financial help of any kind?"

"No."

"Please describe your relationship with your daughter Amelia."

"I would describe it as typical."

"Were you close?"

"Close enough."

"Why did Amelia move out of your house – her family home?"

"She didn't say."

"Did you ask her Mrs. Blake?"

"I attempted to, but she stormed out of the house."

"And again, for my clarification, that was fourteen years ago?"

"Correct."

"How many times did you see Amelia or contact her after she left the house?"

"I did not see or contact her."

"So the last time you saw your daughter she was eighteen and leaving the only home she ever knew?"

"Yes if you choose to see it like that."

"Why do you say that Mrs. Blake?"

"Look – she was a Daddy's girl from day one. When William died she seemed to want nothing to do with me. He left her enough money to take care of herself and she chose to leave – I never asked her to do that."

"When Amelia moved out, how did that make you feel Mrs. Blake?"

"Relieved, but sad of course."

"Why relieved?"

"We did not have a happy relationship – it was stressful."

"How did you learn of your daughter's death?"

"The Covington Police came to my home to tell me."

"And what was your reaction to that news?"

"I was shocked, of course."

"What did the officers tell you about her death?"

"That she was found dead with no identification in the Tampa Bay Area."

"And is it true that you were upset that an autopsy had been preformed?"

"Yes – it was done without my permission."

"And isn't it also true that you were told by the Covington police that an autopsy was standard operating procedure when there is no identification found with a victim?"

"Yes."

"What happened next, Mrs. Blake?"

"I contacted funeral directors in Covington and asked that they have Amelia's body sent there as soon as possible."

"And as a result, was Amelia's body returned to Covington and ultimately laid to rest?"

"Yes, adjacent to her father's grave."

"Did you have a public service for Amelia?"

"No. It was private."

"And how are you coping with the death of your daughter now, Mrs. Blake?"

"I am dealing with it."

"Isn't it true that you telephoned every police agency in the area about your daughter's death – and getting her body returned to Kentucky?"

"I telephoned until I got a satisfactory answer."

"And Mrs. Blake, please tell me why it was so important for you to have the body of Amelia returned without delay?"

"She deserved a proper burial – in her hometown."

"Did you view the body Mrs. Blake?"

"Yes."

"And it was important - for your peace of mind – to bury your estranged daughter in your family plot – is that true?"

"Yes."

"Were you aware that Amelia was pregnant?"

"No – not until she died."

"And do you have any idea who the father of her unborn child might be?"

"No."

"Where did Amelia work prior to her death?"

"At a restaurant named Mike Fink's in Cincinnati."

"And why was she in the Tampa Bay Area in February?"

"I have no idea."

"Do you know if Amelia has any friends who live in this area?"

"I don't know – perhaps."

"Do you know anyone in this area Mrs. Blake?"

"Yes."

"Please give us their name(s) for the record."

"Daniel Blair."

"Anyone else?"

"I recently met a woman named Sophia Newton."

"And how did you meet Ms. Newton?"

"She was visiting the Cincinnati area and we met over drinks in one of the local bars."

"And what was the name of the bar?"

"Mike Fink's."

"I see, and how do you know Daniel Blair?"

"Daniel Blair and I have been friends for several years. We were introduced to one another at a Cincinnati Reds baseball game."

"And do you recall who may have introduced you?"

"No I do not recall."

"How would you describe your relationship with Daniel Blair?"

"Friends."

"So there was no romantic or physical attraction between the two of you?"

"No, not really."

"Are you aware that Daniel Blair is a member of the Florida Highway Patrol?"

"Yes."

"And are you also aware that he was the first officer on scene when your daughter's body was discovered?"

"Yes."

"Do you find that odd or the least bit curious?"

"Objection to form," Morrison said.

"Does the fact that a friend of yours is involved in this case cause you any concern Mrs. Blake?"

"No. I trust that Officer Blair will do his job."

"Have you spoken with Daniel Blair since the death of your daughter?"

"Yes."

"And did you discuss anything about this case with Officer Blair?"

"No."

Heather stated that they would take a fifteen minute break.

Shirley came in the conference room, refreshed the water and coffee and removed the dirtied cups.

Morrison went out into the hallway with Mrs. Blake; Heather sat at the conference table next to Bascom.

Whispering to Heather, Bascom said – "You've got her right where you want her; great job."

Heather smiled but shook her head.

"Having recessed for fifteen minutes, we are now on record and in continuation of the deposition of Barbara Blake, "the stenographer said.

"Mrs. Blake, have you had an occasion to visit the Tampa Bay Area before this trip?"

"Once I believe."

"For the record Mrs. Blake, does that mean you aren't sure, or you don't know? Clarify please."

"I'm not sure, I may have. I really don't remember."

"Please tell me how you know Sophia Newton."

There was a long pause, almost as if Blake was trying to tie the two questions together.

"Mrs. Blake, would you like me to repeat the question?"

"As I said earlier I actually met Ms. Newton in Cincinnati."

"You eluded earlier in the deposition that you met Sophia Newton in the bar at Mike Fink's."

"Correct."

"Was that a chance meeting, or was it pre-arranged?"

"Ms. Newton invited me to meet her there."

"So you knew her and thereby accepted her invitation?"

"No. I did not know her before that meeting."

"I see, then could you share the reason you agreed to meet with an out-of-town stranger in a bar in Cincinnati?"

"Sophia Newton telephoned me earlier in the day saying that we had mutual acquaintances, and that she would like to meet with me while she was in town."

"Who are those mutual acquaintances Mrs. Blake?"

"Daniel Blair."

"But you said acquaintances implying more than one person. Who is the other person Ms. Newton wanted to see you about."

"Amelia."

"Your daughter – Amelia Blake?"

"Yes."

"When was the meeting at Mike Fink's?"

"December of last year – December of 1999."

"Did you see Amelia at the restaurant on that night in December?"

"No. I don't believe she was working that night."

"At this meeting what did you discuss with Sophia Newton?"

"Ms. Newton asked me how I knew Daniel Blair."

"And what else?"

"She also asked how Amelia knew him."

"And how did you answer her queries Mrs. Blake?"

"I told her that Daniel and I had known each other for years. I also told her that I was not aware that Amelia and Daniel knew one another."

"And did that satisfy Ms. Newton's curiosity?"

"No."

"How so?"

"She wanted to know if Daniel and Amelia were 'involved', and I told her I had no idea."

"And did Ms. Newton give you any reason for asking you these questions?"

"She told me that she and Daniel were dating."

"And did Ms. Newton appear threatening in any way toward you or Amelia as a result of your meeting?"

"Her threats were not apparent."

"Are you saying you sensed unspoken threats?"

"Yes."

"Can you pinpoint anything in that conversation that could have been interpreted as 'threatening'?"

"Sophia Newton made it perfectly clear that Daniel Blair was now romantically involved with her and that her desire was to have a mutually exclusive relationship."

"Thank you. How did you meeting with Ms. Newton conclude?"

"Ms. Newton told me I should relay our conversation to my daughter the next time I spoke with her."

"And you agreed?"

"I simply nodded my head – I didn't say anything at all to her."

"Did you communicate any of this information to Amelia?"

"No."

"Have you spoken to Ms. Newton since that time?"

"Yes."

"When and under what circumstances?"

"I telephoned her yesterday when I arrived."

"Why?"

"To let her know I am filing a civil suit in the wrongful death of Amelia naming her company, Big Haul, as negligent."

"And what was her reaction?"

"She hung up on me."

"Have you seen or spoken with Daniel Blair since your arrival?"

"No."

"Did you advise Officer Blair that you were coming to Tampa?"

"No."

"Mrs. Blake, have you ever been physically or romantically involved with Daniel Blair?"

"We are friends."

"How do you define friends, Mrs. Blake?"

"We are not romantically involved."

Heather took a long pause.

"Have you and Daniel Blair ever engaged in any sexual activity?"

"Yes. I would like to take a break now please."

Heather said: "We will take a fifteen minute break."

All was silent as Mrs. Blake and Attorney Morrison left the conference room.

Heather quickly walked to her office – purposely ignoring everyone including Bascom. She needed to be alone with her thoughts knowing what line of questioning she had ahead of her. She closed her door and sat at her desk for ten minutes.

###

"We are now on record in the deposition of Barbara Blake after a fifteen minute recess," said the stenographer.

"Mrs. Blake, when did you and Officer Blair first engage in a sexual relationship?"

"About two years after the death of my husband."

"And has your intimate relationship with Daniel Blair continued?"

"No."

"When did that relationship end?"

"I ended it when I learned that Daniel was involved with other women."

"I see. And when you learned of these other women, did you know that Amelia was one of them?"

"No, absolutely not."

"Do you think that your daughter Amelia was intimately involved with Daniel Blair?"

"I don't know."

"Do you believe Amelia *could* have been intimately involved with Daniel Blair?"

"I do now, but I would have never considered that until Sophia Newton tracked my daughter down the way she did."

"Do you have any idea who might want to harm Amelia?"

"I can only say that if Amelia were seeing Daniel and Sophia Newton found out about it, she could have brought harm to Amelia."

"Why do you think Amelia came to Tampa in February?"

"I think she may have wanted to reveal her pregnancy to the father."

"And was Amelia the type of individual who would do that in person rather than over the telephone?"

"Yes."

"And you know of no one in the Tampa Bay Area that Amelia knew, is that correct?"

There was a long pause. Barbara Blake's face was ashen.

"Mrs. Blake? I need a verbal response please."

"I'm sorry. I am just realizing that it may have been Daniel she was coming to see."

"Did you kill your daughter, Amelia?"

"Absolutely not."

"Are you attempting to set up Sophia Newton as the killer?"

"No, that's preposterous."

"Did you have anything to do with the murder of Amelia?"

"No."

"I remind you that you are under oath."

"I did not kill my daughter nor did I have anything to do with it."

"Mrs. Blake, I have a copy of an airline ticket that you purchased from Delta Airlines for a round trip ticket to Tampa on February 19, 2000 with a return on February 20, 2000. Why did you come here then, and why did you testify that you didn't recall coming here prior to yesterday?"

Blake dropped her head.

"Mrs. Blake - why did you make that trip and with whom did you see while you were here?"

"I came here at Daniel Blair's request."

"So you saw Daniel Blair while you were here?"

"Yes."

"What reason did he give for requesting that you come here?"

"He said he had to talk with me in person."

"Mrs. Blake, I am finding it difficult to believe that you would purchase a round trip ticket to Tampa at the request of a man whom you say you were no longer involved with just because he said he wanted to talk with you. What, if any reason, did he give you?"

"He said it was about my daughter, and that it was extremely important."

"And what did Daniel Blair tell you once you arrived?"

"He said that Amelia called, wanting to see him even though he had broken things off with her in December. He said she was in town and he was avoiding her."

"And this is what he had to tell you in person?"

"He was afraid that she was pregnant and that it might be his child."

"What did he ask you to do?"

"He asked me to talk to her – and to get her to leave town."

"And did you?"

"I went to the hotel where she was staying, but she wasn't there."

"And did you share this with Daniel Blair?"

"Yes, I phoned him."

"And what happened next?"

"He told me he was on patrol and couldn't talk. He promised to call me later."

"When did you speak with Daniel Blair again?"

"He telephoned me at the end of his shift and I agreed to meet him at his apartment."

"And all this transpired on February 19, 2000, correct?"

"Yes."

"Please tell me what happened when you met with Daniel Blair?"

"He wasn't there."

"And what did you do next?"

"I waited in the parking lot of his apartment complex. I saw Daniel pull in and park. Another car pulled in immediately after he did – it was Sophia Newton. She followed him into his apartment."

"And what did you do?"

"I waited five minutes and then knocked on his door."

"Did you enter his apartment?"

"I did and he and Sophia Newton were obviously arguing. He asked her to leave and she refused. He took her by the arm and pulled her to the door. She left crying."

"And what happened then?"

"Daniel was very upset. He asked me to leave and said I should take my daughter home with me."

"What did you do then Mrs. Blake?"

"I got in my car, drove to the Comfort Inn where Amelia was supposed to be staying. I knocked on her door several times, but there was no answer. I gave up and left."

"So you left without seeing Amelia?"

"That's right."

"Did you speak with Daniel Blair again?"

"I phoned him from the airport and left a message saying that I was going home."

"And have you spoken to him since then?"

"No."

"And you left Tampa on February 20, 2000, correct?"

"Yes."

"And you state that you never made contact with your daughter, correct?"

"That's correct."

"Thank you Mrs. Blake. I have no more questions at this time. If additional information is needed from you, we will be in touch."

###

Heather waited until everyone left the conference room except the stenographer.

"May I get an expedited transcript of Mrs. Blake's deposition, please?"

"Certainly," the court reporter answered.

When Heather went to her office, Bascom was nearby.

"Come on in," said Heather "we're in the deep end of the pool now."

"Shall we call Matt and Pete?"

"Let's wait until after we get the expedited transcript which I just requested. I'll send a copy to them and then we'll review it."

"Good call" said Bascom "you've earned a few minutes of silence." He winked at Heather and walked out of her office closing the door behind him.

"Good man Bascom..." said Heather under her breath.

CHAPTER SEVENTY-NINE

Heather Howell's Office
The Following Day

The deposition transcript of Barbara Blake had been delivered by messenger first thing. Realizing what it was, Shirley immediately made enough copies to share with Bascom, Matt and Pete. When Heather walked in the door, Shirley met her with coffee and the transcript copies.

"Shall I fax this to Matt and Pete, or would you prefer that I scan it and send it to them via email?"

"Scan it please; it is probably the more secure way to transmit it. And thanks Shirley – you are always a step ahead of me!"

Heather had thought about little else than Blake's testimony. Something was troubling Heather, and she hadn't yet put her finger on it. The brainstorming session would most likely clear it up. Four heads were better than one.

Setting up a session via Skype allowed the participants of the brainstorming meeting to now only hear but also see one another. After making a secure connection, Shirley left Heather's office.

"Have you two had time to review Mrs. Blake's deposition?" Heather asked.

Both Matt and Pete affirmed they had.

Pete was the first to make any comment. "Heather, first of all you did a great job in conducting this deposition. It couldn't have been pleasant. My initial take on it is that Blake gave two distinct depositions. The first part – deposition number one – was given to save face, positioning herself as an injured party. Although she lied under oath several times, she did so without flinching. She was clearly pointing blame on Newton. The second part – deposition number two – was to point blame directly on Daniel Blair; maybe with Newton as an accomplice, but directly on Blair."

Bascom added "I think we got exactly what we wanted; definitive love triangle. And depending on what we can believe to be the true parts of her deposition, Mrs. Blake gave us means, motive and opportunity for more than one suspect. "

"I see that also," said Matthew "but I am probably most bothered by Mrs. Blake's attempt to push the blame away from her while having her own means, motive and opportunity. This was a woman who had been jilted by Blair – who had probably impregnated her daughter- and she learns all of it from a woman who drove a zillion miles to tell her and her daughter to back off."

Heather had been quietly taking all this information in when she asked the guys to look at the last part of the deposition. She referred to her question about why Blake had come to Tampa in February.

"Mrs. Blake says that Daniel asked her to come here. That seems odd to me, since neither Daniel nor Mrs. Blake knew a) that Amelia was pregnant; and b) Daniel did not know about the meeting Mrs. Blake had with Sophia Newton."

"You think Newton might have told Blair about that meeting in Cincinnati?" Bascom posed.

"No way Sophia Newton would have let Daniel know about that. He would have thrown a fit knowing that she checked into his life." Heather stated. "I sense a change in Mrs. Blake's responses beyond that point in the deposition. Suddenly this strong-willed independent woman becomes a 'whatever you say I'll do' sort of character."

Matt interjected, "I can't envision that scene between Blair, Newton and Blake. I doubt that ever took place. There is too much drama in that dialog and for Blair to man-handle Newton to remove her from the scene is overkill. My guess is that Barbara Blake is writing her own ending to the play."

"And let us not forget," Pete added, "someone killed Amelia that night or the next morning. I know that Mrs. Blake said she never saw Amelia while she was here, but she stated that she went to her hotel room twice. Where would Amelia have been other than with Daniel or in her hotel room? She didn't know anyone else in town."

"She knows Melanie Sergeant," Bascom said, "but I don't believe she knew that Mel was in Tampa. Guess we'd best check that out."

"Has the plot just thickened?" Pete asked.

"I hope not," said Matthew. "The last thing we need is another suspect."

"Before we go down another rabbit hole, let's get telephone records for Barbara Blake's cell phone," Heather said "I want to see who she called while she was here."

"I will get Michael on that right away." Bascom said. He excused himself to do that.

"Heather – what is your gut saying to you?" Matt asked.

"My gut says Barbara Blake is the killer. I just can't prove it – yet. Does your gut have anything to add?"

"I believe she is guilty as well, but I don't see how she could have pulled this off without Blair's help." Matt answered.

Bascom re-entered Heather's office. "What did I miss?"

"We've been spilling our guts." said Pete "What does your gut say?"

"Barbara Blake; in tandem with Daniel Blair."

"It's time for you to weigh in Pete – what do you think?" Heather asked.

"I see Barbara Blake, incensed and angered by Sophia Newton to the point that she probably came here, confronted Daniel about Amelia *and* Sophia and assured him that their 'friends with benefits' time was over. Daniel then breaks off his relationship with Amelia, thinking that will smooth things over with Barbara. He probably saw no need to stop seeing Sophia – Barbara wouldn't know about it anyway."

"Then Amelia learns sometime in January that she is pregnant. She knows that it is Blair's child and wants him to know about the pregnancy. She comes here in February to tell him. When she does, he explodes – tells her it's not his problem and asks her to leave. She leaves – highly emotional – and goes to her hotel room."

"Blair probably called Barbara, tells her Amelia is pregnant and she takes the first plane to Tampa. Barbara gets in

Blair's face about it and he tells her to mind her own business and get out. From there, it's a bit sketchier. Barbara probably went to find Amelia – they argue – ugly things are said and in the heat of the argument, Barbara hits her daughter with something. When she realizes what has just happened ..."

Matt says, "So once Barbara realizes what she has done, she has no other recourse than to involve Blair."

"Right," said Heather, "and Blair just agrees to help? That doesn't fly. Why wouldn't he simply arrest her and have no other involvement?"

"If Barbara had anything on Blair that she could use against him..." Matt stopped in mid sentence. "Tell me again what the markings were on Amelia's scull."

"Cylindrical object ... 12 to 18 inches in length...." said Bascom.

"Of course – a night stick" said Pete.

"Barbara could have taken Blair's night stick when she was at his apartment." Matt said. "That would mean pre-meditated murder."

"So in anger, Barbara strikes her daughter with Daniel Blair's night stick, and then threatens Blair to enlist his help in disposing of Amelia," says Bascom.

"What about fingerprints on the night stick?" Heather posed.

"Barbara is no dummy. She probably told Daniel Blair that she wore gloves and the only prints that would be there were his own." Pete answered. "Or that her prints ended up there when she struggled with him to stop him from killing Amelia... playing the dutiful mother card."

Heather sat quietly for a couple of minutes. "So the rest of the story falls into place with the help of one Anthony Martinez – who we've already linked to Blair."

"There are holes to fill in, but it appears we are onto something here." Bascom smiled.

"And all of the back matter exonerates Tim" said Heather. "There's not a judge or jury in the world that would suspect he had anything to do with this sinister plot."

"Our next steps must be carefully executed," said Matthew. "We don't want to slip on anything here. After all, we are dealing with an FHP Officer who isn't well liked, but hasn't been involved in prior illegal activity. We're also dealing with a calculating shrew that is on her way back to Kentucky by now."

Heather stood up from the table and walked around to the white board on the wall. "Let's just go over what Matt said. We're dealing with a police officer who we believe is being implicated, threatened and made an accomplice to murder by his jilted lover. What would make him roll over on her?"

"A deal," Matt said quickly. "If we could offer him a significantly lesser charge in exchange for his testimony against Barbara Blake, he might just jump at the chance. I personally don't think Blair wanted Amelia dead; I think he wanted her out of his life – pregnancy and all. He doesn't seem to be the fatherly type."

Bascom spoke up to say that he had experience with a similar situation where a cop was being framed. "Cops like dealing with cops in these situations. They don't like outsiders messing with their careers. I would vote to involve his 'go to guy' - Darrell Dunn and get his take on our hypothesis."

"But if Dunn is his buddy, would he have gone to him already?" Pete asked.

"I don't think so," said Heather. "Keeping in mind that we have just put these pieces together, Blair probably thinks he's in the clear at this point. He wouldn't be feeling the pressure to find a confidante, *yet*."

"Excellent Heather – you're spot on" said Matthew. "And we can either opt to put some pressure on Blair or share our findings with FHP Officer Dunn."

"Bringing charges against Blair would be headline news," Bascom said. "Talk about pressure..."

Michael Trimmer knocked on the door of Heather's office.

"Come in Michael" said Heather.

"I have Mrs. Blake's cell phone records."

"Excellent work Michael," said Heather. "Thank you."

Quickly reviewing them, Heather turned to the group. "Since Michael was thorough – giving me the number as well as the name of who was called, I can quickly summarize this for you guys. According to the telephone records, in December of 1999, Barbara Blake called Daniel Blair, Sophia Newton and the prosecuting attorney's office. Moving to February of this year, on February 19, 2000, Barbara Blake telephoned Sophia Newton – which she alleged in her deposition, two calls to the Comfort Inn – where Amelia was staying, and a late night call to Daniel Blair."

"It all fits." Bascom said. "What about February 20, 2000?"

"Interesting," Heather said "it appears that Mrs. Barbara Blake placed a call to the FHP Dispatch at 6:15 pm. It's most likely the anonymous 'tip' that Blair got."

Everyone sat in silence for a few moments – taking in another piece of the puzzle.

"I guess that clears up our next steps" said Matthew. "We need to have Barbara Blake taken into custody for the murder of her daughter."

"Agreed" said Heather "and that will be the impetus for exerting a little pressure on Daniel Blair."

Pete spoke up. "Let's give Blair a day or so to sweat before we make a move on him. Barbara will throw him under the bus so quickly, his head will be spinning. That's when he will be most apt to consider our deal."

"My pal Pete is correct, but we need to carefully word the deal – before we pass it through the prosecuting attorney."

"Right Matthew - I think we need to set up a meeting with Kevin Morrison right away."

"Want Pete and I there for that?" asked Matthew.

"I think we should invite him here and Skype you two in as we did today," Heather suggested.

"Okay – let us know when. We'll be ready."

"Great work guys." said Heather.

Heather placed the call to Kevin Morrison, getting his voice mail. She asked that he return her call at his earliest opportunity.

CHAPTER EIGHTY

Melanie Sergeant
Just Us Bar & Bistro
Tampa, Florida

Bascom had to satisfy his curiosity, and the only way to be non-threatening was to casually ask Melanie if she had spoken to Amelia during Amelia's February visit to the area.

They had developed a rapport over the past few weeks, as had he and Bob Zee. Walking into the bar at happy hour wasn't surprising either. As Bascom entered, he saw Bob at the bar and Melanie behind it. He nodded to both, took a seat next to Bob and before he was settled, Mel had brought him a drink.

The three exchanged pleasantries and Bob asked if Heather would be joining them.

"She might – I guess I should have invited her, but when I left the office Heather was waiting for an important phone call from the Prosecuting Attorney," Bascom said, sipping his drink.

Bob said, "I'll give her a call and let her know we're all here. Maybe she can come by after she talks with Morrison. Be right back – I'll call from outside."

Seizing the opportunity Bascom said, "I meant to ask you Mel, did you hear from Amelia when she came here in February?"

"No," said Mel, "I moved here in February. The last time I spoke to Amelia was in January. As far as I know, she didn't know I had moved to Tampa."

"You don't think Sam would have told her?" Bascom asked.

"I doubt it. The only reason Sam knows where I landed is because the owners here talked with my previous employer before hiring me."

Satisfied that Melanie was telling the truth, Bascom enjoyed his drink and some ordinary conversation with Bob. Bob had phoned Heather but she was busy and wouldn't make it to happy hour.

On the way home that evening, Bascom decided he would check the telephone records from the hotel where Amelia had spent her last nights. He had Mel's phone number and would recognize it had Amelia phoned her. He could then put his suspicion to rest. Logging onto his secured computer at home, he ran the check. To his relief the only telephone call made from Amelia's room at the Comfort Inn was to Daniel Blair.

Bascom sent a secure email to Heather letting her know what had transpired. He sent blind carbon copies to both Matthew and Peter.

CHAPTER EIGHTY-ONE

Howell Legal Services & Investigations
Tampa, Florida
August 2000

Kevin Morrison arrived right on time, accompanied by an associate from the prosecutor's office. As a result of a Heather Howell's short telephone briefing, both had high hopes for a resolution in the case of Timothy Tyler.

Shirley ushered everyone into the conference room where Heather, Bascom and via Skype Matthew and Pete – were set to go. Heather started by saying that the meeting would be videotaped for the benefit of everyone involved. And for the record, she identified all of the participants in attendance.

Heather thoroughly yet succinctly described all the information and evidence the team had garnered. Avoiding too much speculation, yet delivering their findings in an organized manner, Heather allowed the County Prosecutor(s) to arrive at their own conclusion.

"My first reaction," Morrison said "is to recommend that all charges against your client, Timothy Tyler, be dropped. He was obviously the unwitting pawn in this crime. But – before I can make that recommendation, I propose that we indict Barbara Blake and Daniel Blair on charges of murder."

"Mr. Morrison – if you will indulge me for a moment," Pete Sutherland interjected, "It appears that while involved in the disposal of the body, Officer Blair *may not* have been involved in the actual murder of Amelia Blake."

Pete continued, explaining that logic dictated Blair may have been set up by Mrs. Blake, mentioning her access to the night stick, how she could have threatened Blair and while far from innocent, it was plausible that Blair was not a murderer.

"What we would propose – in an effort to uncover the true act perpetrated on Amelia Ann Blake – is to make an offer of a reduced charge to Officer Blair if he will testify against Barbara Blake." Heather paused to see the reaction of the Prosecutor. "We believe once Officer Blair is made aware of the arrest of Mrs. Blake, he will be more than willing to cooperate."

Morrison was silent for a short time. "While I do not know Officer Blair personally, I do know that he is *not* highly regarded among his peers; which more than likely stems from personality issues rather than legal ones. As County Prosecutor I am compelled to err on the side of law enforcement. And, I do see this proposal as a means to getting to the truth."

"I would like to have a warrant issued for the immediate arrest of Barbara Blake," said Heather. "I would ask that all charges against Timothy Tyler be dropped."

"My office will be happy to oblige, Ms. Howell," Morrison said, "Well done."

"Thank you," Heather said.

"We will also issue a warrant for Officer Daniel Blair, on a charge of accessory to murder."

"And your office will facilitate the plea bargain?" Heather asked.

"We will handle it from here and keep your office advised." Morrison responded.

"Anything else before we adjourn, gentlemen?"

"Yes," said Morrison, "go call your client."

"With pleasure" said Heather.

CHAPTER EIGHTY-TWO

Residence of Barbara Blake
Covington, Kentucky
September 2000

The Covington Police once again arrived at the home of Barbara Blake. When Mrs. Blake answered the door, she was arrested for the premeditated murder of her daughter Amelia Ann Blake.

Try as she might to make them listen to reason, the policemen had none of it and after handcuffing her, read her rights to her. "Anything and everything you say can and will be used against you in a court of law. You have the right to have an attorney; if you cannot afford to hire an attorney one will be appointed to you. Do you understand these rights as I have read them to you?"

Barbara Blake said nothing but "yes". She was then escorted to the police cruiser in front of her house and loaded into the back seat.

Reaching the jail, Barbara Blake was fingerprinted, frisked and given an orange jumpsuit for clothing. Barbara Blake was given the right to make one telephone call. She made that call to Daniel Blair. Receiving no answer – rather an answering machine – Barbara Blake said "See you in St. Pete, then hell" and hung up.

She was then transferred to a holding cell where she would remain until she was remanded to the Pinellas County Police for transfer to St. Petersburg, Florida.

CHAPTER EIGHTY-THREE

Daniel Blair, FHP Officer
Tampa, Florida
September 2000

With precise timing, Officer Daniel Blair was arrested by the St. Petersburg Police and charged with being an accessory to the murder of Amelia Ann Blake.

The squad room was full to overflowing but you could have heard a pin drop as the St. Petersburg Police read Blair the same rights he had administered to others hundreds of times. Quietly, they took Daniel Blair into custody.

Blair made no outburst – no comment. He simply lowered his head and left a handcuffed man.

After being processed, Blair was allowed his one phone call. He telephoned Kevin Morrison's office only to learn that his arrest had been ordered by the Prosecuting attorney. This meant he would now need to find another attorney to represent him, or fall into the lottery of court-appointed counsel.

Blair knew he would have to wait for his formal arraignment to request an attorney.

CHAPTER EIGHTY-FOUR

Arraignment Hearing of Daniel Blair
Pinellas County Courthouse
Clearwater, Florida

The Prosecuting Attorney, Kevin Morrison was present when Daniel Blair entered the courtroom. Without making eye contact, Kevin Morrison presented the charges that had been levied against Blair.

The presiding judge asked Blair if he had an attorney, to which Blair simply stated "I do not, your honor."

Being informed that the court would appoint an attorney for him, Blair simply dropped his head.

"Until then, Daniel Blair, you will be remanded to the Pinellas County Jail. Once you have had the opportunity to speak to your attorney, we will return to this courtroom to continue your arraignment and will at that time allow you to respond to the charges that have been levied upon you. Do you understand?" asked the presiding judge.

"Yes, your honor."

The judge struck his gavel and moved on to the next arraignment hearing.

CHAPTER EIGHTY-FIVE

FHP Headquarters
Tampa, Florida

Word of Blair's arrest traveled quickly through the post. Probably most surprised by the arrest was Darrell Dunn, who had worked with Blair for over a decade. Florida Highway Patrol Officers were a close-knit group, regardless of the circumstance, and Dunn was quick to remind his fellow officers of this.

"Innocent until proven guilty" Dunn said quietly but firmly. "Let's not rush to any judgment here but instead look for facts as they come forth. In the meantime, one of our own has been charged with a crime and needs both our support and best wishes for the truth to be known."

All the officers expected that an official announcement would be made at daily roll-call. Dunn hoped there would be more information provided, but also knew little could be reported that would not amount to hearsay.

Indeed, the Captain delivered a written statement that had been prepared in conjunction with a media press conference. The wording was precise, non-committal and non-inflammatory. No questions were entertained and the Captain urged each officer to be diligent in their assignments, conscientious in their demeanor and work with a heightened awareness of their sworn duty to uphold the law.

Shortly after roll-call Dunn was summoned to the Captain's office. There he was briefed on the personnel changes that would be necessary to adequately cover his patrol with backup.

"If I may Captain," said Dunn, "is there anything that I can do to assist Officer Blair at this juncture?"

"I know you are most likely Blair's closest confidante, and I respect your allegiance to your partner, but as things stand now, I think it best that you keep your distance from him," said the Captain. "Once he is represented by counsel that may change, but for now, Officer Blair is on his own."

"As you wish; thank you Captain." Dunn said.

"Oh – and Dunn, I heard about how you quieted things down out there in the squad room. Thanks for that."

Dunn nodded his head and left the Captain's office.

CHAPTER EIGHTY-SIX

Arraignment Hearing of Barbara Blake
Pinellas County Court House
Clearwater, Florida
September 2000

Barbara Blake entered the Court room wearing her issued orange jumpsuit and was brought before the presiding judge on the charge of premeditated murder in the death of her daughter, Amelia Ann Blake.

Blake recognized Kevin Morrison at the prosecutor's table and gave him a long, indignant stare.

Morrison presented the charges levied by his office to the court.

The presiding judge asked Mrs. Blake if she was represented by counsel to which she responded "No, not yet."

The judge asked if she would require a court-appointed attorney to which she said "No, I will hire my own."

"Very well, we will reconvene when the defendant has secured legal counsel. Until that time, Mrs. Blake will be held in the Pinellas County Jail."

"What about bail?" Mrs. Blake screeched.

"Mrs. Blake, you are out of order. Once you secure legal counsel you will be brought back to court and an arraignment hearing will take place. It will be up to you and your attorney to decide whether or not bail should be requested."

The presiding judge dropped the gavel and said, "Next case please."

Barbara Blake was led away screaming and hurling obscenities at the judge.

"One more word Mrs. Blake and you will also face charges of contempt."

Sitting in her cell, Blake reluctantly decided she must secure her attorney friend in Covington to represent her. She requested a telephone call and was told that she would be given that opportunity within twenty-four hours.

CHAPTER EIGHTY-SEVEN

Offices of the Prosecuting Attorney
Pinellas County
St. Petersburg, Florida

Kevin Morrison was contacted by the court-appointed attorney for Daniel Blair. The attorney Jonathan Green, was relatively new in the Tampa Bay Area, but appeared to be a quick study.

Jonathan had thrown himself into the court-appointed attorney pool just five months ago, which was ironically about the same time the murder of Amelia Ann Blake had occurred. He was aware of that, but had vowed to do his best to represent the FHP Officer who was now charged as an accomplice to murder.

After his initial discussion with his new client, Green approached Kevin Morrison and asked that his client be arraigned in court where he would ask that his client be released on his own recognizance. Blair had never been charged with a crime; he was gainfully employed by the Florida Highway Patrol and did not pose a flight risk.

Surprisingly, Morrison agreed that the hearing be held without delay – with one stipulation. Blair had to agree to testify against Barbara Blake, and plead guilty to a lesser charge - assault after the fact, a second degree misdemeanor. That charge carried a maximum sentence of 60 days in jail and a $500 fine - (FL Statute 784.011).

Jonathan Green told Morrison he would discuss the 'deal' with his client and get back to him.

Later that afternoon, the deal was struck.

CHAPTER EIGHTY-EIGHT

Arraignment of Daniel Blair
Pinellas County Courthouse
Clearwater, FL

Officer Blair appeared for his arraignment wearing a suit and tie. He was accompanied by his court-appointed attorney, Jonathan Green and the hearing was called to order.

The presiding judge asked Daniel Blair to stand.

"Mr. Blair, you have been arrested on charges of complicity to murder in the case of Amelia Ann Blake. How do you plead?"

"Not guilty your honor," Blair responded.

"So, entered into record. Mr. Morrison?"

"Your honor," Kevin Morrison responded "the people believe that Officer Daniel Blair was unduly coerced – even threatened by another defendant in this case, to assist in an attempt to cover up this crime. As a result, we have spoken with opposing counsel and have reached an agreement."

"And that agreement is what Mr. Morrison – Mr. Green?" asked the presiding judge.

Jonathan Green said, "Your honor my client is willing to plead guilty to the charge of Assault after the fact, as he was threatened by the other defendant in this case. He has also agreed in exchange to testify against that defendant, serve any mandatory time and pay any mandatory fine associated with that charge."

"Mr. Blair," said the judge "is this correct? Are you willing to plead guilty to the charge of Assault as defined by Florida Statute 784.011 in exchange for your testimony?"

"I am your honor." Blair said.

we are all in agreement I personally thank all parties for saving the court a great deal of time in this case."

"Anything further from counsel?" asked the judge.

"I would respectfully request that the $500 fine be waived and the 60 day jail sentence be reduced to community service" Green said.

The judge looked to the prosecutor's table.

"We have no problem with that your honor," said Morrison.

"Very well" said the judge. "Mr. Blair, this court finds you guilty of assault after the fact in the murder case of Amelia Ann Blake, and orders you to 60 days of community service to be completed within the next three months."

"Thank you your honor," said Blair. It was unbelievable, but he was free. "Thank you Jonathan," he said.

Walking over to the prosecutor's desk, Blair thanked Morrison as well.

"We will expect both you and Green for preparation to testify against Barbara Blake. No other thanks are needed." Morrison said.

"Mr. Morrison, you have my word on that." Blair said.

CHAPTER EIGHTY-NINE

Timothy Tyler

Tim's relief at having all charges dropped against him was obvious. He walked more erect and had a constant smile on his face.

When Heather gave him the good news, he wept openly. He was free. He had been victimized but he vowed not to dwell on that. In the future, Tim would purposely be more aware of his surroundings, and he would begin each day as an opportunity to be the best person he could be.

Tim could now share his story with Natalie Graham. They were growing closer day by day and Tim realized that without having gone through this process, he might have never met her.

CHAPTER NINETY

The Trial of Barbara Blake
Pinellas County Courthouse
Clearwater, Florida
October 2000

The jury trial lasted three weeks. Heather Howell, Steven Oliver Bascom, Matthew Winters and Peter Sutherland were daily fixtures in the court room gallery. Not one of them wanted to miss a word of testimony, even though they all had to work overtime to take care of their other clients.

Barbara Blake was accompanied by Julius Brooks acting as her attorney. He hailed from Cincinnati, Ohio and had been a defense attorney for over twenty years.

Barbara Blake was unaware of his presence until Daniel Blair took the stand. She had no idea he was turning state's evidence in exchange for a plea of guilty to a lesser charge.

Blair was sworn in and the day's questioning began by Kevin Morrison. Taking an unexpected tact, Morrison asked for the indulgence of the judge and opposing counsel and requested a side-bar conversation.

The judge agreed, calling both Brooks and Morrison to the bench. The attorneys returned to their respective sides, and Morrison said: "Office Blair, you are under oath, so in your own words – please provide this court with exactly what transpired on February 19, 2000 and February 20, 2000 in regards to the death of Amelia Ann Blake."

Barbara Blake was livid and stood up in open court to challenge what was happening. Yelling at her attorney, Barbara hurled insults toward her counsel and the judicial system. She gained nothing for her efforts other than an additional charge – contempt of court.

The judge said "Mr. Brooks, if you cannot control your client, she will be removed from the courtroom."

"I understand your honor," said Julius Brooks as he glared at the now silent Barbara Blake.

CHAPTER NINETY-ONE

Daniel Blair's Testimony Against Barbara Blair

"Mr. Morrison, you may proceed with this witness," said the judge.

"Thank you your honor" and turning once again to Daniel Blair, he said "You may proceed."

Daniel Blair spoke clearly. "Amelia drove to St. Petersburg to see me. We had broken off our relationship toward the end of 1999, and she had telephoned me a couple of times but I refused her calls and never called her back. On February 19, Amelia drove to my apartment, waited in the parking lot and when she saw me arrive, she came up and knocked on my door. I let her in; she told me she was pregnant and that the child she was carrying was mine. I basically told her it was not my problem and we argued. Amelia was crying when she left me there."

"Shortly after that I left but noticed a car following me. I assumed it was Amelia, took evasive action to throw off the vehicle and pulled off on a side street where I waited for the car to pass by. I then pulled out, hit my lights on the cruiser and pulled the car over. Instead of finding Amelia behind the wheel, the driver was Barbara Blake, who insisted on talking to me. We then met in a nearby parking lot."

"Barbara was angry and accused me of sleeping with Sophia Newton as well as her daughter Amelia. I told Barbara that the best thing for her to do was to get out of town and forget she ever knew me...that I never wanted to see her (Barbara) or her daughter again. She went into a rage and started hitting me, which must have been when she took the night stick off my belt. There was a lot of pushing and shoving going on at the time. I told her I could arrest her for assaulting an officer – and in hind sight, I should have. I literally pushed her toward her car and told her to leave town and leave me alone. That's when Barbara Blake drove away."

"By this time it was roughly ten o'clock in the evening. I drove home and arrived to hear my telephone ringing. It was Barbara and she was hysterical. She told me she had gotten a key to Amelia's room at the Comfort Inn and had gone there to confront her. The two of them argued and as the argument escalated, Amelia slapped her mother across the face. Enraged, Barbara then struck Amelia with my night stick she had taken earlier. When Barbara bent over to help Amelia up, she realized her daughter was no longer breathing. Amelia was bleeding profusely from the back of her head. Barbara told me she had wrapped Amelia's head in towels from the room and then called me...."

"I went to the Comfort Inn to see for myself what had happened. I found Amelia dead on the floor and Barbara - wearing bloody gloves - standing over her. Barbara insisted that I help her dispose of Amelia's body. Instead, I told Barbara that she was under arrest in the death of Amelia Blake. She shoved me, raised the night stick as if to strike me and told me that the only fingerprints on the club were mine. Barbara Blake then threatened to accuse me of her daughter's death if I did not help her...."

"Barbara knew that Amelia was pregnant, assumed it was my child and threatened to expose me as an outraged killer. Barbara also told me that she had shared our intimate relationship with her daughter, and that's when Amelia slapped her. Barbara insinuated this argument turned fatal because of me..."

"I obviously was not thinking clearly. I know Barbara Blake to be a vindictive woman who was envious of her daughter. I knew Barbara would accuse me of Amelia's death. While not my best choice, but seemingly my only recourse, we placed Amelia's body in a black garbage bag, put it in Barbara's rental car and drove the body to Toy Town. I knew from regular patrol in that area that it was not unusual to find bags alongside the road. My intention was to simply leave the bag in or near the roadway, and wait for the bag to be picked up and dumped at Toy Town. As ludicrous as it sounds now, I thought neither of us would be implicated....or perhaps no one would ever discover Amelia's body..."

"Barbara wanted assurances that her daughter's body would not be traced back to her. So, she devised a plan to have a dump truck physically hit the garbage bag, sending it onto the shoulder of the road, or better, into oncoming traffic. That's when she involved a mutual acquaintance of ours - Anthony Martinez - who was currently operating a large hauler for a company called Site Select in Clearwater. I later learned that Barbara had an ongoing sexual relationship with Anthony Martinez. She felt that she could trust him to hit the black bag and ask no questions...and now having admittedly met Sophia Newton and tying us together, she would use one of *her* drivers to get back at me - or Sophia – or both."

"Barbara made her arrangements with Martinez as to time and place. He would strike the bag with his hauler and then simply drive off. She assured Martinez that's all he had to do. What she didn't choose to tell him is that she planned to place an anonymous phone call to FHP saying that there was a dump truck driving erratically on the street leaving Toytown. She knew that dispatch would likely come to me – and it indeed did..."

"The only thing Barbara did not take into account was the commuter - Timothy Tyler, innocently driving home from work. When Martinez hit the black bag, he sent it careening into Tyler's vehicle. When I arrived at the scene, I was forced to inspect the car and take Tyler's statement of what had happened. It was then that

I realized how Barbara's plan had escalated and I felt compelled to radio for backup..."

"I sent Officer Dunn to inspect the bag and its contents...I placed Mr. Tyler under arrest and Barbara Blake took an evening flight back to Cincinnati believing she had pulled off the perfect crime...Barbara Blake bashed in the head of her only child, tried to implicate me in the act of murder, and left a trail of destruction in her wake. The woman has no remorse, and in my opinion, no conscience."

"I regret my admitted involvement in this heinous crime. It has cost me my reputation in the police community, my job and what little dignity I had left. My professional losses cannot be regained. And I reluctantly must say that my personal losses – that of a lovely innocent young woman who was carrying my child – will forever weigh heavily on me."

"What I have gained in this process is a new respect for life – and a new respect for what love means – neither of which I had until now." Blair lowered his head and had no more to add.

Barbara Blake sat silently in the courtroom. She had nothing left – no daughter, no lover(s), and no grandchild. Worst of all, Barbara Blake had no way out.

Barbara Blake was remanded into custody and placed on a suicide watch pending her sentencing hearing to be held in ninety days.

Barbara Blake was sentenced to life in prison without the possibility of parole for the pre-meditated murder of her daughter Amelia Ann Blake. A civil suit was never filed.

Daniel Blair completed his community service and immediately left the Tampa Bay Area.

Howell Legal Services & Investigations continues to utilize the investigative services of Steven Oliver Bascom. Matthew Winters and Peter Sutherland continue to consult with the firm on an as needed basis.

Michael Trimmer finished his law degree at Stetson and is interning with the firm.

Jonathan Green left the public defender's office and now practices law as an associate with Heather Howell in Tampa.

Made in the USA
Columbia, SC
18 March 2019